Grasmere 2013

Selected Papers from the Wordsworth Summer Conference

Grasmere, 2013

SELECTED PAPERS FROM
THE WORDSWORTH SUMMER CONFERENCE
AT RYDAL HALL

COMPILED BY RICHARD GRAVIL ON BEHALF OF
THE WORDSWORTH CONFERENCE FOUNDATION

𝓗𝓔𝓑 ☼ Humanities-Ebooks, LLP

First published by *Humanities-Ebooks, LLP,*
Tirril Hall, Tirril, Penrith CA10 2JE

PDF Cover: 'Piers Ghyll' (Jamie Castell)
Paperback Cover: one of the 'Borrowdale Yews' (Richard Gravil)

Images in this not-for-profit publication are understood to be in the public domain. If this is not so please notify the publisher.

The Pdf Ebook is available to individual purchasers exclusively from
http://www.humanities-ebooks.co.uk
and can be supplied to libraries by EBSCO, Ebrary and MyiLibrary.

The paperback is available exclusively from Lulu.com

ISBN 978-1-84760-330-2 PDF Ebook
ISBN 978-1-84760-331-9 Paperback

Contents

Foreword   7

Heidi Thomson
A Perfect Storm: The Nature of Consciousness on Salisbury Plain   8

Peter Larkin
Wordsworth's City Retractions   29

Tom Clucas
'On these two pillars rested as in air / Our solitude': Wordsworth's
     use of Plutarch's *Parallel Lives* in *The Excursion*   41

Simon Swift
Wordsworth and Charles Le Brun: Expression, Colour, Sensation   50

Rowan Boyson
Wordsworth's Anosmia: pleasure, scent and the later poetry   63

Daniel Robinson
'Unrememberable Being': Wordsworth Writing about Writing
     about Memory   74

Christopher Simons
Wordsworth in *Geste:* Dissolving the *Ecclesiastical Sketches*   88

Richard Gravil
Wordsworth's Sacred Sites: a Short Tour   121

Kimiyo Ogawa
Embodying Disinterest: William Godwin and William Hazlitt   146

Richard Lansdown
Coralline Geohistory in James Montgomery's
Pelican Island   158

Alexandra Paterson
'The Atmosphere of Human Thought': Atmospheric Science
     in Shelley's *Prometheus Unbound*   175

Deirdre Coleman
Keats, India, and the Vale of Soul-Making   184

Previous Items in this Series

The following volumes, containing these and many other fascinating essays, are still available in PDF and paperback formats:

Grasmere 2008
John Beer, 'Coleridge's Paradoxical Nature'
Judith Thompson, 'John Thelwall in the Lake District'

Grasmere 2009
Gillian Beer, 'Darwin and Romanticism'
Nicholas Roe, 'John Keats and the Elgin Marbles'

Grasmere 2010
Simon Bainbridge, 'Romantic Mountaineering'
Kenneth Johnston, 'Memoirs of Lost Generation'

Grasmere 2011
Ann Wroe, 'The Necessity of Atheism'
Stephen Gill, 'Wordsworth's Sequels'

Grasmere 2012
Heather Glen, '"We are Seven" in the 1790s'
Pamela Woof, 'Dorothy Wordsworth, Writer: the Midde Years'

http://www.humanities-ebooks.co.uk

Foreword

This selection of three lectures and eight papers from the 42nd Wordsworth Conference is the sixth such to be published on behalf of the Wordsworth Conference Foundation.

It opens with Heidi Thomson's new approach to Wordsworth's Salisbury Plain poetry, emphasising the domestic rather than the Gothic, and closes with Deirdre Coleman's fascinating research on the Keats Circle's response to India. In a third keynote lecture, Christopher Simons recovers the personal poetry running through 'Ecclesiastical Sketches'. Also on Wordsworth, Peter Larkin pursues Wordsworth in the city with his customary finesse; Tom Clucas considers how Wordsworth's Cumbrian characters are dignified by association with Plutarch's parallel lives; and Rowan Boyson explores his most famous disability, his deficient sense of smell, while Daniel Robinson elucidates some issues in textual editing. Kimiyo Ogawa writes on what 'disinterestedness' in Godwin may owe to Hazlitt, whose philosophical stock is steadily rising, and in two scientific papers, Richard Lansdown introduces James Montgomery's remarkable poem, *Pelican Island*, and Alexandra Paterson writes on on Shelley and atmospheric science. Together they give a good sense of the variety and the quality associated with the Wordsworth Summer Conference. An unexpected gap has been plugged by a hastily 'finished' Winter School talk from 2011, on 'Wordsworth's Sacred Sites'.

Richard Gravil, *1 December 2013*

Heidi Thomson

A Perfect Storm: The Nature of Consciousness on Salisbury Plain

The Salisbury Plain poems were on Wordsworth's mind for half a century. Stephen Gill starts off his Cornell edition of these poems with this brief chronology: 'In 1793 and 1794, partly as a result of experiences while wandering over Salisbury Plain, Wordsworth composed the poem he called *Salisbury Plain*. Between 1795 and 1799 this work was transformed into the more ambitious *Adventures on Salisbury Plain*.... In 1841 he returned to this early work and revised it for publication in 1842 as *Guilt and Sorrow*' (xv). My focus in this talk will be primarily on the mental adventures of the long suffering Sailor turned murderer in *Adventures on Salisbury Plain*, the story which embeds the narrative of *The Female Vagrant*. The importance of the Sailor's inner life is affirmed by the 1842 title in which paired emotions are juxtaposed with casual occurrences: *Guilt and Sorrow; or, Incidents upon Salisbury Plain*. Wordsworth's poem *Resolution and Independence* gives us a similar twin pairing of emotions in a poem which started off as *The Leech Gatherer*. During the course of that poem the speaker's encounter with the Buddhistic leech gatherer prompts him to rephrase the question about purposeful labour 'What kind of work is that which you pursue' (263, l. 95) into the existential query 'How is it that you live, and what is it you do' (264, l. 126). Similarly, *Adventures on Salisbury Plain* provides the opportunity for a range of questions which may complicate our view of the characters involved.[1]

In *Adventures on Salisbury Plain* we witness a transition from

---

[1] For readings of the Salisbury Plain poems, see primarily Averill, Bailey, Fosso, Gill (*Wordsworth's Revisitings*), Gravil, Hartman, Jones, Modiano, Potkay, Sheats, Swann, Trott, Ulmer, Wiley.

fugitive entrapment into a state of enlightenment. What that enlightenment consists of relates to the guilt for the murder which the Sailor has committed, but it also incorporates the sorrow of the Sailor's fundamental loss, the loss of his family. Most readings emphasize the Sailor's conscientious awareness of guilt as opposed to his mere submission to the operations of the judicial system. The discussion as to whether the Sailor goes to his execution because he has been betrayed into doing so or because he fully realizes that this is the price he has to pay for his crime revolves around the characterization of the Sailor as a murderer. A similar contrast is suggested by the difference between the translated titles of Dostoyevski's great novel: we think of Raskolnikov differently if we read his narrative under the banner of *Crime and Punishment* (in English) than if we consider it under the heading of *Guilt and Repentance* (as you would in the older Dutch and German translations).

Without discarding readings with an ethical emphasis, I will read *Adventures on Salisbury Plain* in terms of the Sailor's most grievous loss, the loss of his wife and family, and how the realization of that loss through a process of physical trances amounts to the loss of his own life. The convergence of justice, conscience, and, I add, overwhelming consciousness of loss within the poem reminds me of a perfect storm, in which the calamitous outcome through 'a rare combination of adverse … factors' (*OED*) is offset by an earlier use of the phrase, in a 1718 quotation by Hubert Stogdon, a Presbyterian minister: 'There was a rushing mighty wind, a perfect storm, and tempest before the descent of the Holy Ghost' (*OED*). In *Adventures on Salisbury Plain* the rise and fall of the storm coincides with the turbulent behaviour of the Sailor's body which, in successive trances, expresses and rehearses the loss of life he has experienced and will experience. He dies before he dies, in the same sense that Wallace Stevens writes in the final part of 'Thirteen Ways of Looking at a Blackbird': 'It was evening all afternoon. / It was snowing / And it was going to snow' (76). In his essay 'On Chaucer and Spenser' Hazlitt defines the strength of Spenser, who presides strongly over the Salisbury Plain poems, as follows: 'His strength … is not strength of will or action, of bone and muscle, nor is it coarse and palpable—

but it assumes a character of vastness and sublimity seen through the same visionary medium, and blended with the appalling associations of preternatural agency' (203). Wordsworth manages to graft this effect on the Sailor whose body is subject to fits, trances, and tremors. Moreover, Wordsworth incorporates those events into a vision of the Sailor's purpose and direction.

When Coleridge reminisces fondly about the recitation of *Salisbury Plain* in *Biographia Literaria* he also includes a meteorological element when he refers to 'the union of deep feeling with profound thought' and singles out 'above all the original gift of spreading the tone, the *atmosphere*, and with it the depth and height of the ideal world around forms, incidents, and situations, of which, for the common view, custom had bedimmed all the lustre, had dried up the sparkle and the dew drops' (*BL*, 1.80). Coleridge's use of 'atmosphere' here is invoked as an early example of the figurative use of the word in the *OED* in which the whole body of terrestrial air is extended into a 'prevailing psychological climate', 'a pervading tone or mood'. In *Adventures on Salisbury Plain* the effect of the Sailor's suicidal vision accompanies the moral purpose of justice, and the profound thought which underlies the deep feeling is the awareness that life is not worth living without 'the things worth living for'. The Female Vagrant says as much when she talks about the 'dreadful price of being to resign / All that is dear *in* being' (*ASP*, 137, ll. 379–380), but Wordsworth uses the actual phrase, 'the things worth living for', in the 1797 *Argument for Suicide* (included as an Appendix in the Cornell edition of *The Borderers*) which ends on: 'strange it is / And most fantastic are the magic circles / Drawn round the thing called life – till we have learned / To prize it less we ne'er shall learn to prize / The things worth living for.— ' (811). In the manuscript the last phrase is repeated below the lines, by itself, in pencil. The Sailor's full realization of the 'things worth living for, is intimated by the reactions of his body at crucial moments in the poem, and most strikingly in reaction to the Female Vagrant's tale.

I agree with Richard Gravil who refers to the Sailor's execution by the justice system as 'self-chosen' (254). My focus is on how that choice is revealed to the Sailor himself, and how it is a choice which combines profound thought about guilt with a deep feeling of sorrowing loss. In a variation on the French phrase for suicide, *il se donne la mort*, the Sailor gives death to himself, or death swims into his ken at the right moment, for the reason that life, for lack of his family, has been stripped of meaning. This realization, and its poetic expression, is not only meaningful in itself; it is also a blueprint for Wordsworth's poetic of domesticity which I see as an imaginative settlement project of inventing and claiming a chosen home, as 'Home at Grasmere' (1800) indicates. *Adventures on Salisbury Plain* confirms Wordsworth's most fundamental conviction, above and beyond any beliefs or philosophies, namely that solitary homelessness, existential vagrancy in the sense of separation from one's loved family is a fate worse than death. This fundamental belief in the domestic affections and its moral implications distinguishes Wordsworth most clearly from Godwin and his Philosophy of Necessity.[1] While the story of the social and political underpinnings of the Sailor's crime invites a Godwinian reading, Wordsworth also provides us with a parallel story of loss which cannot be cast in rational terms. *Adventures on Salisbury Plain* illustrates the limits of reason as 'a principle of human cognition and motivation' (Ulmer, 174). The epigraph from Pope's *Epistle to Cobham* to *The Borderers* could also be the epigraph to *Adventures on Salisbury Plain*. The actual epigraph is italicised, but it makes sense to quote the adjacent lines as well:

> Our depths who fathoms, or our shallows finds,
> Quick whirls, and shifting eddies, of our minds?

---

1 Philosophically, the influence of Coleridge was considerable in this instance. See, for instance, Coleridge's letter to Southey in 1794: 'The ardour of private Attachments make Philanthropy a necessary habit of the Soul. I love my Friend – such as he is, all mankind are, or might be! Philanthropy (and indeed every other Virtue) is a thing of Concretion – Some home-born Feeling is the center of the Ball, that, rolling on thro' Life collects and assimilates every congenial Affection.' (*CL* 1: 86). Also: 'Jesus knew our nature – and that expands like the circles of a Lake – the Love of our Friends, parents and neighbours lead[s] us to love of our Country to the love of all Mankind' (*Lectures 1795*,163). In *Conciones ad Populum*, he wrote that 'general benevolence is begotten and rendered permanent by social and domestic affections … The intensity of private attachments encourages, not prevents, universal Benevolence … The paternal and filial duties discipline the Heart and prepare it for the love of all Mankind' (*Lectures 1795*, 46).

> *On human actions reason though you can,*
> *It may be reason, but it is not man:*
> *His principle of action once explore,*
> *That instant 'tis his principle no more.*
> Like following life through creatures you dissect,
> You lose it in the moment you detect. (Pope, 320, ll. 23–30)

The Salisbury Plain poems were conceived in the wake of Wordsworth's second stay in France in 1792. Now separated by the Channel from his lover Annette Vallon, their child Caroline (who had been born in December 1792), Wordsworth would have been contemplating the terrible loss of his French family as he observed the preparations for war of the British fleet from the shores of the Isle of Wight throughout July 1793. Annette's passionate letter of March 1793 in response to Wordsworth's indicates clearly how they thought of themselves as a young family temporarily separated by war. The letter was intercepted and he never saw it, but we can read it in Appendix II of Emile Legouis' book, and in that fiery letter to her 'mari', her husband, her friend and lover, Annette is a version of the Sailor's wife, of the Female Vagrant, of Margaret, of all those women who start off warm blooded and fulfilled as wives and mothers in reciprocated love. When William Calvert and Wordsworth made their way back towards Wales in late July or early August 1793 their whiskey (light one-horse carriage) broke down near Salisbury and Wordsworth 'wanders about (probably between Salisbury and Bath) two or three days, probably at least two days mainly on Salisbury Plain. He naps in Stonehenge c noon of one day' (Reed, 145).

The empty hollowness of loss and despondency which character-ized Wordsworth's Salisbury Plain experience became the crucible of artistic creation. Wordsworth singles out the hallucinatory Salisbury Plain experience as a, if not *the*, defining moment of his early artis-tic development in the final 80 lines of Book 12 of the 1805 *Prelude*. The process of poetic imagination which Wordsworth describes in this *Prelude* passage mirrors, to a significant extent, the imaginative enlightenment which the Sailor in *Adventures upon Salisbury Plain* experiences. M. H. Abrams' idea that *The Prelude* 'incorporates the

discovery of its own *ars poetica*' (78) extends to the Sailor's self discovery in terms of his loss in the course of *Adventures on Salisbury
Plain*, and in particular in response to the Female Vagrant's narrative.
Both the Sailor in *Adventures on Salisbury Plain* and the speaker in the
self-fashioning *Prelude* share, in different ways, a 'peculiar dower',
namely 'a sense / By which he is enabled to perceive / Something
unseen before' (12. 303–305). That kind of talent is conducive to
the production of a work '[p]roceeding from the depth of untaught
things, / Enduring and creative' which 'might become / A power like
one of Nature's' (12. 310–312). The mood which makes this artistic
feat possible is based on directionless, despondent wandering:

> To such mood,
> Once above all—a traveller at that time
> Upon the plain of Sarum—was I raised:
> There on the pastoral downs without a track
> To guide me, or along the bare white roads
> Lengthening in solitude their dreary line,
> While through those vestiges of ancient times
> I ranged, and by the solitude o'ercome,
> I had a reverie and saw the past, (12. 312–320)

The absence of purposeful direction in this passage ('without a
track / To guide me') is nevertheless combined with a powerful suggestion of emotionally informed aesthetic form ('the bare white roads
/ Lengthening in solitude their dreary line'). That absence of direction, combined with the overpowering solitude leads to the loss of
rational consciousness in which the reverie substantiates the vision of
Britain's barbaric past. That vision is interrupted by the poet's god-
like command:

> I called upon the darkness, and it took—
> A midnight darkness seemed to come and take—
> All objects from my sight; and lo, again
> The desart visible by dismal flames! (12. 327–330)

The authoritative shaman-like invocation of darkness creates the
necessary void for the imagined gruesome vision of the sacrifices at

Stonehenge, at which the living victims were imprisoned in a gigantic wicker effigy in a human form which is then set on fire.[1] The grim sight of immolating human beings within a wicker structure shaped like a human being, surely symbolic of humanity destroying its own, hovers over *Adventures on Salisbury Plain* when the narrator invokes the same ritual in stanza 18, only four stanzas after the Sailor has been profoundly affected by the eighteenth-century equivalent of ancient sacrifices, the exemplary public hanging in irons of executed criminals. In those stanzas the Sailor hears the 'sudden clang / A sound of chains along the desart' (126, ll. 112–113). The view of the executed body on the gibbet, circled by ravens, horrifies the Sailor and causes him to stumble in a scene which attributes malicious motivation to some rolling stones:

> The stones, as if to sweep him from the day,
> Roll'd at his back along the living plain;
> He fell and without sense or motion lay,
> And when the trance was gone, feebly pursued his way.
> (126, ll. 123–126)

The trance recurs, poignantly, later on, in response to the Female Vagrant's tale.

The conclusion to Book 12 of *The Prelude* is a typical example of what Stephen Gill calls the 'signature' of Wordsworth's philosophic verse: 'It is that his poetry shifts continually on the axis between the exultantly affirmative and the hesitantly exploratory' ('The Philosophic Poet', 152–3). The final image is 'exultantly affirmative' in its harmonious portrayal of the interaction between subject and object:

> A balance, an ennobling interchange
> Of action from within and from without:
> The excellence, pure spirit, and best power,
> Both of the object seen, and eye that sees. (12. 376–379)

The poetic essence which is distilled from this balance between object seen and seeing eye incorporates the 'hesitantly exploratory',

---

1   See also Duggett, 86.

the reluctant experience of the void, of intimations of the unspeakable, of horrific violence on a range of scales, present and past. The affirmation of reluctance, the necessary vision of what we don't want to see is part and parcel of Wordsworth's poetry and poetics. I wanted to start with this excursion to *The Prelude* because it articulates poetically what happens in *Adventures on Salisbury Plain* with the Sailor whose body moves from doubt to decision, whose body knows before his mind fully grasps, when the darkness takes over before, unbidden but inevitably, the vision of his loss emerges more clearly.

In *The Prelude* Wordsworth stages the 'transforming and organizing energies' (Rudy, 11) of a creative self explicitly. In *Adventures on Salisbury Plain* he stages those energies through the portrayal of the Sailor. In a crucial moment the Sailor recovers from a trance and states simply 'I have been / I know not where'. The enjambment separating 'I have been' and 'I know not where' points to not only the separation between 'being' and 'knowing' but also to the precedence of 'being' over 'knowing', with the assertion of positively having been somewhere without knowing precisely where that is. Throughout the poem the Sailor's consciousness catches up with his body which absorbs and transforms vital information in its surrender to various bouts of unconsciousness.

Now to the poem: first and foremost the Sailor embodies what Wordsworth wrote about in his famous letter to Charles Fox (14 January 1801), namely that 'men who do not wear fine cloaths can feel deeply' (315). The dissolution of the family is what Wordsworth, and by extension his poetic characters, feel most deeply about. It is no surprise that in the opening scene of *Adventures on Salisbury Plain* we witness a Traveller who is instrumental in reuniting an old Soldier with his friends and family by putting him on the mail coach. The Traveller's self-esteem is boosted by his ability to bestow generosity on the old man who prefigures the Sailor's own wife at the end of the poem. After this reassuring set-up 'evening came with clouds and stormy fire' (124, l. 46). The verse suggests various landmarks or signs of human activity, but the signs only point at absence, with the frame recording the loss of the actual object of focus: the 'distant spire [of Salisbury Cathedral] / That fix'd at every turn his backward eye / Was lost, though still he turn'd, in the blank sky' (124, ll. 48–50). As even the crows are 'homeward borne' (125, l. 67), the Sailor cannot discern a hovel on the 'wild, forlorn, / And vacant' (ll. 70–71) 'huge plain' (125, l. 71). In this vacant setting Wordsworth strips all tourist connotations from the Traveller. He had been a home-bound Sailor who 'enflamed with long desire' for the wife he'd left behind was press ganged into warfare, 'the work of carnage' (l. 82). Upon his release as Soldier he was denied his victory earnings by the 'slaves of Office' (125, l. 91). Destitute and depressed the Sailor heads home in a mood which foreshadows the abusive father later in the poem; he is 'in such a mood / That from his view his children might have run' (125, l. 96). That casual reference to the threat of violence within the domestic circle immediately precedes the succinct summing up of the actual murder: 'He met a traveller, robb'd him, shed his blood' (125, l. 97). When he hears the rattling sound of the gibbet's chains on the empty plain, emblems of his own future fate, to which I already referred, he falls into a trance which is followed by a 'deepest calm', with his mind 'still as a deep evening stream' (127, l. 132). That calm should not be mistaken for emotional tranquillity.

The storm gains momentum and the Sailor now seemed 'the only creature in the wild / On whom the elements their rage might wreak' (127, ll. 147–148) on a stage where the absence of earlier pastoral figures is now replaced with the absence of more marginal figures: no gypsy, no labourer, no light from sick man's room. The darkness is 'void as ocean's watry realm' (128, l. 174). Yet, at this point, totally unexpectedly, the word 'pleasure' appears, only to reappear, for the Sailor, at the very end of the poem when 'not without pleasure' he turns himself in to the authorities:

> Once did the lightning's faint disastrous gleam
> Disclose a naked guide-post's double head,
> Sight which, though lost at once, some glimpse of pleasure shed.
> (128, ll. 169–171)

On 8 June 1794 Wordsworth wrote to his friend William Matthews about his plans for a radical journal *The Philanthropist a monthly Miscellany*. Just before suggesting this title he writes: 'I know that the multitude walk in darkness. I would put into each man's hand a lantern to guide him and not have him to set out upon his journey depending for illumination on abortive flashes of lightning, or the coruscations of transitory meteors' (125). A puny glimpse of wry pleasure, with an abortive flash of lightning revealing a Janus-faced guide-post, with each head pointing into the darkness, is all we get in *Adventures on Salisbury Plain*.

Very soon afterwards the Sailor seeks refuge in the ruinous Spital, 'the dead house of the Plain' (128, l. 189) where he encounters, reluctantly, 'one who mourn'd in sleep' (129, l. 200), a Female Vagrant whom he wakens. Setting and characterization are entirely coloured in a posthumous hue. The portrayal of the encounter emphasizes the horror of the woman who has been thinking about a story related to the ruin in which a man lifts up a stone which reveals the 'grim head of a new-murder'd corse' (129, l. 216). In her excellent reading of the poem Karen Swann makes the point that the woman may be afraid that she is seeing that very corpse when she opens her eyes and confronts the Sailor. I would argue in addition that she could also be afraid of seeing the murderer (after all the view was of a new-murdered corpse). The Sailor of course *is* a murderer, but his characterization is such that we do not consider this his defining trait. With 'low words of chearing sound' (129, l. 221) the Sailor reassures the terrified woman. The notion of the Sailor as the comforter of the woman, soon to be confirmed by his sympathetic response as a listener to her tale, already indicated by his kindness to the old Soldier at the very beginning of the poem and later affirmed again as the protector of the abused child, reinforces our reading of him as a kind, altruistic human being. Yet it is a role which also made me realize that he himself is beyond consolation. The Sailor's altruism is yet another marker of his existential loneliness.

The bond between the Vagrant and the Sailor is instant and suggestive of marital harmony: as vagrants their lives run parallel, but more importantly, as widowed wife and fugitive husband, these two strangers mirror *both* each other and each other's spouses. The Female Vagrant and the Sailor both complement and mirror each other; their absent spouses are ghosts of remembrance in their interaction with each other. In this interaction, already tinged by death, they both see their former lives and 'the things worth living for' embodied in each other. Their tender interaction, redolent of easy marital intimacy, underlines their respective isolation.

The Female Vagrant's tale (which I cannot go into any detail about) could be the story of the Sailor's wife. The break-up of the family figures throughout, beyond life itself even when she refers to how her father's wish that 'his bones might there be laid, / Close by my mother in their native bowers' has been denied (134, ll. 320–321). She interrupts her narrative at the moment that she herself wakes up on a British ship 'as from a trance restored' (138, l. 396). This moment triggers a trance in the Sailor. The jumble of pronouns in the lines that follow makes it almost impossible to distinguish between the Female Vagrant and the Sailor:

> She paused—or by excess of grief oppress'd,
> Or that some sign of mortal anguish broke
> In strong convulsion from her comrade's breast—
> She paused and shivering wrapp'd her in her cloak
> Once more a horrid trance his limbs did lock.
> Him through the gloom she could not then discern
> And after a short while again she spoke;
> But he was stretch'd upon the wither'd fern,
> Nor to her friendly summons answer could return.
> (138, ll. 397–405)

She shivers, his limbs lock in trance. In contrast with their first encounter when the Sailor's cheering words managed to reassure her, she cannot coax a response out of him. Now that the storm is setting, the inner storm in the sailor is subsiding as well. When he wakes up he asks 'if she had nothing seen' (138, l. 416)? to which the Vagrant replies that she hadn't:

> "'Tis well. I am a wretched man I ween.
> Your tale has moved me much and I have been
> I know not where." Quoth she, "Your heart is kind,
> And if no wish of sleep should intervene,
> Till we by morning light some track can find,

I will relate the rest, 'twill ease my burden'd mind.
(139, ll. 418–423)

The Sailor professes that he has been somewhere under the influence of her story, but he doesn't know where. The Female Vagrant continues with her account, both indulging in and mocking her suicidal state on the ocean, her 'ready tomb' (141, l. 465). Back in England, the absence of a domestic context is the defining aspect of her desolation: she is 'homeless near a thousand homes' (141, l. 467). Treated sympathetically by gypsies, she realizes acutely that she is the outsider among these outsiders. In-laws do not match the ties of blood: 'kindred of dead husband are at best / Small help' (145, l. 534). The conclusion of her aimless wandering on the moor is entirely connected with the lack of a human relationship: 'Oh! tell me whither—for no earthly friend / Have I.'" (146, l. 554). The request for an indication of direction rekindles the image of the 'naked guide-post's double head', the Janus-faced indication to nowhere for an individual without familial context.

In the stanzas dealing with the morning after the storm the full extent to which Wordsworth experiments with the limits of consolation in *Adventures on Salisbury Plain* becomes clear. In this version, in contrast with the earlier *Salisbury Plain* and the later *Guilt and Sorrow*, Wordsworth resists the more affirmative portrayal of bestowing and receiving comfort, an interaction which creates the illusion of a mutually satisfying situation of sorts. Instead, we get two stanzas where syntactic consistency is not entirely observed through alternation between pronouns.

Stanza 63 starts off with the stillness after the Female Vagrant's narrative: 'She ended, of all present thought forlorn, / Nor voice nor sound that moment's pang expressed' (146, ll. 559–560). The blankness of the moment and the use of 'thought forlorn' and 'that moment's pang' anticipate that most moving sonnet of a later date 'Surprised by joy' in which the forlorn speaker articulates the moment's thought, the guilty awareness of feeling joy, as the worst pang save the one of the actual moment of loss of his child. After that stillness, the cathartic tears flow, and the Sailor wisely maintains a silence: 'He sate and spake not, ere her weeping ceased' (146, l. 563).

The following line diverges from the two other versions in which it is the Sailor who moves towards the portal of the ruin to watch the dawn. In *Adventures* the woman cries, he sits quietly, but, in contrast with the two other versions, she, and not he, gets up and goes towards the door where she observes the dawn, and in the process of it all her acute grief diminishes.

The following stanza portrays a logical progression in the earlier and later versions: the Sailor, who has moved to the door, now invites the Female Vagrant to join him in watching the sun rise, an experience which restores the colour to her cheek and some cheer to her heart. The Sailor is very clearly cast in the role of comforter who contributes, in both versions, 'words of hope' (32 and 249). In the *Adventures* version those roles are more ambivalent, even reversed, which points, I believe, to a different effect of the Vagrant's tale on the Sailor. In the Reading Text lines 568–570 are recorded as:

> "But come," she cried, "come after weary night
> Of such rough storm the breaking day to view."
> So forth he came and eastward look'd: the sight
> (146, ll. 568–570)

'"But come," she cried' is Gill's reading version, and his footnote to line 568 indicates: 'she] Written "he" by mistake.' I looked at the photograph of MS 2, largely in the hand of Dorothy Wordsworth (but with many bold changes by Mary Wordsworth dating of 1841, though not to these particular lines). The MS shows the line as '"But come," he cried' (184). This would make sense in the context of the two other versions where it is very clearly the Sailor who is exhorting the Vagrant to pull herself together. Gill's emendation, however, makes sense syntactically because of the preceding stanza, which clearly indicates that 'she' and not 'he' rose. In addition, in response to the woman's invitation, we find out that '[s]o forth he came': 'he' and not 'she' as in the other versions. The slip in the MS, or in the dictation, indicates the wavering between 'he' and 'she' in their roles. The hesitation or ambiguity is also visible in the incomplete line 571, which Gill identifies as a later addition, and which is recorded in the Reading Text as, starting from 570:

> So forth he came and eastward look'd: the sight
>   Into his heart a [   ] anguish threw;

The picture of the MS on page 184 show this:

> So forth he came, & eastward look'd the sight
>   Into his art   anguish threw

Structurally the incomplete and inserted line 571 has much in common with an equivalent line in the earlier version in which the effect of the sight applies to the woman and not to the Sailor: 'O'er her moist eyes meek dawn of gladness threw' (32, l. 337) or 'Over her brow like dawn of gladness threw' (l. 249).

In the reversal of the pronouns, though, the consolation does not happen. In line 572 the Sailor's cheek is revealed to be of 'ashy hue', and this deadly association is further reinforced by his trembling with grief and fear. The substitution of 'gladness' (in the case of the woman) with 'anguish' makes sense, but it is as if the poet had not made up his mind yet what to make of the rest. I quite like the mark of hesitation or dithering in the word 'art' for 'heart', as if indeed any thought about the Sailor's frame of mind threw a dimension of anguish over the poet's art. How does one write about the realization that mutual comfort is not necessarily an outcome or an option of this encounter? The reassuring comfort which the Sailor manages to bestow in the other versions is a reflection and assertion of the inner strength of his own identity, but in this version Wordsworth wanted to experiment with a point of no return.

The story of the disintegration and death of the Female Vagrant's family, the necessary domestic context which Wordsworth always upholds as the basis of any society, has made the Sailor aware that removing himself from the scene of the murder, so close to his home, is not just an act of self preservation but also one of destruction, the abandonment and ruin of his family. The encounter with the woman itself is loaded with the memory of, and also charged with the energy of, domestic attachment. One may go as far as to see an erotic tinge in greeting the dawn together as the lark sings near. Her efforts to cheer up the Sailor 'with affectionate and homely art' (1. 590) make it worse, because 'deep into his vitals she had sent / Anguish [again that word] that rankled like a fiery dart' (147, 1. 589). As a result 'still the more he griev'd, she loved him still the more' (1. 594). As the Sailor's thoughts remain fixed on 'the murder'd man' (147, 1. 597), the woman's final resort to the commonplace of the afterlife as a comfort sounds particularly fraught, as if these words were spoken by a spouse and not a random stranger: '"Why should you grieve," she said, "a little while / And we shall meet in heaven"' (147, ll. 599-600). Wordsworth's affinity for the graveyard as a communal site of familial kindness in his second Essay upon Epitaphs is well known, but it is worth repeating that the comforting prospect of domestic reunion in heaven, somehow prefigured in proximity in the graveyard, is a very powerful notion in Wordsworth. As a sinful murderer the Sailor would be denied the illusion of this comfort.

The visceral awareness that his life is over for lack of a domestic context, the fiery dart of anguish which rankles in the Sailor's vitals, is compounded by the next horrific encounter which serves two related purposes: it exposes the tragic vulnerability of the weak, in the context where they should be protected most, the family, and in addition, it associates the beaten child with the murdered man, an association which steels the sailor's death-wish.

The momentary pleasant prospect of the new day is shattered by a dire cacophony of human sounds: the shrill screams of a child, the hoarse blasphemy of a man beating the child, the cries of a distressed mother assault the ears of the Female Vagrant and the Sailor. They come across a scene of domestic abuse, triggered by the child's innocent clumsy act:

> He was not five years old, and him to trail
> And bruise, as if each blow had been his last,
> She knew not what for life his brain might ail.
> Shuddering the soldier's widow stood aghast
> And stern looks on the man her grey-hair'd comrade cast.
> (148, ll. 626–630)

In a defamiliarizing move the widow and the sailor, both loners but presented here as if they were an observant couple, of one mind and heart, are juxtaposed with the dysfunctional family in which cruel abuse is inflicted on its weakest member. The initial ranting, counter-accusing reaction of the father against the sailor who urges the man to stop his beating highlights the sailor's appearance as a vagabond who has no business interfering with so-called normal people's families. There is no doubt that Wordsworth is drawing attention to the poten-tial and prevalence of domestic violence in these unsettled, impover-ished contexts. The passage, we may recall, echoes the Sailor's des-titute homecoming from the wars which was cast in 'such a mood / that from his view his children might have run' (125, ll. 95–96); no one is immune to inhumane behaviour.

The fiery dart which had already found its way into the sailor's vitals through the vagrant's narrative, is now, figuratively, supple-mented by a 'griding iron' (149, l. 646) finding passage through his brain when he comforts the boy and notices that the child's head wound is in exactly the same spot 'where he that deadly wound / Had fix'd on him he murder'd' (149, ll. 644–645): 'Through his brain / At once the griding iron passage found; / Deluge of tender thoughts then rush'd amain / Nor could his aged eyes from very tears abstain' (149, ll. 645–648). Mortally wounded, one could argue, by the fiery dart and the griding iron, in his vitals and his brain, the Sailor now makes his only extended speech within the whole poem. It is the speech of a dead man. The sailor executes himself before the gallows merci-fully finish him off (otherwise he 'was resolved to turn towards the seas / Since he that tale had heard', and that was obviously not with a view to join a ship again, but, more likely, to follow the desperate idea of the Female Vagrant when she was 'in deep despair by fright-ful wishes stirr'd, / Near the sea-side' [142, ll.480–481]).

The incantatory address of stanza 74 reminds me of the rhythm of François Villon's valedictory *Ballade des pendus*, a poem which I believe Wordsworth may very well have encountered during his stay in France and upon which he drew for the Salisbury Plain poems. The Sailor's speech is only seven lines long and framed with signs of a body in extremis:

Then with a voice which inward trouble broke
In the full swelling throat, the Sailor them bespoke.

"'Tis a bad world, and hard is the world's law;
Each prowls to strip his brother of his fleece;
Much need have ye that time more closely draw
The bond of nature, all unkindness cease,
And that among so few there still be peace:
Else can ye hope but with such num'rous foes
Your pains shall ever with your years increase."
While his pale lips these homely truths disclose,
A correspondent calm stole gently on his woes.
(149, ll. 656–666)

The sailor's address reveals both the Hobbesian (homo homini lupus) predatory state of the world and the desperate need for domestic harmony if one is going to have a life worth living. But above all, they are the words of a man for whom all is over already, who, with belaboured breath, finally articulates what has been troubling him all along and for whom these 'homely truths' have now become his own with full force. The calm after his pale lips pronounce this speech is deadly.

The closing scenes mirror the opening passage, but now the rustic inn is hospitable, staging domestic contentment with the Female Vagrant and the Sailor joining the family for breakfast, and the cottage children clustering spontaneously and playfully around the Sailor's knees. And again, in a mirroring of the opening of the story, a cart appears wherein there is a 'single woman, lying spent and gone' (l. 698). In her near posthumous state the woman is beyond seeking support herself: 'No pity asking, on the group she gazed / As if with eye by blank suffusion glazed, / Then sunk upon her straw with feeble moan' (151, ll. 715–717). The way she is tended to resembles the preparation of a corpse for a wake rather than the resuscitation of a patient. Her story is the Female Vagrant's hallucination about the murdered man in the ruinous spital come alive: life was hard but she coped until 'one was found by stroke of violence dead / And near my door the Stranger chanced to lie' (152, 752–753). Part of the horror in the dying woman's account revolves around the juxtaposition of the suspicion on her husband and the idea that he would have committed this crime so close to his own home, all so contrary to how she knew him: he would 'not have robb'd the raven of his food' (153, l. 763).

In the final section of the poem the Sailor breaks down and addresses his wife, 'weeping loud, in this extreme distress': 'O bless me now, that thou should'st live / I do not wish or ask: forgive me, now forgive' (153, ll. 773–774). The Sailor asks for forgiveness, not for her life. Their lives ended a long time ago already, and the dissolution of their family had amounted to death for the characters in this poem. I am again reminded of the fraught emotion, against all reason, in 'Surprised by joy' when in the dying wife '[a] sudden joy surprised expiring thought, / And every mortal pang dissolved away' (153, ll. 777–778). While the poem indicates that her expression communicated comfort to the Sailor, he does not interpret it that way. His wish for death has become absolute, as 'in his breast a dreadful quiet reign'd' (154, l. 801).

In this version he cottagers resolve to report the Sailor to the authorities ('Most fit it is that we unfold this woful tale' (154, l. 810). In terms of plot this makes it look as if the world is bringing the criminal to justice, but, just like Thomas Hardy's Tess at the end of a novel which closes upon a similar setting, the Sailor has taken the initiative towards his death much earlier:

> Confirm'd of purpose, fearless and prepared,
> Not without pleasure, to the city strait
> He went and all which he had done declar'd.
> (154, ll. 811–813)

The final line of *Elegiac Stanzas* puts it that 'not without hope we suffer and we mourn'. The way in which Wordsworth uses the 'not without' construction is not so much an understatement or litotes but an affirmation of the strange confluence of contradictory emotions: hope and loss, pleasure and death. The recurrence of the word 'pleasure' in *Adventures on Salisbury Plain* is both surprising and logical: the glimpse of pleasure brought about by the momentary illumination of the naked guide-post's double head in lines 170–171 on page 128 is here confirmed in the active choice of his destiny. Regardless of the cottagers' suggested intention of intervention we know that the Sailor has chosen his direction. Justice prevails in the wake of the profession of guilt of the criminal, but, in addition, the poem also suggests something different: namely that life is not worth living when one is divorced from the domestic context of love. Death is a site of release rather than of punishment. That it is a preferable, rational choice to leave this bad world is confirmed by a final grotesque scene which highlights how vulnerable domestic harmony is within a disintegrating society:

> They left him hung on high in iron case,
> And dissolute men, unthinking and untaught,
> Planted their festive booths beneath his face;
> And to that spot, which idle thousands sought,
> Women and children were by fathers brought;
> And now some kindred sufferer driven, perchance,
> That way when into storm the sky is wrought,
> Upon his swinging corpse his eye may glance
> And drop, as he once dropp'd, in miserable trance.
> (154, ll. 820–828)

The juxtaposition of the gibbet and the fair is emblematic of inhumane voyeurism dressed up as family entertainment (as in the case of the fair further explored in Book 7 of *The Prelude*). The warning and reflection on a 'kindred sufferer' (and note, not criminal, but sufferer) in the final lines also serves as an explanation why a situation like that would put one for whom emotion and thought about family and society are deeply connected in a 'miserable trance'.

Bibliography

Abrams, M. H. *Natural Supernaturalism: Tradition and Revolution in Romantic Literature*. New York: Norton, 1973.

Averill, James H. *Wordsworth and the Poetry of Human Suffering*. Ithaca and London: Cornell UP, 1980.

Bailey, Quentin. "'Strike not from Law's firm hand that awful rod':

Wordsworth's Salisbury Plain and the Penalty of Death." *European Romantic Review* 21.2 (2010): 235-49.

Beer, John. "The Paradoxes of Nature in Wordsworth and Coleridge." *The Wordsworth Circle* 40.1 (2009): 4-9.

Duggett, Tom. *Gothic Romanticism: Architecture, Politics, and Literary Form*. Houndmills and New York: Palgrave Macmillan, 2010.

Fosso, Kurt. "The Politics of Genre in Wordsworth's Salisbury Plain." *New Literary History* 30 (1999): 159-177.

Gill, Stephen. "The Philosophic Poet." *The Cambridge Companion to Wordsworth*. Ed. Stephen Gill. Cambridge: CUP, 2003. 142-160.

———. *William Wordsworth: A Life*. Oxford: OUP, 1990.

———. *Wordsworth's Revisitings*. Oxford: OUP, 2011.

Gravil, Richard. *Wordsworth's Bardic Vocation, 1787–1842*. Basingstoke and New York: Palgrave, 2003.

Hartman, Geoffrey. *Wordsworth's Poetry 1787–1814*. New Haven and London: Yale UP, 1977.

Hazlitt, William. *The Selected Writings of William Hazlitt*. Volume 2. *The Round Table. Lectures on the English Poets*. Ed. Duncan Wu. London: Pickering and Chatto, 1998.

Jones, John. *The Egotistical Sublime: A History of Wordsworth's Imagination*. London: Chatto & Windus, 1960.

Legouis, Emile. *William Wordsworth and Annette Vallon*. Hamden, Conn.: Archon,1967.

Modiano, Raimonda. "Recollection and Misrecognition: Coleridge's and Wordsworth's Reading of the Salisbury Plain Poems." *The Wordsworth Circle* 28 (1997): 74-82.

Pope, Alexander. Alexander Pope. The Oxford Authors. Ed. Pat Rogers. Oxford: OUP, 1993.

Potkay, Adam. *Wordsworth's Ethics*. Baltimore: Johns Hopkins UP, 2012.

Reed, Mark L. *Wordsworth: The Chronology of the Early Years 1770-1799*. Cambridge, MA: Harvard UP, 1967.

Roe, Nicholas. *Wordsworth and Coleridge: The Radical Years*.

Oxford: Clarendon, 1988.

Rudy, John G. *Wordsworth and the Zen Mind: The Poetry of Self-Emptying.* Albany: SUNY P, 1996.

Sheats, Paul. *The Making of Wordsworth's Poetry, 1785-1798.* Cambridge: Harvard UP, 1973.

Stevens, Wallace. *Collected Poetry and Prose.* Eds. Frank Kermode and Joan Richardson. New York: Library of America, 1997.

Swann, Karen. "Public Transport: Adventuring on Salisbury Plain." *ELH* 55.4 (1988): 811-34.

Trott, Nicola. "The Coleridge Circle and the 'Answer to Godwin.'" *Review of English Studies* 41 (1990): 212-29.

Ulmer, William A. "William Wordsworth and Philosophical Necessity." *Studies in Philology* 110 (2013): 168-98.

Wiley, Mike. "Wordsworthian dystopia: The spatial play of Salisbury Plain." *Nineteenth-Century Contexts* 21.1 (1999): 89-114.

Wordsworth, William. *The Borderers.* Ed. Robert Osborn. Ithaca: Cornell UP, 1982.

——. *The Letters of William and Dorothy Wordsworth. The Early Years 1787-1805.* ed. Ernest de Selincourt. Second Ed. Rev. Chester L. Shaver. Oxford: Clarendon, 1967.

——. *The Prelude 1799, 1805, 1850.* Eds. Jonathan Wordsworth, M. H. Abrams, Stephen Gill. New York and London: Norton, 1979.

——. *The Salisbury Plain Poems of William Wordsworth.* Ed. Stephen Gill. Ithaca: Cornell UP, 1975.

——. *William Wordsworth: The Major Works.* Ed. Stephen Gill. Oxford: Oxford UP, 1984.

Peter Larkin

Wordsworth's City Retractions

I

What is Wordsworth doing *to* the city as it overwhelms him in the midst of his attempts to recuperate its temporal excess and spatial conglomeration, as such impossible to redistribute, being simultaneously everywhere and nowhere? The poet's joyous relief in quitting the town at the opening of the *Prelude* eventually demands a narrative revision of what is also a resubmission *to* London. He must re-betray himself before he can mark out a retraction from its invasive margins, before he can re-offer the city to its own underlying geophysical 'tract' as not coinciding with its surface mappings. This is not just to re-imagine London satirically or by pastoral contrast but to inscribe on it a topography of its own local impossibilities and subtractive interludes.

By the early 1800's Wordsworth is proleptically reading the city as a total immersion, a metropolis impossible to escape on foot (a commonplace later in the century) to the extent he traces the city's own failure to take its leave according to more singular leavings or retractions of his own. As Raymond Williams knew, the pollution of industrial society is found not only in infected products as everyday objects but in ourselves in relation to them.[1] A linked idea is that of 'metabolic rift', the historically unprecedented rupture of nutrient flows between town and country in which the acceleration of capital outweighs any exchange with a hinterland.[2] The city as a concentrated geospatial accumulation hasn't simply displaced nature

---

1   *Problems in Materialism and Culture* (London: Verso, 1980), 83–4.
2   Jason W. Moore, 'Transcending the Metabolic Rift: a Theory of Crises in the Capitalist–World Ecology', *Journal of Peasant Studies*, 38 (2011), 12.

but becomes the acutest means of representing nature in crisis. What were earlier city/hinterland relations intensify as tensions between town and country, and Wordsworth is one of the first to plot lines of resistance to town and country being reducible to core and periphery.[1] The drama of urbanisation can be seen as literally geological in scale, where humans have become the premier geomorphic agent sculpting the landscape. But cities, precisely as 'smart mountains of accumulation' remain in disequilibrium unable to absorb their own expansive scale.[2] The rule of temporal acceleration and exception itself remains temporary as it contracts its own capacity to experience slow duration or low density. This suggests a paradox to which Wordsworth was alert: human adaptability to the city is ambivalent: resistance to constructed grandeur of scale goes as deep as the impulse towards acceleration and agglomeration. It is not just self-invention which is speculative—so also is retraction across the lineaments of what is irreversible. Wordsworth discovers that a sense of being nowhere has itself to be invented complicitly in order to experience from within the crush of the city.

II

The 'Westminster Bridge' sonnet ponders what a sleeping city can mean—not just as dreaming of its own elsewhere but one that lays bare its own exteriority which seems able (while remaining inert) to re–encounter its interior life:

> This city now doth like a garment wear
> The beauty of the morning; silent, bare
> Ships, towers, domes, theatres, and temples lie
> Open unto the fields, and to the sky;
> All bright and glittering in the smokeless air.
> *Never did sun more beautifully steep*
> *In his first splendor valley, rock, or hill;*
> *Ne'er saw I, never felt, a calm so deep!*
> The river glideth at his own sweet will;

---

1   Jason W. Moore, 'Marx's Ecology and the Environmental History of World Capitalism', *Capitalism, Nature, Socialism*, 12 (2002), 137–9.
2   Mike Davis, *Dead Cities: a Natural History* (New York: New Press, 2002), 361–2

> Dear God! the very houses seem asleep;
> (4–13; My emphasis)[1]

Henri Lefebvre's hypothesis of urban 'rhythmanalysis' identifies 'strong times' and 'weak times' within everyday space–time structures of repetition.[2] It is during a 'weak time' that a city might release a distinctive slipstream picking up its own underlying layout. If Wordsworth's foundational childhood memories can be 'doomed to sleep / Until maturer seasons called them forth' (*Prelude* 1: 622–3), here city buildings sleep off their own post–maturity or are dreaming forward, reposing on an inference for which they do not have a narrative, simply a location that has lapsed functionally. My italicised passage highlights the gesture of retraction: once a pristine moment is recognised as belonging *here* urban primacy paradoxically surrenders its exclusivity and allows the poet to carry away with him a London immersion exceeding overt urban privilege.

For Maurice Merleau–Ponty a lived body is embedded in a pre–objective (which I read as a pre–constructed) world. Historicity itself and the advent of meaning are maintained through periods of unconsciousness like sleep.[3] With Geoffrey Hartman phylogenetic regression can evoke a species of poetic intercession;[4] one might even say an 'inter–ceasing', a holding back which allows a retraction in the midst of or an arrest detecting underlying traces moving through it, but which are usually obliterated by surface movement. The city's openness 'unto the fields, and to the sky' (7) glimpses an obstructive skyline's self–dissolution at the moment in which it catches the light: what is offered is radiant disappearance inhabiting the open rather than being voided by it. The city becomes a pastoral population of itself, its diversity a divestiture counter–ornamented by the beauty of

1   William Wordsworth, *William Wordsworth*, ed. Stephen Gill (Oxford University Press, 1984), 285. Henceforth *WW*.
2   Quoted in C. R. Stokes, 'Sign, Sensation and the Body in Wordsworth's "Residence in London"', *European Romantic Review*, 23 (2012), 208.
3   *Institution and Passivity: Course Notes from the Collège de France*, trans. Leonard Lawler and Heath Massey (Evanston: Northwestern University Press, 2010), 122–32.
4   'Wordsworth and Metapsychology' in *Wordsworth's Poetic Theory*, ed. Alexander Regier and Stefan H. Uhlig (Basingstoke: Palgrave, 2010), 209.

the morning. It is not the built environment but the air which confers bareness, the result of lying open. The rhyme locking 'wear' onto 'bare' converges on a chiasmus whereby a secondary quality now become primary (the capacity to receive a garment) overlaps with a primary as secondary (bareness is not a condition but a pastoral act). Even the problematic epithet 'smokeless' bespeaks an atmosphere productively less than smoke (which normally renders it 'unbare') but which is here suspended as unprivileged within what bears and distributes it. The suspension is itself retracted as the touching sight is recognised as what enabled a disappearance to bring about a resurfacing of the city: sleep needs no witness of smoke.

III

Anne-Lise François warns us that genetically engineered plant defence systems 'never sleep', are always switched on whether beneficial or not.[1] A city that does sleep can still be diverted between strong and weak states of itself. As London stands open it can also figure a marginal repose, retracting in favour of an interstice placed exactly where what is a built environment constitutes an ancillary response in waiting. The city dreams of being enough at home to receive itself but only through a self-abstinence, comprehending its own duration as punctuated by episodes of discontinuous withdrawal outside normative appropriation. Wordsworth's London is an argument between bodies in and beyond the city, implicated in humanity's apparently infinite drive to finitely over-exist. If London seems infinite in the appearances it can adopt, it offers no face to put before such faces, remaining more like a face-off of representation against itself. Only new impossibilities are able to keep time with the pace of urban innovations. Here, face dissolves into face as excess encounter cancels out before a plethora of disparate counters and momentary contingencies, all under high-pressure contiguity. Nonetheless, I read *Prelude* VII in terms of three facial planes: the theatre proscenium, the face-after-face of the crowd and the labelled stare of the blind beggar.

1 ' "O Happy Living Things": Frankenfoods and the Bounds of Wordsworthian Natural Piety', *Diacritics*, 35 (2003), 56.

Mary Jacobus sees the whole of London as an open–air theatre;[1] however, the city's self-performance may be as much framed behind myriad prosceniums, a product of projection and recession but lacking the incidental mutations of obliquity or reserve:

> He was in limbs, in face a Cottage rose
> Just three parts blown; a Cottage Child,but ne'er
> Saw I, by cottage or elsewhere, a Babe
> By Nature's gifts so honored. Upon a Board
> [...................] had this Child been placed,
> And there he sate, environed with a Ring
> Of chance spectators [.......................]
> While oaths, indecent speech, and ribaldry
> Were rife about him as are the songs of birds
> In spring-time after showers.
> (*Prelude* VII: 378–92; *WW*, 478)

The babe on his own board is juxtaposed with the theatre. If his board suggests a retraction from the life of the boards themselves, his cottage–life is half-smothered by spectators whose oaths are 'rife about him as are the songs of birds / In spring–time after showers' (391–2). Though the child is 'as if embalmed / By Nature'(400–01) the simile has already contaminated nature as another rifeness but retracts to what can do more about its multiplicity than can the urban theatre. Nature can acknowledge delay and interruption: if bird–song is another sort of clamour it retrieves another sort of purification 'after showers' (392). Though the theatre never lacks animation and its waves of stimulus are rhythmic enough to be 'tide[s] of pleasure', no interstice is offered between ebb and return by the 'ever-shifting figures of the scene' (*Prelude 1850* VII:412).

Walter Benjamin notes that it is through the crowd that nature exercises its elemental rights over the city.[2] Crowd–nature is a solitary insulation (rather than shared isolation) from within a uniformly generated indeterminacy compared to 'sea–shells that bestud the sandy

---

1   *Romanticism: Writing and Sexual Difference: Essays on The Prelude* (Oxford: Clarendon Press, 1989), 52.
2   *Selected Writings*, trans. Edmund Jephcott et al., 4 vols (Cambridge, Mass: Harvard University Press, 2003), 4:187.

beach, / Or daisies swarming through the fields in June' (587–8).

> Here, there, and everywhere, a weary throng,
> The Comers and the Goers face to face,
> Face after face; the string of dazzling wares,
> Shop after shop,   (*Prelude* VII: 171–4; *WW*, 472)

The uncountable state of the London crowd is over-determined by natural imagery at once contaminated and held in reserve. The natural offers a basis of comparison because it *can* count on itself despite its own myriad manifestations. Comers and goers in the crowd, however, resemble self–cancelling tides lacking any point of turn and so embodying the ideality of the city.[1] A missing 'face to face' inherits the massing of 'face after face' and is commodified in the answering phrase 'Shop after shop'. The moment of retraction both displaces and reinstalls in withdrawal by lending the urban a promordiality it cannot bear: 'but ne'er / Saw I, by cottage or elsewhere, a Babe / By Nature's gifts so honoured' (380–3). The untransposable simultaneity of the crowd imposes not only on faces unfaced but a defacing totality creating a common but unshared nothing that Wordsworth has to co–invent in order to detect. This will provoke a retraction to a nature whose plurality is given and re–offerable: 'the forms / Perennial of the ancient hills' can be such through the 'changeful language of their countenances' which is what 'Gives movement' as something implicitly participative rather than an auto–competitive drive (726–9). Countenance is refaced as offering an exchangeable mutability, retracting from novelty so that form is both what its own changefulness passes by and leaves behind, the deference of one face scaled to the after–length of another face.

Wordsworth's self-parodic overview of Bartholomew Fair upon 'some Showman's platform' (659) is ordained by a stagey muse. An arbitrary construction enables a perspective on arbitrary consumption, and as Simon Jarvis comments, 'it is only from this no–place that the whole view has been delivered' (Jarvis, 143). This is a wholeness Wordsworth simultaneously retracts from in order to lessen the

---

1   For 'ideality' in this context, see Simon Jarvis, *Wordsworth's Philosophic Song* (Cambridge: Cambridge University Press, 2007), 142.

collusive draw of the spectacle itself. He dramatises himself as a weak visionary visible as another competing platform which must pass through (rather than by) the transgressive advertising of an obsolete muse. Pre-*flaneur* as he is, he needs to be bewitched by the Fair because this is how it works: it is the only way he can know it by being drained enough to glimpse how to post-know it, while admitting he can teach it nothing new about its own vortex of self-exhaustion.

The blind beggar can only stand by being propped but has an 'upright face' (612).

> beyond
> The reach of common indications, lost
> Amid the moving pageant, 'twas my chance
> Abruptly to be smitten with the view
> Of a blind Beggar, who, with upright face,
> Stood, propped against a Wall, upon his chest
> Wearing a written paper, to explain
> The story of the Man, and who he was.
> My mind did at this spectacle turn round
> As with the might of waters, and it seemed
> To me that in this Label was a type,
> Or emblem, of the utmost that we know,
> Both of ourselves and of the universe;
> And, on the shape of the unmoving man,
> His fixèd face and sightless eyes, I looked,
> As if admonished from another world.
> (*Prelude* VII: 608–23; *WW*, 483–4)

His handicap means there is no face-to-face but the way the spectacle 'turns' the mind also suspends the repetition of face after face. The labelled 'utmost that we know' interrupts indifferent crowd equivalences with a new mode of exception, an abrupt transition from bustle to stasis, from vacuity to the promise of a hollow interstice that is attentive (though blank) and can be attended to. To learn the city anew may mean a purgative blindness by which any sounding out of city interactions has to be groped towards and cannot be signalled overtly. Here is another asymmetrical encounter which interrupts the work of poetry itself;[1] it is an exception that gestures towards an exemption. The beggar has intercepted the poet's own speculative recreation of urban disorder with a partly submerged but distinct non-order, and not outside the city. The beggar offers a contrary vacuum as usable interstice in the midst or 'eye' of the crowd, an emptiness paradoxically visible above the jostling. The beggar's withdrawn presence is a mysterious non-absence; it is his 'unmoving' quality which is cast up on the surface of the crowd where it is untouchable. His being stranded within the city is a mode of defeat directly feeding Wordsworth's own retractive contra-flow. Here, a stasis can register what gets to be marked down by being passed over as what diverts in retraction the pattern and grain of acceleration itself. The 'might of waters' counter-turns or re-rifles the urban vortex where a levity of self-invention is over-written by a burden of the given showing up through the arrested exception of sensory deprivation. It is this blockage which indicates. Hartman discerns an embodiment of immutability rather than immunity in the blind beggar.[2] Retraction will withdraw immunity for all who enter or inhabit the city (it is too late to do otherwise) but will also explore that latent mutability that allows the city's self–fulfilment to be negotiated in a non-expansive way following a different pattern of the unstable provision that underlies it. If the crowd is too fragmentary to accommodate any stable horizon, the creases of a trampled earth are too singular to be permanently passed over.

IV

In his 'St Paul's' fragment, Wordsworth, guided only by his feet encounters another exceptional city moment:

> Press'd with conflicting thoughts of love and fear,
> I parted from thee, Friend! and took my way
> Through the great City, pacing with an eye
> Down cast, ear sleeping, and feet masterless,

1   See William Galperin, 'Wordsworth's Double–Take', in *Romanticism and the City*, ed. Larry H. Peer (New York: Palgrave, 2011), 36.
2   *Wordsworth's Poetry, 1787–1814* (New Haven: Yale University Press, 1964), 235.

That were sufficient guide unto themselves,
And step by step went pensively. Now, mark!
Not how my trouble was entirely hushed,
(That might not be) but how by sudden gift,
Gift of Imagination's holy power!
My Soul in her uneasiness received
An anchor of stability. It chanced
That, while I thus was pacing, I raised up
My heavy eyes and instantly beheld,
Saw at a glance in that familiar spot
A visionary scene—a length of street
Laid open in its morning quietness,
Deep, hollow, unobstructed, vacant, smooth
And white with winter's purest white, as fair,
As fresh and spotless as he ever sheds
On field or mountain. Moving Form was none,
Save here and there a shadowy Passenger,
Slow, shadowy, silent, dusky, and beyond
And high above this winding length of street,
This noiseless and unpeopled avenue,
Pure, silent, solemn, beautiful, was seen
The huge majestic Temple of St. Paul
In awful sequestration, through a veil,
Through its own sacred veil of falling snow.
(*WW,* 332–3; my emphasis)

Here is granted an auto–recessive city as 'sudden gift' (8) of Imagination. Rather than 'blank confusion' as a type of what the 'mighty City' is in itself, a snow blankness intervenes with the poet himself the 'straggler here and there' (*Prelude* VII: 697). The pristine swarming of snow disperses any other crowd. This, though held in the heart of the city, seems numbered among one of those 'scenes different there are / Full-formed, which take, with small internal help, / Possession of the faculties' (VII: 652–4) which the *Prelude* identifies with 'nature's intermediate hours of rest' or with 'empty streets and sounds / Unfrequent as in deserts' (VII: 634–5). Any city desert will be either blanked out by crowds or by snow, but remains an index of human presence or the gaps within human self–presence, that lack of internal resource which can nonetheless become a gift to the imagination. The unpublished 'St Paul's' fragment is lightly sketched despite its sense of revelation and preserves some spontaneously reoccurring epithets figuring recessive surprise and inauguration. So 'shadowy' via 'silent' finds the obliquity of a 'shadowy Passenger' which further recedes through 'slow' before recapitulating 'shadowy' as 'dusky' (21–2). The adjective 'silent' recedes from its sparse middle ground to alight on St Paul's itself as part of a now 'solemn' train. Such concise, reiterated epithets constitute a sort of mutter of relief before the feeling of snow which relays a renewed matter of topographic relief: here is pure outline, a sort of city scarp with all intermediate circuits blanked out. London is whited out but not dissolved; rather, it is able to mean its own reserved configuration, or occupy a tract or parcel of itself which bear the marks of what might be given to it in addition to any overt design frequencies. This might elicit Gilles Deleuze's 'white spaces of conjunctions' which constitute that 'whatever' or event not reducible to the state of things but which inaugurate a mysteriously 'begun-again-present'.[1] With Wordsworth what is begun again is found out beyond any normative participation and which opens it, not so much to the status of event, as to field. The city has become its own type of weather-system as it distributes snow along 'a length of street / Laid open in its morning quietness' (15–16): what the snow can be to the surface suggests both depth and hollowness. This is not another instance of the trope 'beautiful because dead' that critics have noted, given that the scene, once shrouded against a 'hideously living city'[2] and no longer succumbing to its own norms, summons back images of life or is asleep to its own death in life. As Anne-Lise François urges us, we should learn to relate to 'partial blankness, other than as a deficiency to be filled' (François, 68). 'St Paul's' figures a new surface which is not a further accretive layer but a veil delineating what cannot be sealed off from the earth's crust: all activity sooner or later is interrupted by being laid out anew across such an underlying field, capable of mysterious decompressions.

---

1   Quoted in Ash Amin and Nigel Thrift, *Cities: Re–Imagining the Urban* (Cambridge: Polity, 2002), 46.
2   See John Plotz, *The Crowd: British Literature and Public Politics* (Berkeley: University of California Press, 2000), 32.

V

How comes it that, for the *Prelude*, the ever-changing scenes of a theatricalising city 'Passed not beyond the suburbs of the mind' (VII: 507), a trope that re-centers the moral imagination within a monumental urban fastness? Is urban disorder resisted by an internalised urban core, or has the mind performed its own retraction in favour of a hinterland of the spirit? To pass beyond the suburbs is reversible in terms of what they are trying to emerge *towards*. Wordsworth already knows the city cannot naturalize itself; in fact it problematizes any naturalization outside or anterior to it. Simon Jarvis ponders how the accelerative city-idea's 'illimitable walk' might differ from an 'endless way' of spiritual growth (Jarvis, 148). One answer might be that what is endless retracts before an imposed illimitation so as to offer the city a paradoxical containment against the grain of its own expansive lineaments. The inescapable city is recapitulated as that which admits to be withdrawn *from* across its own dynamically self-enveloping fabric via those spatial tracts that actively neglect their roles within urban logic. Retraction does not so much pacify any central ferment, but is a 'ferment quiet and sublime' which offers the city a 'Canopy / Of shapes' (*Prelude* VIII: 720–23) Nothing can rest on and acknowledge a given context without retraction to what functions like a city canopy, whether it be sleep or snow. For Foucault life's own limit is its capacity for error, whereby the human is never altogether in its place (Amin and Thrift, 80). Thus, the city can be seen as a set of ecologies of ignorance through its gaps, blind spots, anomalies, invisibilities (Amin and Thrift, 92). Wordsworth's city retractions are stimulated by such anomalies but as reserved counter-norms in attendance rather than the sheerly disparate. For Merleau-Ponty what allows itself to be put in question is prior institution, so that what can be engaged is a 'field defined by what has been surpassed' (Merleau-Ponty, 11–12). What is surpassed leaves its own indicative residue as a revisionary horizon rather than inert sediment. The new human dimensions provoked by the sheer scale of London also declare their own unstable after–burn or a wake of retro–innovation across which Wordsworth's city imagination actively retracts. To retract is not a private event but a way of re-tracing the city in terms of a topography of self-exception: how the city henceforth can map not of its own provision but rather a proviso against urban self-sufficiency. What Wordsworth discovers in the city is neither his failure alone nor his future outside it but fresh chiastic ranges between primary and secondary. Arbitrary human self–invention discovers that its own interruptibility is imagining a new primary whereby what is peripheralized as secondary within city space/time becomes a pathway of autonomous retraction, one no longer reducible to either furtive denial or aborted escape.

Tom Clucas

'On these two pillars rested as in air / Our solitude': Wordsworth's use of Plutarch's *Parallel Lives* in *The Excursion*

The death of Thomas Wordsworth on 1 December 1812 stunned his family, especially since it followed so closely upon that of Catherine, who had died on 4 June. At the same time, it led them to reflect with wonder on the character of the child they had just lost. On 27 December, William wrote to Basil Montagu that Thomas 'was a Child of heavenly disposition, meek, simple, innocent unoffending affectionate tender-hearted, passionately fond of knowledge, and ardent in his duty, but in every thing else mild and peacefull.'[1] Dorothy wrote with equal feeling to Catherine Clarkson on 5 January 1813: 'Thomas was the darling of the house, and of everyone who looked at him—he was innocent as a new-born Babe—with a heavenly light on his countenance.' (*Letters*, vol. 3, 61) His character, reminiscent of the child in the 'Immortality Ode', strikes Dorothy as being so remarkable that she finds herself drawn to compare it with those of William and Mary's other children:

> [Dorothy] has great sensibility with liveliness in the extreme which is attended with its frequently accompanying fault, restlessness; and at times unquietness of manners. John and she are opposites—Thomas was between them—he had not the faults of either. (*Letters*, vol. 3, 64)

Dorothy treats Thomas's character as a puzzle, trying to define his

---

1   William Wordsworth and Dorothy Wordsworth, *The Letters of William and Dorothy Wordsworth*, ed. Ernest De Selincourt, rev. Chester L. Shaver, Mary Moorman, and Alan G. Hill, 2nd edn, 8 vols (Oxford: Clarendon Press, 1967–93), vol. 3, 56.

qualities in relation to those of his siblings. Following his death, the Wordsworths seem to have found it helpful to celebrate Thomas's remarkable disposition and to consider how it was formed.

William and Dorothy's tributes to Thomas might be read as rehearsals for his epitaph. Fittingly, for a child who lived 'Six months to six years added', the epitaph that William composed for Thomas's grave was six lines long.[1] It contains two references to his character, echoing Dorothy's claim that he 'was the darling ... of everyone who looked at him' in the line 'A Child whom every eye that look'd on lov'd' (l. 4), and encapsulating his 'heavenly disposition' in the epithet 'by sin unstain'd' (l. 2). By paring down the lists of adjectives which he and Dorothy had originally used to describe his son, William conforms to the principles that he had set out in his 'Essays upon Epitaphs' two years earlier. These 'Essays' are ambivalent on the subject of character. In the first, Wordsworth argues that '[t]he character of a deceased friend or beloved kinsman is not seen, no— nor ought to be seen, otherwise than as a tree through a tender haze or a luminous mist'.[2] He argues that

> minute distinctions in individual character ... will, even when they are true and just, for the most part be grievously out of place; for, as it is probable that few only have explored these intricacies of human nature, so can the tracing of them be interesting only to a few. (*Prose Works*, vol. 2, 59)

On this basis, he rejects Pope's epitaphs, which convey a 'mere character' ('Essay II', *Prose Works*, vol. 2, 77), in favour of John Weever's view that 'an Epitaph was not to be an abstract character of the deceased but an epitomized biography' ('Essay III', *Prose Works*, vol. 2, 89). The character is to be communicated precisely by moving it out of the centre of the focus so that, like the tree in the 'luminous mist', it can be clothed with the imagination.

Wordsworth upheld these convictions when he wrote Thomas's epi-

---

1   William Wordsworth, 'Six months to six years added, He remain'd', in *Shorter Poems, 1807–1820*, ed. Carl H. Ketcham, The Cornell Wordsworth (Ithaca and London: Cornell University Press, 1989), 123.

2   William Wordsworth, 'Essays Upon Epitaphs, I', *The Prose Works of William Wordsworth*, ed. W. J. B. Owen and Jane Worthington Smyser, 3 vols (Oxford: Clarendon Press, 1974), vol. 2, 58.

taph, paring down the description of his character. Yet this left much unsaid, and Wordsworth's redoubled interest in character seems to have found an outlet in his reading. Duncan Wu notes that in 'March 1811' and again 'by May 1814' Wordsworth was reading Sir Thomas North's translation of Plutarch's *Parallel Lives*—the same translation used by Shakespeare.[1] In Plutarch, Wordsworth found a writer who shared his deep-seated interest in character. By pairing up the lives of noble Greeks with those of noble Romans, Plutarch explored the formation of character and the role it plays in shaping people's actions and experiences. After each pair of lives, he wrote a comparison (σύνκρισις or *synkrisis*) in which he compared and contrasted the characters of his Greek and Roman subjects. 'The main purpose of the comparisons,' as Alan Wardman explains, 'is to point out the differences between men of similar achievement and similar virtue'.[2] There is certainly some sense of an *agon* or competition between the paired lives, but this takes place primarily in the reader's mind, as he or she deduces from each pair of examples the extent to which 'true happiness consisteth in the vertue and qualities of the mind'.[3] Plutarch makes the instructional nature of his work clear at the beginning of his 'Life of Alexander', where he states that:

> [M]y intent is not to write Histories, but onely Lives. For the noblest deeds do not always shew mens vertues and vices, but oftentimes a light occasion, a word, or some sport, makes mens natural dispositions and manners appear more plain…. For like as Painters or drawers of Pictures, which make no account of other parts of the body, do take the resemblances of the face and favour of the countenance, in which consisteth the judgement of their manners and disposition: even so they must give us leave

---

1   Duncan Wu, *Wordsworth's Reading 1800–1815* (Cambridge: Cambridge University Press, 1995), 168–9. Wu posits that Wordsworth obtained his copy of the 1676 edition of North's translation of *The Lives of the Noble Grecians and Romans* 'some time between 1808 and 1810'. He suggests that Wordsworth read copies of North's translation in 1804, 1806, 1808, 1811, and 1814, but notes that there was also a copy at Hawkshead Grammar School in 1788.
2   Alan Wardman, *Plutarch's Lives* (London: Elek, 1974), 237.
3   Plutarch, *The Lives of the Noble Grecians and Romans,* trans. James Amiot and Sir Thomas North, revised edn (London: George Sawbridge and Thomas Lee, 1676), 699; Life of Demosthenes, I.1.

to seek out the signs and tokens of the mind onely, and thereby shew the life. (Plutarch, 559; Life of Alexander I.2–3)

Like Wordsworth in the third of his 'Essays upon Epitaphs', Plutarch thinks in terms of an 'epitomized biography', emphasising the 'manifestation of virtue or vice' and the 'revelation of character' that can be gleaned from small details of a person's life. His attempt to make the 'signs of the soul in men' shine through by shifting the focus away from their 'deeds' is not dissimilar from Wordsworth's attempt to reveal the character like a tree through a 'luminous mist'. In this respect, the form of the *Parallel Lives* offers an extension of the epitaphic mode, a chance to explore all of the 'intricacies of human nature' which, according to Wordsworth, had to be left off a monument ('Essay I', *Prose Works*, vol. 2, 59).

The dates when Wordsworth was reading Plutarch correspond to the 'Fifth' and 'Sixth Stage[s]' of his work on *The Excursion*, during which he worked chiefly on Books Three, Six, and Seven.[1] In many ways, the passages which Wordsworth wrote between 'January 3, 1813, and May 1814' can be seen as continued tributes to Catherine and Thomas. Plutarch's influence can perhaps be felt in the Solitary's epitaph to his own two children in Book Three, particularly in the lines 'On these two pillars rested as in air / Our solitude' (III, 606–7), which reflect a wish to put his children's lives in parallel, as Dorothy had done in her letter to Catherine Clarkson. However, it is in the 'epitaphic stories' told by the Pastor in Books Six and Seven that the structure of Plutarch's *Lives* comes to the fore. Sally Bushell has shown the extent to which these narratives are rooted in Wordsworth's 'Essays upon Epitaphs' and in his poem 'The Brothers'. She describes how, in *The Excursion*, Wordsworth develops the epitaphic mode in the direction of the 'oral epitaph', a mode perfectly suited to show the deceased 'through a tender haze or a luminous mist', by creating 'a loving context of recollection which both veils and enhances the figure'.[2] The effect of the Pastor's narra-

---

1   William Wordsworth, *The Excursion*, ed. Sally Bushell, James A. Butler, and Michael C. Jaye with the assistance of David Garcia, The Cornell Wordsworth (Ithaca and London: Cornell University Press, 2007), 427–8.

2   Sally Bushell, *Re-Reading The Excursion: Narrative, Response and the Wordsworthian Dramatic Voice* (Aldershot: Ashgate, 2002), 187.

tives, she argues, is 'cumulative':

> The Pastor articulates the individuals of the churchyard as a multitude of lives which are held together and feed off each other in the mind, like the turf which rolls over them and makes of them one landscape. It is through this 'conglomerate', at times so frustrating to the listener, that the Pastor most clearly asserts the value of the spoken over the epitaph: the heterogeneous mixture of related lives over the engravings of cold stone. (Bushell, 208)

Drawing on this sense of the Pastor's narratives working in unison, I would suggest that Plutarch's *Parallel Lives* served as a further contributory source to their genesis. Like Plutarch, the Pastor pairs up his lives in order to draw implicit and explicit comparisons between them. Wordsworth clarifies this pattern in his 'Summary of Contents' for *The Excursion*, which foregrounds the similarities and differences between pairs of lives. In his summary of Book Six, for example, he describes how 'The lonely Miner, an Instance of Perseverance … leads by contrast to an Example of abused talents, irresolution, and weakness' in the life of 'The Adventurer, or The Prodigal Son' (*The Excursion*, 45). Similarly, the 'Instance of a Marriage Contract broken is contrasted with one of a Widower, evidencing his faithful affection towards his deceased Wife', while in Book Seven an 'Instance of less exalted excellence in a deaf Man' is paired up with the 'Elevated character of a blind Man' (*The Excursion*, 45–6). The effect of these juxtapositions is very much like that of Plutarch's 'comparisons' between lives. Wordsworth's sense that one life can answer another, and that the qualities and faults of one character can best be understood in contrast with its counterpart, can both be likened to Plutarch's method in the *Parallel Lives*.

Wordsworth had, of course, written oral epitaphs before beginning work on *The Excursion*. The stories of Wilfred Armathwaite and The Widower with six daughters had emerged as early as 1801, in MS. B of *Home at Grasmere*. The structure of the *Parallel Lives*, however, was clearly prominent in his mind as he wrote and arranged more stories in 1813. By superimposing this structure of parallels and comparisons onto the churchyard at Grasmere, he created a moral narrative which shows how people's characters shape, and are shaped by, the events in their lives. This is the case, for example, in the lives of the two Clergymen which the Pastor delivers at the beginning of Book Seven. Wordsworth tells us that the first Clergyman, modelled on the Reverend Joseph Sympson, was 'A Priest ... by function' (VII, 112), but that he was equally at home 'in the jolly hall / Of country Squire; or at the statelier board / Of Duke or Earl' (VII, 124–6):

> With these high Comrades he had revelled long,
> Had frolicked many a year; a simple Clerk
> By hopes of coming patronage beguiled
> And vexed, until the weary heart grew sick. (VII, 129–32)

On a small scale, Sympson resembles Cicero, of whom Plutarch writes that 'the great pleasure he took to hear his own praise, and to be over-much given to desire of honour and estimation ... continued with him even to his dying day, and did eftsoons make him swerve from justice' (Plutarch, 713; Life of Cicero, VI.5). By saying this, I do not mean to offer Cicero as a source for the life of Joseph Sympson; rather, I wish to compare Plutarch and Wordsworth's didactic treatment of the lives of two men, one a Roman Orator and one a Grasmere Clergyman, who shared the dream of political greatness. Wordsworth describes how, even in middle age, Sympson's

> harsher passions kept their hold,
> Anger and indignation; still he loved
> The sound of titled names, and talked in glee
> Of long-past banquetings with high-born Friends:
> Then, from those lulling fits of vain delight
> Uproused by recollected injury, railed
> At their false ways disdainfully. (VII, 216–22)

Here, Sympson resembles Cicero when he was banished from Rome by Clodius. Plutarch describes how Cicero 'was always sad, and could not be merry, but cast his eyes still towards ITALY, as passionate Lovers do towards the Women they love: shewing himself faint-hearted, and took this adversity more basely then was looked for in one so well studied and learned as he' (Plutarch, 723; Life of Cicero, XXXIII.4). Sympson's life begins similarly, but then bears out the claim in Gray's 'Elegy' that the humble lives of the villagers 'circumscrib[e]' their 'crimes' as well as their 'virtues'.[1] Whereas Cicero's outspoken love of fame made him enemies and led to his being put to death by Antony for composing the *Philippics*, Sympson lived innocently in Grasmere Vale 'From vice and premature decay preserved' (VII, 319). There is a sense that the flaws in his character bring about his disappointments, but that these disappointments eventually function as a kind of 'apt admonishment', correcting the flaws that caused them.[2]

The Pastor follows Sympson's life with that of a second Clergyman, modelled on Wordsworth's friend Robert Walker. This account is shorter than its counterpart, but it shows Plutarch's principle of comparison at work in *The Excursion*. The Pastor ends his re-telling of Sympson's life by considering how far character 'is but the blind result / Of cordial spirits and vital temperament, / And what to higher powers is justly due' (VII, 321–33). Plutarch pairs his life of Cicero with that of Demosthenes, at the beginning of which he also speculates on the formation of character. '[V]ertue,' he claims, 'like a strong and fruitful plant, can take root, and bring forth in every place, where it is graffed in a good nature, and gentle person, that can patiently away with pains.' (Plutarch, 699; Life of Demosthenes, I.3) The life of Demosthenes bears witness to such patience, as Plutarch describes how Demosthenes lived frugally and laboured at his oratory. Six days after the death of his daughter, Plutarch claims, Demosthenes appeared in public to rally the Athenians after Philip of Macedon's death. He commends this action highly, commenting that 'he did therein act like a man of courage, and worthy to be a Governour of a Common-wealth, rejecting all his troubles, cares, and affections, in respect of the service of his Countrey' (Plutarch, 707; Life of Demosthenes, XXII.4). Much the same may be said of Robert Walker, who, according to the Pastor, demonstrates 'a temper-

---

1   Thomas Gray, 'Elegy Written in a Country Churchyard', *The Poems of Thomas Gray, William Collins, Oliver Goldsmith*, ed. Roger Lonsdale (London: Longmans, 1969), ll. 65–6, 129.

2   William Wordsworth, 'Resolution and Independence', *Poems, in Two Volumes, and Other Poems 1800–1807*, ed. Jared Curtis, The Cornell Wordsworth (Ithaca, New York: Cornell University Press, 1983), l. 119, 1827 variant, 128n.

ance—proof / Against all trials; industry severe / And constant as the motion of the day' (VII, 342–4). In this selflessness, Walker excels Sympson as Demosthenes excelled Cicero. Yet Plutarch is typically even-handed in his comparison of the two orators and concedes that, although Demosthenes showed more temperance, Cicero deserves praise for putting himself through the test of holding public office: 'nothing sheweth a mans nature and condition more ... then when he is in authority, for that bewraieth his humour, and the affections of his mind, and layeth open also all the secret vices in him' (Plutarch, 731; Comparison of Demosthenes and Cicero, III.2).

Ultimately, neither Plutarch nor Wordsworth attempts to favour one life over another. Their aims are both more sympathetic and more subtle. In Book Six, the Pastor promises that 'when / I speak of such among my flock as swerved / Or fell, those only will I single out / Upon whose lapse, or error, something more / Than brotherly forgiveness may attend' (VI, 671–4). Faults are revealed so that the reader may sympathise with the suffering that they cause; virtuous lives are offered by contrast to show that the faults in people's characters can be overcome. The Pastor proceeds to explain that the 'native grandeur of the human Soul' is often exemplified 'no less / In the grey cottage by the murmuring stream / Than the fantastic Conqueror's roving camp, / Or in the factious Senate' (VI, 684–8). By saying this, he hints at the Classical source for the lives that he is narrating. Moreover, he affirms the universality of suffering and reveals the 'common nature' that Wordsworth prioritised over 'individual character' in his 'Essays upon Epitaphs' ('Essay I', *Prose Works*, vol. 2, 59). In the Pastor's stories, Wordsworth bodies out the 'village-Hampden[s]' and 'mute inglorious Milton[s]' of Gray's 'Elegy' (ll. 57–9), as well as providing evidence for Plutarch's belief that 'vertue, like a strong and fruitful plant, can take root, and bring forth in every place' (Plutarch, 699; Life of Demosthenes, I.3).

Earlier in Book Six, the Solitary responds to the paired lives of the Jacobite and the Hanoverian Whig by observing: 'Exchange the Shepherd's frock of native grey / For robes with regal purple tinged; convert / The crook into a sceptre;—give the pomp / Of circumstance, and here the tragic Muse / Shall find apt subjects for her highest art' (VI, 563–7). It is tempting to read these lines as a clue linking the people buried in Grasmere churchyard to the Roman senators who were, in some sense, their counterparts. Whether or not this is true, there are definite similarities between Wordsworth's epitaphic stories and Plutarch's *Parallel Lives*, both in terms of their patterning and in terms of their narrative voice and didactic function. As a final example, we might consider Oswald, the young 'Patriot' whose life the Pastor narrates towards the end of Book Seven. It would be difficult—and perhaps unnecessary—to single out from Plutarch's Greek and Roman generals one whose life most closely resembles that of 'young Oswald, like a Chief / And yet a modest Comrade' (VII, 794–5), who captained a group of ten militiamen during the Napoleonic Wars. Yet Wordsworth affords Oswald's life the same treatment, and the same lofty tone, that Plutarch gives to his noble Greeks and Romans. The Pastor describes how 'The Shepherd's grey to martial scarlet changed' (VII, 786) and how Oswald trained his men like a 'true Patriot' 'with kindling brow' (VII, 826–7). He claims that 'England, the ancient and the free, appeared, / In [Oswald], to stand before my swimming eyes / Unconquerably virtuous and secure' (VII, 876–8). In this respect, Oswald seems to resemble Theseus, the legendary founder-king of Athens, who also came to symbolise his country, so much so that at the Battle of Marathon many Athenians shared a vision in which they 'thought they saw his shadow and image in arms, fighting against the barbarous people' (Plutarch, 14; Life of Theseus, XXXVI.1). When the Pastor finishes his story, the Pedlar feels an 'awful power' descending 'and supporting his pure heart / With patriotic confidence and joy' (VII, 920–3); even the Solitary responds similarly. Like Theseus, Oswald seems capable of uniting the people of Grasmere in a spirit of *synoikismos* (συνοικισμός, or 'dwelling together'). Prompted by the death of Thomas, and his reflections on character, Wordsworth fills Books Six and Seven of *The Excursion* with his own set of parallel lives. I would argue that it was in tribute to Thomas and Catherine that he spent 1813 writing and re-ordering these lives, showing that the characters of Plutarch's noblest Greeks and Romans found their equals in the churchyard among the mountains.

Simon Swift

Wordsworth and Charles Le Brun: Expression, Colour, Sensation

Figure 1 is a reproduction of the painting that Wordsworth records having sought out as he passed through Paris on his way to Orléans in 1791, early on in Book 9 of *The Prelude*.[1] He recalls a whistle-stop tour of some of the key sights of the early Revolution, including the Champ de Mars, the National Assembly and the Jacobins, and the site of the Bastille. But he writes that these 'spots,' as he calls them,

> Seemed less to recompense the traveller's pains,
> Less moved me, gave me less delight, than did
> A single picture merely, hunted out
> Among other sights, the Magdalene of Le Brun,
> A beauty exquisitely wrought—fair face
> And rueful, with its ever-flowing tears.[2]

The painting captures the Magdalene in transition—renouncing worldly goods for a life of retirement and spiritual devotion, as its full title, *Sainte Madeleine Repentante Renonce A' Toutes Les Vanités de La Vie,* discloses. The restless, energetic zig-zagging of her body across the picture plane gives a sense of its subject caught in transformation. Wordsworth's encounter with the painting forms a linchpin for Alan Liu's and Jerome Christensen's influential readings of the relations between painting and history in his verse.[3] Liu understands Wordsworth's response to the painting as a denial of the sublime vio-

---

1   Permission has been sought for reproduction of Figure 1. Other images in this paper are believed to be free of copyrght and will be removed on application.
2   William Wordsworth, *The Prelude* [1805], ed. by M. H. Abrams, Stephen Gill, and Jonathan Wordsworth (New York: Norton, 1979), 9. 75–80. Cited by line in the text.
3   Alan Liu, *Wordsworth: The Sense of History* (Stanford, CA: Stanford University Press, 1989), 366–380; Jerome Christensen, *Romanticism at the End of History* (Baltimore, Md: Johns Hopkins University Press, 2000), 60–73.

Figure 1

lence of the revolution through an appeal to the aesthetics of the picturesque and beautiful. Christensen claims this moment in the poem
as instead evidence of the "postmodern" way in which Wordsworth's

poetry 'invites misreading rather than suffers from it' (Christensen, 65). I would argue that both approaches block attention to the historical life of paintings as singular, material objects, and fail to pay close enough attention to the peculiar fate of the genre of history painting in this period.[1] What I describe here as the "historical life" of a painting can be tracked through the institutional conditions of its survival, that is to say, where, how and if it gets displayed, as well as in any efforts made to restore it. These institutional conditions might also be taken as an index of, or causal factor in, the growth or decline of public interest in a painting. Debates around the different possible techniques for display and restoration of artworks were in fact important subjects of ideological dispute in the revolutionary decade in France, where they registered a highly visible opportunity for the new political power to define its relationship to the past and to shape an emergent public sphere through its management of public access to newly-nationalised treasures. As I'll suggest in what follows, the singular fate of Le Brun's painting is worthy of closer attention for what it can begin to tell us about Wordsworth, painting and history.

I want to suggest that reading the painting in this way might enable a closer understanding of the embodied, sensory appeals to history that Wordsworth makes throughout *The Prelude*.[2] After all, his being "moved" by the Magdalene stands in for, or in some way recompenses him for the feeling of disengagement or estrangement that he experiences at the monumental sites of recent history in Paris in 1791. If new historicism was guilty of making an 'abstract appeal to history'[3] in its effort to track denials of history across Wordsworth's

---

1 For an influential argument about the re-assertion of the hierarchy of the genres in the second half of the Eighteenth Century in France, which sees this as foundational for the modernity of painting rather than simply backward-looking, see Michael Fried, *Absorption and Theatricality: Painting and Beholder in the Age of Diderot* (Berkeley, CA: University of California Press, 1980), 72. The case in Britain is somewhat different, of course: but it is important to note that key theorists such as Reynolds in the *Discourses* continue to mount a defence of history painting over landscape, while the importance of the genre to Wordsworth's self-conception can be glimpsed in the sonnet to Haydon "High is our calling, friend!"

2 For a full discussion of this topic, see Noel Jackson, *Science and Sensation in Romantic Poetry* (Cambridge: Cambridge University Press, 2008), 23–63.

3 Simon Jarvis, "Wordsworth and Idolatry", *Studies in Romanticism* 38 (1999), 24.

poetry, then the recent turn against new historicism has done little, as yet, to redress this. Closer attention to the place of Wordsworth's response to the painting in the web of reflections on history that constitute a deep structure of *The Prelude*, as well as attention to the fate of the painting itself, can offer ways forward.

According to Liu, the conventions of classical history painting's representation of national history, classical myth and scenes from Scripture, and especially moments of violent or agitated transition, were 'arrested,' first in Claude's landscapes and then in the British picturesque that took him as its model (Liu, 55–137). Picturesque and Claudian landscapes sought instead, according to Liu, to represent a new, post-sectarian model of liberal freedom. In France, however, the religious power of history painting remained a key issue of contestation in the revolutionary decade. The plundered art that began to arrive in Paris after 1792, especially the artworks confiscated from the Church, presented the new public authority with a problem. How was it to use the great masters to foster public instruction— the expressed intention for the Louvre when it was opened in 1793, —without re-subjecting the public to the iconography of Catholic fanaticism, and its association with absolute sovereignty? This conflict, as Andrew McLellan has argued, was solved through investing the museum space itself with secularizing tendencies. The mystical power of individual paintings was disarmed by organising those paintings into different schools and chronologies that turned them into objects of art-historical and aesthetic appreciation, intended to contribute to an enlightenment narrative of the historical progress of the arts.[1]

As McLellan claims, influenced by the new taxonomies of the natural sciences, and the rise of historicism, late eighteenth-century museums initiated the now-commonplace practice of isolating works of art, both from each other, and from the social roles and physical contexts that they originally enjoyed, in the service of direct or transparent viewing. This desire for transparency aimed to erase the his-

---

1   Andrew McClellan, *Inventing the Louvre: Art, Politics and the Origins of the Modern Museum in Eighteenth-Century Paris* (Cambridge: Cambridge University Press, 1994), 91–124.

torical life of the picture, partly through newly-developed restoration techniques that sought to return the painting to the condition that it had been in at the time that it left the artist's studio. These restoration techniques were themselves highly contentious and ideologically— loaded in the 1790s, and might even seem to function as metonyms for the revolution itself, since the line between restoring an artwork to its imagined original purity and vandalising it was not always an easy one to draw.

The Magdalene of Le Brun became a victim of just these radi- cally historicizing tendencies: displaced from the Carmelite Convent in 1792, where the painting had been a witness to the September Massacres a little over a year after Wordsworth saw her, she failed to make the grade for inclusion in the Le Brun collection at the Louvre in 1793. Where Le Brun had carefully matched the light represented in the picture with the real flow of light in the chapel of the Convent dedicated to her and where she had hung, the Magdalene was deemed to look colourless in the Grand Gallery and sent to the lesser museum at Versailles. There, encountered as just another picture in a museum, she became a forgotten classic. At the time Wordsworth saw her, the Magdalene was still just about an unmissable highlight of any tour- ist's itinerary in Paris, but her stock was in rapid decline. Today, she remains in storage at the Louvre.[1]

If the Magdalene was a victim of late Enlightenment exhibition practice as it was adopted by the new French republic, she proves that only certain works of art are amenable to the illusion that their historical life can be stripped away in the name of restoring them to their original context. Others, that can't be separated from that life, are left at the roadside (something that the apocryphal story, associ- ated with the painting into the Nineteenth Century, that the model for the Magdalene was a former mistress of Louis XIV, who herself

---

1   'In times gone by, an informed traveller who would have left Paris without having seen Le Brun's *Magdalene* would have appeared as someone ignorant of the arts; today, if the same person dared to compliment himself on having made the trip to Versailles in order to pay the same homage to this picture as it received generally before '89, he would be considered a rather superficial con- noiseur' writes François Lauzan, a keeper at the Musée spéciale, in 1797. Cited in McClellan, 1994, 203–4.

renounced worldly goods for life in the convent, seems to prove).

I think it's possible that Wordsworth's poem explores a mode of counter—history that has to do with the duration and change of particular objects. This can begin to be glimpsed through the poetic trope invoked in *The Prelude*, and that reaches back to Richard Crashaw's own weeping Magdalene, of her ever-flowing tears. But I want to approach this mode of counter—history sideways through three aspects of the painting's duration; first, through the expressive tradition that Le Brun is often taken to stand for; second, through the issue of colour as a mark of duration and/or decay, as well as identity; and then finally through a reading of sense and sensation that will emerge from this thinking about colour.

Expression

It is partly as a theorist of expression that Le Brun was remembered and still influential across the Eighteenth Century, especially for the extraordinary studies of expression in heads that were still used as a copy-book for students, and that had been made to illustrate a con-

ference on general and particular expression that he had given to the French Royal Academy of Painting in 1668. It is not difficult to understand why the public imagination in the Revolutionary decade should be captivated by Le Brun's studies of isolated heads in states of violent contorted passion as in Figure 2. In 1797, a related aspect of Le Brun's work, that had not gone out of fashion, that is, his curious physiognomic drawings comparing personal-

Figure 2

ity types to animals, were on display at the Louvre. While the effort
to classify human personality types through physiognomy took on
a particular urgency as public life became less rigidly defined with
the advent of newly-permissive conditions of visibility in the 1790s,
the French public's fascination with human-animals also emerges
as a key reflection on the traumatic events of 1792–5. Having visited the Louvre exhibition in 1797, Sébastian Mercier recounts in his
Nouveau Tableau de Paris that, after surveying the drawings, visitors
would furtively sidle towards the mirrors at the end of the gallery to

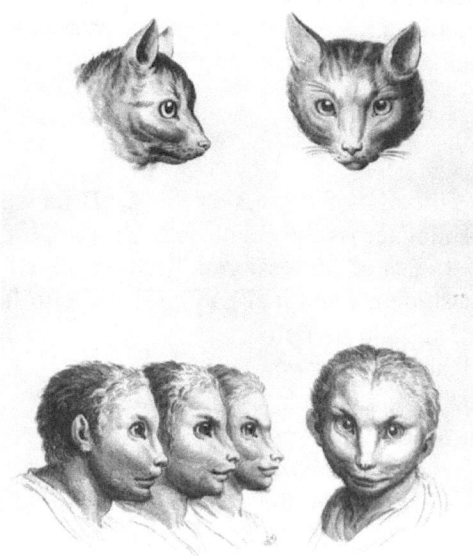

Figure 3

scrutinize their features, and to verify as to whether they resembled
an Indian cock or an eagle, a dromedary or a lion, a monkey or a pig.[1]
The joke is partly one about a new, vulgar public exposed to art, but
the point is also a political one. Mercier recalled that in the context
of recent history, such comparisons seemed valid as Robespierre had

---

1   Sébastien Mercier, *Paris Pendant La Révolution (1789–1798)* vol. 2 (Paris:
1862), 318–318.

resembled a wild cat (fig. 3 shows Le Brun's cat-man) while Marat
had looked like an alarming night-bird (fig. 4 shows Le Brun's man-
owl; a quick glance at David's *Death of Marat* confirms Mercier's
thesis about the birdlike shape of Marat's face).

Figure 4

Le Brun's interest in expression is bound up with his desire to
give history painting the dignity of a liberal art. Through expression,
which relates both to the depiction of passion in the human face, and
the general composition of the picture space, it was hoped that painting, which can only refer to a single moment in time, could capture
something of the dynamic narrative movement of poetry, a movement which renders poetry ripe for employment in the charting of

epic national histories. This association of expression with history painting seems significant for the kinds of history Wordsworth experiences in *the Prelude*. He tells us at the beginning of book 9 that he was drawn to France by a personal wish '[t]o speak the language more familiarly' (9.37), and his linguistic lack gives him a particular view on the atmosphere in Paris. The fact that language is sound rather than fully articulate meaning attunes Wordsworth to mood and sense; in this case the chaotic, hissing fanaticism of the Miltonic swarms of factionists he encounters in the streets. It also cues him to read the expression of faces absorbed in their plots:

> I stared and listened with a stranger's ears
> To hawkers and haranguers, hubbub wild,
> And hissing factionists with ardent eyes,
> In knots, or pairs, or single, ant-like swarms
> Of builders and subverters, every face
> That hope or apprehension could put on—
> Joy, anger, and vexation, in the midst
> Of gaiety and dissolute idleness. (9. 55–62)

The faces whose expressions he reads in fact correspond remarkably well to Le Brun's heads, designed to accompany his conference (fig 5 shows joy, but Le Brun also has heads for hope, apprehension and, as we've seen, anger). If the sounds of Paris are hissing and creaturely, so its faces have the expressive qualities of a LeBrunian history painting.

Colour

While Le Brun's studies of expression remained influential and of general interest into the 1790s in France, his Cartesian theory of expression went out of fashion in the early Eighteenth Century. The rise of Rococo and the cult of sensibility privileged the beautiful and natural over the agitation of violent passions; and even with the turn against the Rococo in the mid-Century, the return to an emphasis on expression in painting and commentary, as Michael Fried has argued, takes place in the context of the absorption and self-forgetting of the

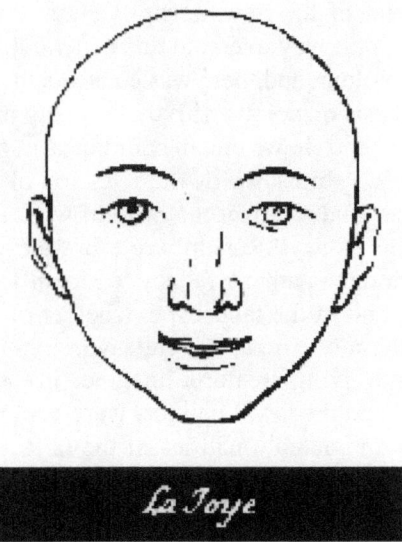

La Joye

Figure 5

subject in particular tasks, where the depiction of specific passions becomes little more than an afterthought (see Fried, 24). Part of this shift also had to do with a new emphasis on the importance of colour in creating painterly effect. While later theorists such as Reynolds in the *Discourses* would still try to defend the narrative form of history painting, and especially the Roman school's use of simple, often discordant colours over the blended, colourful luxuriance of the Venetian school, this was mainly a rearguard effort. Because Le Brun's effort to give painting a literary status had led him to privilege line over colour, and because he consequently often applied paint thinly to the canvas, the colour quality of his own images deteriorated rapidly over the Eighteenth Century, giving rise to frequent puns on his name.

If they departed from the violent contortions of Le Brun's passion heads, Jennifer Montagu argues that Eighteenth Century theorists retained an interest in the other half of expression, general expression, which made a more immediate impact on the spectator, and required less attention and analysis than emotions written on the face.[1] Since the end of the Seventeenth Century, and the work of Roger de Piles, the best way to create this general mood was considered to be through colour, and there was consequently a shift towards a heightened emphasis on colour with the growing mood of sensibility in painting. Montagu shows that in painting as in other arts such as sculpture, there was a shift towards the selection of objects for their expressive qualities, and in effect the birth of what Ruskin was later to call the 'pathetic fallacy.' Ruskin wrote in *Modern Painters* that his reader would find the pathetic fallacy 'eminently characteristic of the modern mind; and in the landscape, whether of literature or art, he will also find the modern painter endeavouring to express something which he, as a living creature, imagines in the lifeless object, while the classical and medieval painters were content with expressing the imaginary and actual qualities of the object itself.'[2] Ruskin has Wordsworth as a key example of what he calls the first order of poets, the man who 'perceives rightly in spite of his feelings, and to whom the primrose is for ever nothing else than itself' (Ruskin, 209). While for Ruskin this capacity has to do with the ability to manage one's emotions in all but the most extreme situations—when it would be psychotic not to break down—it also has to do with the ways in which this emotional restraint gives their own life to objects.

In Book 11 of *The Prelude,* Wordsworth records his having been cured of a tendency, derived from an idolatry of reason in logic and minute analysis, to substitute a perception of general expression for a deeper communion with nature: he records that he had been, in the early 1790s, 'Bent overmuch on superficial things, / Pampering myself with meagre novelties / Of colour and proportion, to the moods / Of Nature, and the spirit of the place, / Less sensible' (11. 159—63). His attunement to the deeper moods of nature enables a sensory encounter with particulars that resist the despotic eye's effort to classify them as parts of an aesthetic effect or a landscape, and to enter into a comparison of scene with scene. In place, he offers his

---

1   Jennifer Montagu, *The Expression of the Passions: The Origin of Charles Le Brun's "Conférence sur l'Expression Générale et Particulière* (New Haven, CT and London: Yale University Press, 1994), 85–100.
2   John Ruskin, *Modern Painters,* in *The Works of John Ruskin, vol. 5,* ed. E. T. Cook and Alexander Wedderburn (London: George Allen, 1904), 221.

lovely homage to his own youthful and Mary Hutchinson's uncorrupted capacity just to receive from nature, which leads to a kind of higher converse with things. Such a converse with things – with the thingly pitcher on the head of the girl ascending a hill in the first spot of time that follows on from this passage, or the garments vexed and tossed by the strong wind, refuses general expression, a mannered aesthetics, in favour of the mood given out by things themselves. It invests in the world of the spontaneous life in things, a world that would need colours and words unknown to man to picture its visionary dreariness.

Sensation

> Colorfulness does not stimulate the animal senses because the child's uncorrupted imaginative activity springs from the soul [...] The order of art is paradisiacal because there is no thought of the dissolution of boundaries—from excitement—in the object of experience. Instead the world is full of color in a state of identity, innocence, and harmony.[1]

Benjamin argues that colour is not a deceptive layer thrown over discrete objects, but rather provides contours that fashion boundaries while giving individual objects a nuanced relation to the world. In place of the Kantian forms of intuition. space and time, that formally determine our experience and downgrade colour to the categories of objective and subjective sense, he imagines a different life in the world, where parts give and receive from an overall complexity. For a Wordsworthian equivalent of this different texture of reality, we could turn to the cave of Yordas in Book 8 of *The Prelude,* that describes the experience of moving through an overwhelming, spectral obscurity into a lifeless, written clarity before waiting for the move back into a kind of moving, living obscurity and complexity of folds. This latter movement is of 'a senseless mass,' that 'In its projections, wrinkles, cavities, / Through all its surface, with all colours

---

1   Walter Benjamin, "A Child's View of Color," in *Walter Benjamin: Selected Writings 1913-1926,* ed. Marcus Bullock and Michael W. Jennings (Cambridge, MA and London: Belknap, 1996), 51.

streaming,/ Like a magician's airy pageant, parts,/ Unites, embodying everywhere some pressure/ Or image, recognised or new, some type/ Or picture of the world' (8. 731–7). This projection offers us a picture of the world, not a world picture: it is not a delusive metaphysics that asks us to act suspiciously towards what it defines as unifying layers of sense that are painted onto a world of discretely defined particulars. This projection can then imagine boundaries as the site of paradisiacal fulfilment, rather than the trauma of an original separation.

Sense in Wordsworth, in fact, is about duration, or perhaps better movement in duration. When he records his complex attraction to a history of *longue durée* just after the Cave of Yordas episode, he writes that both national history and local, familiar, 'extrinsic' history had never delighted him; instead he searches for 'a sense / Of what had been done, and suffered here / Through ages, and was doing, suffering still' (8. 781–3). Sense is, rather than a handmaid to reason, the possibility of our contact with duration, with what goes on—like the Magdalene's ever-flowing tears. Sensation can offer pictures of unity in multitude, as in Wordsworth's record at the end of Book 8 of 'One sense for moral judgments, as one eye/ For the sun's light' (8. 830–1). Consequently, he can offer a post-lapsarian, but also heliotropic image that can stand for a different possible aesthetic account of sense in his recollection of an 'artificer,' who has just left off work and sits on the corner-stone of a low-wall that fenced in the green plot of an open square in London, where he is seen eyeing with unutterable love his sickly babe—'as if he were afraid both of the sun/ And of the air which he had come to seek' (8. 857–9). Expression is this double-edge: dead passion, but also living joy, a sensation of history found in particulars rather than a sensational history, just as the sun can both bleach away the colour of particulars and bring them to light.

Rowan Boyson

Wordsworth's Anosmia: pleasure, scent and the later poetry[1]

'Devotional Incitements'

"Not to the earth confined,
Ascend to heaven."

WHERE will they stop, those breathing Powers,
The Spirits of the new-born flowers?
They wander with the breeze, they wind
Where'er the streams a passage find;
Up from their native ground they rise
In mute aërial harmonies;
From humble violet modest thyme
Exhaled, the essential odours climb,
As if no space below the sky
Their subtle flight could satisfy: [10]
Heaven will not tax our thoughts with pride
If like ambition be *their* guide.[2]

In this paper I wish to explore Wordsworth's late poem 'Devotional Incitements' in relation to the theme of scent in the poet's work. One incentive to do so is the odd biographical anecdote of Wordsworth's anosmia: that is to say, his lack of a sense of smell. Whilst, as far as

---

1 A longer version of this paper, alongside essays by Emma Mason, Adela Pinch, Mark Lussier, Leslie Brisman, Crystal Lake, Giuliana Ferreccio, Donald. J. Moores, Rhian Williams and Alex Benchimol, and Geoffrey Hartman, is forthcoming in early 2014 in 'New perspectives on William Wordsworth', a special issue of *La Questione Romantica* edited by Emma Mason and Elena Spandri.
2 William Wordsworth, 'Devotional Incitements', in *Last poems, 1821-1850*, ed. by Jared Curtis, (Cornell, Ithaca: Cornell University Press, 1999), p.226.

I am aware, Wordsworth never commented on this directly, several contemporary sources attest to this fact, sources which I will discuss at the end of this paper. Despite this perceptual deficiency, scent references abound in Wordsworth's late verse, and my purpose is to use this potential paradox to think about various ways of approaching the senses in literature and criticism. This paper is a small window onto my larger project investigating philosophical, scientific and literary representations of smell in the long eighteenth century. One of the questions that this project has raised for me, and which I think is of particular interest to Wordsworthians, is the critical moralization of a language of the senses. Since the twentieth century, 'sensual' has undergone a full moral shift, so that to 'deny the senses' is bad and to 'celebrate' them is good. In recent years, Wordsworth was criticized for denying the senses, and critics and biographers including Denise Gigante and Hunter Davies went so far as to suggest that this lack of sensuousness might be attributed to his real lack of a sense of smell.[1] Other critics, including Geoffrey Hartman, Kerry McSweeney, Noel Jackson and most recently Adam Potkay, have articulated and defended Wordsworth's engagement with the senses.[2] But all these viewpoints may be critically enriched with a longer history of the concepts of sensuality and sensuousness.

'Sensual' was once a derogatory descriptor, indicating gratification

---

1   Denise Gigante, *Taste: A Literary History* (New Haven, Connecticut, Yale University Press, 2005), p.69. Hunter Davies, *William Wordsworth: A Biography* (London: Weidenfeld & Nicholson, 1980), p.320. Consider also the gentle *LRB* spat between Jonathan Wordsworth and Marilyn Butler in relation to the publication of the 1810 correspondence of William and Mary, which turned on whether Shelley's description of Wordsworth as a 'solemn and unsexual man' was fairly grounded in the poet's life or in his verse. 'Letters', *LRB* 3:21, 19 November 1981, *LRB*, 4:1, 21 January 1982.

2   Geoffrey Hartman, *The Unremarkable Wordsworth* (Minneapolis: University of Minnesota Press, 1987), p.24; Kerry McSweeney, *The Language of the Senses: Sensory-Perceptual Dynamics in Wordsworth, Coleridge, Thoreau, Whitman, and Dickinson* (Liverpool, Liverpool University Press, 1998), p.52; Noel Jackson, *Science and Sensation in British Romantic Poetry* (Cambridge, Cambridge University Press, 2008), pp.70-91; Adam Potkay, 'Ear and Eye: Counteracting Senses in Loco-descriptive Poetry', *The Blackwell Companion to Romantic Poetry*, ed. by Charles Mahoney (London: Blackwell, 2011), p.28. Adam Potkay, *Wordsworth's Ethics* (Baltimore: Johns Hopkins University Press, 2012), p.14.

of the senses often implicitly sexual, an adjective that Milton carefully avoided by inventing the word 'sensuous'.[1] Poetry, he wrote in *Of Education* (1644) is more 'simple, sensuous and passionate' than logic and metaphysics. Coleridge picked this term up again in his *Principles of Genial Criticism* of 1814: 'to express in one word what belongs to the senses, or the recipient and more passive faculty of the soul, I have reintroduced the word *sensuous*, used, among many others of our elder writers, by Milton'.[2] In a footnote to his famous review of Tennyson's *Poems, Chiefly Lyrical*, Arthur Hallam in turn offered as an alternative to 'sensitive' (in the context of Sensitive, Reflective and Passionate poetic emotion) the word 'sensuous', noting that it was 'a word in use amongst our elder divines, and revived by a few bold writers in our own time'.[3] The word then went on to have a highly successful critical career in the nineteenth century: a Google ngram reveals how the word 'sensuous' actually overtook 'sensual' in terms of number of uses in published books in the third quarter of the nineteenth century.[4] In modern English, 'sensuous' tends to denote an aesthetic (rather than a sexual) evocation of the senses, especially those of touch, taste and smell, particularly as against the traditionally privileged sense of sight, and as a style of writing it is often now taken to be a positive or celebratory end in itself.

That sensuousness and sensuality were starting to become significant critical terms in the early 1830s is a useful starting point for considering Wordsworth's 'Devotional Incitements'. The version published in *Yarrow Revisited* in 1835 doubled the length of the first

---

1   "sensuous, adj.". OED Online. September 2013. Oxford University Press. 14 November 2013 <http://www.oed.com/view/Entry/176027?redirectedFrom=sensuous>.

2   'Essays on the Principles of Genial Criticism', in *The Collected Works of Samuel Taylor Coleridge: Shorter Works and Fragments*, ed. by H. J. Jackson and J. R. de J. Jackson, 2 vols (London: Princeton University Press, 1995), II, 350-81, p.

3   Arthur Hallam, "On Some of the Characteristics of Modern Poetry, and on the Lyrical Poems of Alfred Tennyson" (unsigned), *Englishman's Magazine*, I:5, August 1831, 616-628, p.620. http://0-search.proquest.com.catalogue.ulrls.lon.ac.uk/docview/4384993?accountid=14565. Accessed 14 November 2013.

4   I explored this word history in my paper 'The Invention of Sensuousness', delivered at the conference 'Romanticism at the *fin-de-siècle*', Trinity College, Oxford, June 2013.

1832 draft, drawing much more attention to the theme of scent. The earlier version contrasted the stern summons to worship of institutional religion versus the softer incitements offered by the church of Nature, including a line about 'flowerbreathed incense'. Comparisons between incense and plant scents, and scent and religious feeling, had earlier appeared in a few of the *Ecclesiastical Sonnets* of 1822. In one sonnet, Wordsworth quoted the phrase 'incense-breathing morn', which comes from Gray's 'Elegy', and which, as the Cornell editors note, probably itself draws from *Paradise Lost* Book IX: 'humid Flours, that breathd / Thir morning Incense'. So in Wordsworth's earlier religious poetry scent was a useful metaphor for divine communication and for the cognitive work of the senses, as well as evoking his literary precursors. The revised version of 'Devotional Incitements' further asserts the significance of the idea of sensuous communication through the air with that opening epigraph (slightly abbreviated) from *Paradise Lost*: 'Not to the earth confined / Ascend to heaven.' In Milton's poem, Eve is recalling to Adam her dream of Satan's voice, telling her to taste the fruit of knowledge (a fruit with a 'pleasant savoury smell'), so that she will be

> [...] henceforth among the Gods
> Thyself a goddess, not to Earth confined,
> But sometimes in the Air, as we; sometimes,
> Ascend to Heaven [...][1]

Replanted at the opening of Wordsworth's poem, these hubristic lines get an entirely new context as a broader account of scent. Wordsworth personifies scents as wilful, unstoppable emanations from baby flowers, as climbing 'essential odours'. This is a playful and strange reworking of Milton, in that Wordsworth restores Satan's tempting words to a claim that we can rightfully ascend to heaven if our thoughts climb like floral scent. The language also has a natural-philosophical, Lucretian tone: the odours are 'subtle' (like the subtil ether of the previous century) and travel in molecular streams in the breeze. On the other hand, unlike for instance Shelley's synaesthetic

---

1   John Milton, *Paradise Lost*, V, ll.77-80, in *The Portable Milton*, ed. by Douglas Bush (London: Penguin / Viking Press, 1977), p.344.

treatment of scent in which scents *are* sounds, the use of synaes-
thesia (to use an anachronistic term for Wordsworth) is undecided:
'violet' evokes colour as quickly as smell; and scents are only 'mute'
harmonies.

Incense seems to be a particular interest of Wordsworth both here
and in other late poems, partly because of his late poetry's rather historical, dialectical treatment of religion as a whole. Incense itself has
a vexed and fascinating history, sketched wittily by E.G. Cuthbert
F. Atchley in a long 1909 book, which was produced in response
to fraught turn-of-the-century arguments within the Anglican church
as Ritualism gained ground.[1] In ancient pagan and Jewish religion,
incense was supplement, in that Derridean sense, to sacrifice, and so
it was used as a test against early Christians: suspected Christians had
to agree to burn a small piece of incense before a statue of a pagan
deity to avoid martyrdom. Incense seems to have been accepted
into Christian worship from at least the tenth century, for driving
away demons, expelling diseases and restoring health, and was used
for different purposes thereafter by both the Catholic and Anglican
churches. However, it periodically ignited controversies, including with respect to the censing of *images*. Whilst the 1549 Book of
Common Prayer made no specific comments on incense, Edward
VI's 1547 Injunctions had demanded the destruction of images that
were 'abused with pilgrimage or offering of anything made there-
unto, or shall be hereafter censed unto'.[2]

In this context Wordsworth's account of incense as concealing and
revealing the religious paintings – 'curls in clouds / Around angelic
Forms' (ll. 32-37) - evokes questions about the place of sensual ritual
that were very much current in the culture. As Wordsworth explained
in his Advertisement to the *Ecclesiastical Sketches*, he was preoccu-
pied with Catholic Emancipation in the early 1820s.[3] The later 1820s
and early 1830s were times of urgent debate in Anglicanism, not least

---

1   E. G. C. F. Atchley, *A history of the use of incense in Divine worship* (London:
     Longmans, 1909).
2   *Documents of the English Reformation 1526–1701*, ed. by Gerald Bray
     (Cambridge: James Clarke & Co, 1994), p.249.
3   William Wordsworth, *Sonnet series and itinerary poems, 1820–1845*, ed. by
     Geoffrey Jackson (Cornell, Ithaca: Cornell University Press, 2004), p.130.

with the birth of the Oxford Movement, which as Stephen Prickett argued some decades ago, was itself influenced by Wordsworth and Coleridge.[1] In the context of these debates, Wordsworth's friend and patron, the sugar-plantation-heir John Kenyon had published in 1833 a long poem in heroic couplets entitled 'A Rhymed Plea for Tolerance', which offers a mild-mannered support to all forms of institutional religion. In a letter of December that year, Wordsworth complimented him on his line, 'And incense breathes at once thro' sense and soul', highlighting the similarity with his own discussion of incense in 'Devotional Incitements'.[2] As I have mentioned, the revisions he made to 'Devotional Incitements' further emphasized scent, especially in those opening two stanzas.

Those stanzas describe the abundantly rich natural scents and sounds that Nature emits on a May morning: 'With bounty more and more enlarged, / Till the whole air is overcharged' (ll. 21-22). This theme of generous excess and wastage resonates with earlier works like *Home at Grasmere* and 'Stray Pleasures', and is one that Wordsworth picks up again in contrasting the sound and scent produced by church choir and censer (line 43, 44): sensory emanations that are, as the poem somewhat grudgingly puts it, 'not wasted' nor 'wholly lost', on the otherwise indifferent city that weaves around the church. This ambiguous acceptance of the power of institutional incitements turns harsher in the next stanza describing the fate of a religion of 'forms':

> Alas! the sanctities combined
> By art to unsensualise the mind,
> Decay and languish; or, as creeds
> And humours change, are spurned like weeds:
> The priests are from their altars thrust;
> The temples levelled with the dust;
> And solemn rites and awful forms
> Founder amid fanatic storms. (ll.46-53)

---

1   Stephen Prickett, *Romanticism and religion: the tradition of Coleridge and Wordsworth in the Victorian Church* (Cambridge: Cambridge University Press, 1976).
2   *Last poems, 1821–1850*, p.454.

'Unsensualise' is an unusual verb, one that Wordsworth probably borrowed from Coleridge, who used the term positively in his poem 'The Destiny of Nations': 'Fancy is the power, / That first unsensualizes the dark mind, / Giving it new delights' (ll.80-82).[1] But where Coleridge's poem celebrates emancipation from 'the present impulse' (l.86) Wordsworth's is softer in its contrasts, comparing different modes of sensual persuasion rather than decrying sensuality altogether. Whilst ultimately the poem argues that flowers, birds and mists offer a more durable and more accessible encouragement to worship God than 'pomp of sacrifice' and 'solemn Rites', the trope of scent-as-spirituality suggests a continuity between historic forms of worship, and between natural and religious pleasures of sound, art and scent. The church of nature is

> Where flower-breathed incense to the skies
> Is wafted in mute harmonies;
> And ground fresh-cloven by the plough
> Is fragrant with a humbler vow (ll.60-64)

The ancient idea of scent as mode of communion with God was brilliantly analysed in Susan Harvey Ashbrook's *Scenting Salvation*. She describes apocryphal books of the Bible in which Adam pleads to be allowed to take spice seeds from Eden in order to be able to communicate with God from afar.[2] In the final lines Wordsworth emphasizes the role of pleasure and rest beyond work routines and 'bread alone', 'a Sabbath of the heart', which ties back to the earlier idea of the natural generosity of nature. What I still find most interesting about the poem however is the playful provocative and frankly odd opening, 'Where will they stop, those breathing Powers', which animates scent and rather brilliantly evokes the pleasant chaos and urgency of vivid smell perception.

Does Wordsworth's interest in scent look different in light of his apparent anosmia? And if, as I would argue, scent references emerge

---

1   *Poetical Works I*, The *Collected Works of Samuel Taylor Coleridge*, ed. J. C. C. Mays (Princeton, N.J., Princeton University Press, 2001), p.285.

2   Susan Ashbrook Harvey, *Scenting Salvation: Ancient Christianity and the Olfactory Imagination* (Berkeley, Los Angeles: University of California Press, 2006).

more frequently in the later poems than in the earlier part of his writing career, how do we account for this? One might begin with a general answer to that second question by saying that his engagement with current religious debates and church history in *Ecclesiastical Sketches* and elsewhere brings the theme of incense directly into his work. Nonetheless, other scent references, which I cannot enumerate here, encompass flowers and living lawns.[1] Felicia Hemans' poetry is an important influence in this regard; her 'feminine' poetics of flowers and spirituality seems to seep into Wordsworth's 1830s writing in unacknowledged ways. In particular, her terrific poem 'Nightblowing flowers' may well have informed that animation of scent we see in 'Devotional Incitements'.

> Call back your odours, lonely flowers,
>   From the night-wind call them back,
> And fold your leaves till the laughing hours
>   Come forth on the sunbeam's track![2]

The animation of flowers is also a key theme of Shelley's, especially in 'The Sensitive-Plant' about which I have written elsewhere.[3] So what I want to stress is that Wordsworth's language of scent is intertextual and theological, and unrelated to his actual perceptual abilities. It is a kind of borrowed language, but then again, is not all language, and perhaps especially olfactory language, borrowed? Christopher Wordsworth's 1851 *Memoirs* of the poet included William's note on the scent of the Italian broom, for his poem 'Musings in Aquapendente' (1837). Christopher added this comment:

> With regard to *fragrance*, Mr. Wordsworth spoke from the testimony of *others:* he himself had *no sense of smell*. The single instance of his enjoying such a perception, which is recorded

---

1   On Wordsworth's 'This Lawn, A Carpet All Alive', see Timothy Morton, 'Wordsworth Digs the Lawn', *European Romantic Review*, 15:2 (2004), 317-327.
2   Felicia Hemans, *Selected poems, letters, reception materials*, ed. by Susan J. Wolfson (Princeton, New Jersey: Princeton University Press, 2000), p.439. I am indebted to Jeffrey Robinson for pointing me to 'Night-Blowing Flowers'.
3   Rowan Boyson, 'Shelley's Republic of Odours: aesthetic and political dimensions of scent in "The Sensitive-Plant"', *Keats-Shelley Review*, 27: 2, September 2013, 105–20.

of him in Southey's life, was, in fact, imaginary. The incident occurred at Racedown, when he was walking with Miss H - , who coming suddenly upon a parterre of sweet flowers, expressed her pleasure at his fragrance, - a pleasure which he caught from her lips, and then fancied to be her own.[1]

This insistence that Wordsworth *never* smelled does not exactly diminish the curiosity of the anecdote, for what, in ordinary experience, is the difference between suddenly experiencing the 'real' heady pleasure of blooming stocks and merely 'imagining' that pleasure, as if through a fanciful contagion? The occasional hesitance of our own cognition of smell is something well attested to by patients suffering long-term anosmia, where scents may randomly and doubtfully present to consciousness.[2] Indeed, smell is a particularly cognitive and reflective kind of experience, and presents a notorious challenge to language, depending above all on simile: something smells LIKE... thyme, or parma violets. Scent, being, as Isobel Armstrong stresses, both 'highly physical and invisible', is particularly meta-poetic; Hegel made an analogy between scent and metre in his Lectures on Aesthetics, calling metre poetry's 'one and only sensuous fragrance'.[3]

In a letter of 1822 Southey gave a fuller account of the highly curious scented reverie that Wordsworth supposedly experienced:

> Just by the orchard gate was a fine barberry-bush; and that peculiar odor of its blossoms, which is supposed to injure the wheat within its reach, is still fresh in my remembrance. Wordsworth has no sense of smell. Once, and once only in his life, the dormant power awakened; it was by a bed of stocks in full bloom, at a house which he inhabited in Dorsetshire, some five-and-twenty years ago; and he says it was like a vision of Paradise to him;

1   Christopher Wordsworth, Memoirs of William Wordsworth, 2 vols., (London: Edward Moxon, 1851), I, 322.

2   Molly Birnbaum, Season to Taste: How I Lost My Sense of Smell and Found My Way (London: Portobello, 2011).

3   Isobel Armstrong, 'Hegel: The Time of Rhythm, the Time of Rhyme', Thinking Verse, 1 (2011), 124–36 (p. 127); G. W. F. Hegel, Aesthetics. Lectures on Fine Art, trans. by T. M. Knox, 2 vols (Oxford: Oxford University Press, 1975), II, p. 1011.

but it lasted only a few minutes, and the faculty has continued torpid from that time. The fact is remarkable in itself, and would be worthy of remark, even if it did not relate to a man of whom posterity will desire to know all that can be remembered. He has often expressed to me his regret for this privation. I, on the contrary, possess the sense in such acuteness, that I can remember an odor and call up the ghost of one that is departed. But I must return to the barberry-bush.[1]

Southey's prolepsis may suggest the fulfilment of Wordsworth's own claim for the importance of the poet's own 'organic sensibility' in the 'Preface' to the *Lyrical Ballads*. In any case, Southey's curious sympathy about Wordsworth's anosmia seems a better model than the comic derision of later commentators when they attack the poet for a lack of sensuality: a lack sometimes seen now as a quasi-ethical failing. But his self-consciousness about comparing their two abilities also points to something historically interesting. The *OED* gives 1811 as the first use of 'Anosmia', in Robert Hooper's medical dictionary, though the Latin term appeared regularly in the great nosologies (disease classifications) of the mid-eighteenth century.[2] It had certainly been identified much earlier by the tenth-century physician Haly Abbas and the seventeenth century German physician Daniel Sennert. But anosmia, and the sense of smell in general, began receiving a great deal more attention from the 1810s and 20s. For instance, the chemist Wiliam Prout published new research showing the link between smell and taste in 1812.[3] Early nineteenth-century French publications on smell made new arguments about the link between 'savage' life and sensual acuity: the nose thus began to be seen as a source of aesthetic refinement that paradoxically remained undeveloped in civilized man.[4] So the simple point I would like to make is

---

1   'Recollections of the Early Life of Robert Southey, Esq., L.L.D., Written by Himself', in *The Life and Correspondence of Robert Southey* (London: Longmans, 1849-50), p.33.
2   'Anosmia, n.'. *OED* Online. September 2013. Oxford University Press. 15 November 2013 <http://www.oed.com/view/Entry/8100?redirectedFrom=anosmia>.
3   William Prout, 'Observations on the Sensations of Taste and Smell', *The Medical and Physical Journal*, 28 (1812), 457-461.
4   See for instance, Hippolyte Cloquet, *Osphrésiologie, ou Traité des odeurs, du*

that the biographical attention paid to Wordsworth's own nose by his contemporaries might echo the attention paid to smell in other discourses at the same time, and that the whole discussion already carried odd value judgments about differences in human organic sensibility. As sensory disabilities go, anosmia is undoubtedly a minor one, but it is still instructive in terms of, as Sharon Snyder has expressed it, 'the necessity of assessing, for an aesthetic or cultural purpose, the implications of disability as critical insight'.[1] Smell, the senses, and sensuousness have historical and aesthetic dimensions as multi-faceted as their real experience.

sens et des organes de l'olfaction (Paris: Libraire Mequignon-Marvis, 1821).

1   Sharon L. Snyder, 'Infinities of Forms: Disability Figures in Artistic Traditions' in *Disability Studies: Enabling the Humanities*, eds. Sharon Snyder, Brenda Jo Brueggemann, and Rosemarie Garland Thomson (New York: MLA, 2002), p.178.

Daniel Robinson

'Unrememberable Being': Wordsworth Writing about Writing about Memory

We assume that life *produces* the autobiography as an act produces its consequences, but can we not suggest, with equal justice, that the autobiographical project may itself produce and determine the life and that whatever the writer *does* is in fact governed by the technical demands of self-portraiture and thus determined, in all its aspects, by the resources of his medium?

—Paul de Man[1]

In this paper, I want to examine some of the earliest writing Wordsworth did for *The Prelude*: the fragments in the Goslar notebook from the winter of 1798 and 1799, drafting that he revised for the two-part *Prelude* and that some editors have attempted to make coherent. Jonathan Wordsworth even composed a heavily edited version from the fragments that he calls 'Was It For This', his '1798 *Prelude*'.[2] By situating the Goslar fragments within the larger project of *The Prelude*, I want to consider the possibility that editorial interventions have obscured an important concern that is, among the earliest drafts of *The Prelude*, peculiar to the Goslar notebook, although evident elsewhere in Wordsworth's work—that is, the veracity of one's memories and the unavoidable embellishing of them for adaptation as literary art. At the heart of this concern is Wordsworth's larger attempt to fashion a poetic self by reaching back to, and reshaping, the past. In their attempts to render these fragments coherent, Wordsworth's editors may be at odds with the poet's very purpose: to work out how to write about

---

1 'Autobiography as De-facement', *MLN*, 94 (1979), 919–30 (p. 920).
2 'Was It For This', *The Prelude: The Four Texts (1798, 1799, 1805, 1850)*, ed. Jonathan Wordsworth (London: Penguin, 1995), pp. 3–7.

something that is not always coherent, namely memory, as part of shaping something that works at a semblance of coherence, namely a poetic self.

In the Goslar notebook, Wordsworth is particularly concerned with *un*-remembering. In one fragment he is working out a similar notion of 'unremembered pleasure' that he already had defined in 'Lines Written a Few Miles above Tintern Abbey'. Here, however, Wordsworth is writing about writing. More specifically, he is writing about *writing about* memories. These are the 'things' already 'created'—they already exist. Writing them down is the act of 'creating not but as it may / disturbing things created'.[1] This act is comparable to a film adaptation of a literary work: Wordsworth originary text is his memory; the poem is his adaptation of that text into a different medium in an attempt to construct—if not a definitive—a delineated self as a new, discrete work. Moreover, in the Goslar notebook, Wordsworth is working backwards in space and thinking backwards in time. As these new poems written in Goslar show, this association involves more a reckoning of one's debts and other costs than of 'abundant recompense'. The earliest writing for *The Prelude* shows Wordsworth taking account of what he owes, of what he has lost, and of what means he has of paying for it all.

That winter the two Wordsworth siblings even shared a notebook because writing was literally too expensive for them due to the cost of paper. Dorothy filled the first several pages with an account of their journey and notes on German grammar. Starting from the opposite end of the notebook, Wordsworth wrote dozens of lines of poetry recto to verso instead of the other way around. The proper order of this scribbling is discernible because he repurposed much of it later for various drafts of what would become *The Prelude*; in fact, Wordsworth preserved some phrases and lines intact throughout the decades of revision to come. Itself a backwards document, the notebook survives as a synecdochic emblem of the process of writing *The Prelude*. And the fact that it contains Wordsworth's writing literally and materially inter-

---

1   MS. JJ, *The Prelude, 1798–1799*, ed. Stephen Parrish (Ithaca: Cornell University Press, 1977), p. 117. Subsequent citations of the Goslar notebook are to this edition.

twined with his sister's makes it perhaps even more so.

Since the composition of the poem set at least three miles north of Tintern Abbey just a few months earlier, Wordsworth came to associate creativity with memory and *un*-memory. In Goslar he found himself relying on memories of home to supply material for composition, writing 'in self-defence' as he explains in a letter to Coleridge, who, flush with the Wedgwood annuity, had gone on to Ratzeburg.[1] The Goslar poems show Wordsworth at work writing *himself* and writing *his self* during the closing months of 1798, sometime between October and December. Two different entities, or, what he calls 'two consciousnesses'—'myself and some other being'—are at work. The two consciousnesses are, essentially, the now-Wordsworth and the then-Wordsworth. The life writing is asserting its own existence in relation to a fictional, textual self. For the now-Wordsworth, memory is a stimulus to creativity—even when those 'mountings of the mind' threaten to quash it—and that creativity finds expression in the relationship between present and past. The creative moment occurs in Wordsworth when the past becomes present in the act of representing memory as past.

The Goslar notebook reveals Wordsworth's earliest attempts to understand the relationship between memory and creativity for the process of writing *The Prelude*. On the final page of the notebook, facing the inside back cover (on which Wordsworth also has scrawled a few lines), Wordsworth begins his backwards writing with an attempt to figure and thus to understand creativity. The word 'inspiration' appears twice at the top of the page, crammed between two attempts to figure out the relationships between the differing meanings of the Latin sense of *inspirare*, literally 'to breathe in',' as metaphor—'a mild creative breeze', 'a gentle inspiration'. Although the poem is yet unformed, these early jottings would become the opening of *The Prelude*.

On the next page forward in mental space—but actually the recto of the last page—Wordsworth has drafted lines toward what would

---

1   Letter of 14 or 21 December 1798, *The Letters of William and Dorothy Wordsworth: The Early Years, 1787–1805*, ed. Ernest de Selincourt and Chester L. Shaver, 2nd edn (Oxford: Clarendon Press, 1967), 236. This letter includes some fragments that would later appear in *The Prelude*.

become the opening passage of a complete two-part version of *The Prelude* over the next year; the lines would be slightly emended but preserved for the 13- and 14-book version. The poetry on this page begins seemingly in *media res*, emerging from what would appear to be a serious case of writer's block:

> was it for this
> That one, the fairest of all rivers, loved
> To blend his murmurs with my nurse's song
> And from his alder shades and rocky falls,
> And from his fords and shallows sent a voice
> To intertwine my dreams. . . .[1]

In the 13- and 14-book versions of *The Prelude*, these lines appear in a context that clearly establishes a reading wherein the poet is grappling with what he regards as a gift and his own potential unworthiness. In lines preceding those directly above, Wordsworth presents himself trapped in 'indolence', or 'listlessness', and 'vain perplexity', like the servant who hides his one talent in Jesus's parable from Matthew 25: foiled by his own creative inertia, Wordsworth compares himself to 'a false Steward who hath much receiv'd / And renders nothing back'.[2] Wordsworth feels that he has forsaken the blessing conferred on him by nature as a 'chosen son' and judges himself accordingly, in the words of the Gospel, as 'wicked and slothful'.

The crucial opening question—'Was it for this. . . ?'—appears in all versions of *The Prelude*. The Goslar notebooks thus offer evidence for the origins not only of *The Prelude* but of Wordsworth's own sense of himself as a poet: frustration and self-rebuke. Wordsworth echoes a line from Virgil's *Aeneid* ('*Hoc erat. . . ?*' which literally means something like 'Was this all along. . . ?'); it becomes a rhetorical expression of frustration, disappointment, and sarcastic admonishment. In order to further elucidate Wordsworth's tone here, I quote

---

1   MS. JJ, p. 115. For ease of reading and layout, I have normalized Parrish's diplomatic representation of interlinear words and of the relative sizes of the words in the original script.
2   *The Thirteen-Book Prelude*, ed. Mark L. Reed, 2 vols (Ithaca: Cornell University Press, 1991), I, 269–72 (p. 113); *The Fourteen-Book Prelude*, ed. W. J. B. Owen (Ithaca: Cornell University Press, 1985), 266–69, (p. 35).

John A. Hodgson's translation of the relevant passage from Virgil:

> Was it for this, fostering parent, that you brought me through
> spears, through fire?—that I might behold the enemy inside our
> home, and Ascanius, and my father, and Creusa nearby, slaugh-
> tered in each other's blood?[1]

More than twenty years later, Wordsworth himself translated these
same lines more concisely and with some poetic license: 'For this
was Priam slain? Troy burnt? The shore / Of Darden seas so often
drenched in gore?'[2] In having Aeneas rebuke Venus for not aiding
him more directly—basically 'where were you when I needed
you?'—Virgil here imitates Homer's Odysseus expressing similar
dismay when Athena appears to him in Book 13 of *The Odyssey*.
Both protagonists doubt the providential hand that would guide
them through such horrors and hardships without intervening. The
tone established through the choice of phrase is important—frustration, disappointment, wrath, despair consonant with feeling destitute
of divine favour. For Wordsworth writing in the formative year of
1798, that favour was bestowed, consecrated by his native river, the
Derwent, which still flows behind the Cockermouth house where he
was born. The river, an agent of Nature, a muse itself perhaps, 'loved'
to blend its own natural music with the nursery lullabies that form the
ontology of Wordsworth's creative self. Has he forsaken it? Implicit
in this question is another, more formidable and fundamental question—*erat*? It was? Was it? The 'it' is more mysterious than the 'this'
even though the antecedent effectively *follows* with the list of things
that were presumably for 'this', the creative torpor for which the poet
is admonishing himself.

The rest of *The Prelude*—in all its variations—strives to understand precisely what 'it' is, even here where 'this' remains somewhat
indeterminate in the draft. One of the most provocative questions
The Prelude raises concerns, if not the veracity of one's memory, the
accuracy of it and whether or not that even matters in the construction

---

1   '"Was It for This . . . ?": Wordsworth's Virgilian Questionings', *Texas Studies in Literature and Language*, 33 (1991), 125–36, 130.
2   *Translations of Chaucer and Virgil*, ed. Bruce E. Graver (Ithaca: Cornell University Press, 1998), lines 780–81, p. 238.

of a poetic self. This page of the notebook also has several struck-through lines marked for deletion as Wordsworth works at defining through trial and error the processes of 'it' figured as the waters of the Derwent as they have shaped his developing mind—just as the course of a river defines the shape of the land as much as various landmasses may determine the path of the river. Wordsworth imagines the 'ceaseless music' and 'steady cadence' of the river 'tempering / Our human waywardness'.[1]

The Goslar notebook provides a tiny but, I think, crucially significant example of Wordsworth writing about writing about memory, an act in which any writer may find himself at odds with his own creativity. This is reflected in the writing and rewriting, the drafting and deletions.[2] One passage in particular poses a problem Wordsworth's editors have had representing what Wordsworth has written and demonstrates how difficult it has been to maintain the integrity of what the poet was trying to work through: half-remembering and half-creating the past as part of the process of envisioning the poet he was to become, of writing that self into existence.

Transcripts of poetry from the Goslar notebook were first published by Helen Darbishire in her 1959 revision of Ernest De Selincourt's groundbreaking edition of the 13-book *Prelude*. I will do my best here to replicate in print what appears as script in the notebook:

> it for these perhaps [interlinear phrase]
> Was for this & now I speak of things
> [a line vigorously deleted]
> Complacent fashioned fondly to adorn
> years [interlinear word]
> The time of unrememberable being

---

1   MS. JJ, p. 115.
2   In *Text as Process* Sally Bushell reads carefully the notebook fragments in various stages to demonstrate how, as she puts it, 'the detailed study of composition can provide an alternative perspective on the completed text' (97). From the perspective of genetic criticism, Bushell helpfully considers drafting and redrafting—the kinds of things that editors have a difficult time representing when they want to produce a 'reading text' of unpublished, and thus in some ways unauthorized, manuscript materials. *Text as Process: Creative Composition in Wordsworth, Tennyson, and Dickinson* (Charlottesville: University of Virginia Press, 2009).

Editors since and including Darbishire have represented this passage
on the assumption that the obviously deleted line, which I find difficult to make out, is essential to the meaning. Darbishire provides in
brackets her reading of the deleted line: '[That have been & that are,
no gentle (dreams?)]'. The comma is not apparent in the manuscript,
however, so Darbishire is suggesting an independent clause—'&
now I speak of things that have been and that are'—with 'no gentle
dreams / Complacent . . .' functioning as an appositive asserting the
veracity of the poet's assertions.[1] On this reading, 'Complacent' is an
inverted adjective modifying the already modified 'dreams', which is
itself a conjectural noun. More recent editors have more been more
confident: Stephen Parrish provides a photograph of the page plus a
diplomatic transcription of the deleted line, unpunctuated, as "~~That
have been & that are no gentle dreams~~," which is a more accurate
printed representation; the entire passage appears as

> it for these perhaps
> Was for this & now I speak of things
> ~~That have been & that are no gentle dreams~~
> Complacent fashioned fondly to adorn
> years
> The time of unrememberable being[2]

However, when Parrish provides his 'Reading Text' of the Goslar
passages, he presents a conjectural assemblage of the disjointed fragments that is on the whole justified by the poet's later ordering of
them. But because of his editorial principle, which requires representing the poet's earliest intentions, the passage I have attempted to
replicate above appears as the following:

> Was it for this & now I speak of things
> That have been & that are no gentle dreams
> Complacent fashioned fondly to adorn
> The time of unrememberable being[3]

---

1   *The Prelude or Growth of a Poet's Mind*, ed. Ernest de Selincourt and Helen
     Darbishire, 2nd edn (Oxford: Clarendon Press, 1959), p. 633.
2   'MS. JJ Transcriptions', *The Prelude, 1798–1799*, p. 115.
3   'MS. JJ Reading Text', *The Prelude, 1798–1799*, p. 124.

Parrish refrains from speculating on punctuation but, without any, the passage reads more or less the same as Darbishire's text. Yet here Parrish has determined that the deletion must have been made so late as to invalidate its authority—which may be the case, or not.

Jonathan Wordsworth takes this revisionary editing to an extreme by presenting the lines as fully formed and finished, determining that the lines are parenthetical in context and making them visually so:

> Was it for this (and now I speak of things
> That have been, and that are, no gentle dreams
> Complacent, fashioned fondly to adorn
> The time of unrememberable being)[1]

The punctuation here amounts to the same reading implied by Darbishire and Parrish. Plus, I see no reason to de-emphasize this statement by placing the lines in parentheses; indeed, I would prefer dashes for emphasis. Furthermore, for his Penguin Classics edition of *The Prelude*, Jonathan Wordsworth presents fragments from the note-book as a coherent 1798 version of *The Prelude*, a standalone work he dubs 'Was It For This', making the essential rhetorical question into the title of a poem he conjures out of sheer editorial chutzpah.

In the desire to present 'reading' texts of the notebook, these three editors want to ignore the fact that Wordsworth—or, admittedly, somebody else perhaps—struck through the line. The uncertainty regarding the authority of the deletion granted, I think what is important here is that Wordsworth's editors appear to have been uncomfortable with the possibility that Wordsworth might be admitting to having embellished some of his memories, which, as I will explain below, is what the passage says without the contested line. Of course, Wordsworth frequently admits this as a possibility in his poetry; therefore, if we situate this textual moment within the rest of Wordsworth's writing, we find that such 'embellishment' is important to his poetic. The difficulty in resolving this textual crux is that Wordsworth did not use *this* particular passage when he came to revise the opening for the two-book version of *The Prelude*—he used the one I quoted at the start, 'the fairest of all rivers'—so we

---

1   *Prelude: The Four Texts*, p. 3.

do not have another authoritative version with which to compare the notebook jottings which have been the subject of so much editorial manipulation.

But what if the deletion is authoritative? What if Wordsworth struck through the line in the initial act of writing (a distinct possibility, in this instance, since Wordsworth is clearly drafting and not dictating already composed lines to his sister). Let's take something else from this passage in order to discern the poet's larger point: what if we read it as, '& now I speak of things / Complacent, fashioned fondly to adorn / The years of unrememberable being'. On my and the previous editors' readings, 'complacent' works as an inverted modifier, an adjective modifying either 'dreams' (previous editors' readings) or modifying 'things' (my reading). But the sense is greatly different if one reads the passage with the deleted line, as previous editors have insisted that we do. Here is a proposed (and certainly not definitive) reading text of the passage which takes for granted that the interlinear words and the deletion are authoritative, admitting also that the interlinear 'these' is an unfortunate alteration to the symmetry—and perhaps to the presumed antecedent(s). However, if I admit one correction, I ought to admit them all, although 'this' works better because the pronoun 'these' would seem to refer to the forthcoming 'things', which, in order for the passage to agree with the received reading, must refer to the memories bundled together as the benedictory 'it' with which the passage—and the entire two-part *Prelude* begins.

> Was it for these[this?]—perhaps I speak of things
> Complacent, fashioned fondly to adorn
> The years of unrememberable being—
> Was it for this[these?] that I, a four-years child,
> A naked boy among thy silent pools,
> Made one long bathing of a summer's day. . . ?

In the previous editors' readings, the deleted line involves both the past and present, neither being 'no gentle dreams complacent', when, even if the line is preserved, it could just as easily convey the sense that the 'things that have been' are 'no [not] gentle dreams complacent'—given the absence of punctuation in the original manuscript. But, honestly if we must *stick to* what Wordsworth originally wrote in the notebook, we'd be *stuck with* 'Was for this?' Nobody wants that, so we must allow for some moderate correction: if it does not happen on the page, the reader make the adjustment as he or she sees fit in his or her own head while reading.

Either way, these editors go to great lengths to preserve the deleted line, thus making Wordsworth assert a veracity that seems incongruous with this poetry he presents as recollections of the years of 'unrememberable being'. When he writes that he 'now' speaks of complacent things, he could be referring to the preceding lines; or, if the lines on the next page follow from this, then he is about to launch into a passage that describes the poet at the age of four and thus takes its origin in experiences the poet cannot possibly recall with any kind of precision. It seems perfectly reasonable for Wordsworth to admit that these recollections may be 'fashioned fondly' by the later mind as a way of compensating for that which is 'unrememberable'. These things are 'complacent' because they are pleasing and thus crafted to be so. Incidentally, Wordsworth rarely uses the word 'complacent'— only four times in the complete corpus—and it always means pleasing and not so much the negative sense we have today of being smug or dully self-satisfied.

The 'years of unrememberable being' is not the only subject of *The Prelude*, nor of this passage. Grammatically speaking, the *subject* is the poet trying to make those years past recollection realizable in words. He is the one doing the fashioning—and doing so 'fondly', both affectionately and perhaps foolishly. The accessory *object* of the poem is also that 'unrememberable being', the then-Wordsworth. In lines Wordsworth dictated to his sister, he posits what will become the thesis of his entire life, the biological and the poetical:

> I believe
> That there are spirits which when they would form
> A favor'd being open out the clouds
> As at the touch of lightning
> Seeking him with gentle visitation. . . .[1]

---

1   MS. JJ, p. 83.

Even in the first drafts of *The Prelude* dating from 1798–99, Wordsworth recognizes—with more gratitude than pride—that he was 'a favor'd being'. Note that the being already exists—but he is not "formed" as a 'favor'd being' until the spirits find him and consummate their will with 'gentle visitation'. Wordsworth envisions other spirits, 'aiming at the self-same end' as these but who 'use . . . Severer interventions' and 'ministry / Of grosser kind'. He notes that 'of their school was I'.[1] His schooling by these spirits is the main subject of the first book of the two-book *Prelude*. Wordsworth must figure himself as a 'favor'd being' in order for the admonishment of the 'was it for this' passage to carry its weight. But this figuring of the 'unrememberable being', the writing of one's self, is also the way around—if not effectually the way out of—the paralysis brought about by the pressure to write 'The Recluse'.

A few months later, when he begins developing fragments of the Goslar notebook into the two-part *Prelude*, he frames this passage differently, nearly as a non sequitur: after describing some of his earliest memories, those that are contiguous with the 'unrememberable' ones, Wordsworth pauses abruptly to explain the fashioning of his being:

> The mind of man is fashioned and built up
> Even as a strain of music: I believe
> That there are spirits, which, when they would form
> A favored being, from his very dawn
> Of infancy do open out the clouds
> As at the touch of lightning, seeking him
> With gentle visitation. . . .[2]

As a 'history of Poet's mind', Wordsworth's primary interest in *The Prelude* is 'the mind of man', specifically a man-poet, but what does it mean for the mind to be fashioned even 'as a strain of music'? Does he mean that the mind is fashioned as a strain of music is fashioned? Or that the mind is made to be similar to a strain of music. The subsequent lines don't really explain, but the 1799 draft, to

---

1   *Ibid.*
2   *The Prelude, 1798–1799*, ed. Parrish, 67–73 (pp. 44–45).

me, favours the former meaning, by emphasizing the fashioning in the subsequent lines, where Wordsworth describes the 'gentle visitation' of the spirits who will that mind into being. Those visitations extend the melody. And they visit everyone, Wordsworth goes on to assert. These are 'quiet powers' that are 'retired, and seldom recognized, yet kind, / And to the very meanest not unknown'. By 'meanest' Wordsworth means the most ordinary people, although the double negative makes the sentiment seem a bit stinting. But Wordsworth writes that these spirits 'rarely' communed with him as a boy. Other spirits 'aiming at the self-same end'—that is, the making of a 'favored being'—administer the 'severer interventions' first developed in the Goslar notebook but which is now 'ministry / More palpable' than the 'gentle visitation' of the former spirits.[1] But what does this have to do with music? It is the fashioning. For example, when he revised the above passage for the 13-book draft completed in 1805, Wordsworth decided on the second reading proposed above, asserting that 'The mind of man is framed even like the breath / And harmony of music'.

For the 13- and the 14-book versions, Wordsworth would clarify just in what those 'severer interventions' consist. 'Fair seed-time had my soul', he explains, 'and I grew up / Foster'd alike by beauty and by fear'.[2] His most formative experience of nature, therefore, is akin to what Edmund Burke writes about in his *Philosophical Enquiry into the Origin of Our Ideas of the Sublime and Beautiful*. But instead of working upon him in the development only of an aesthetic, the sublime and beautiful nurture Wordsworth's poetic. Wordsworth goes on to describe the famous episode in which the boy rows out on Ullswater in a stolen skiff but haunted by guilt believes the mountains to be pursuing him. Afterwards, Wordsworth writes that 'for many days my brain / Worked with a dim and undetermined sense / Of unknown modes of being'. He becomes aware, due to the 'severer interventions' of those other spirits, of the *thingness* of those Wordsworthian things. It sounds like an epiphany of Platonic idealism but it disturbs him in the same way as the creative power he

---

1   *Ibid.*, 78–80 (p. 45).
2   *Thirteen-Book Prelude*, 306–7 (p. 114); *Fourteen-Book Prelude*, 301–2, (p. 36).

elsewhere describes as 'disturbing things created': 'huge and mighty Forms that do not live / Like living men mov'd slowly through my mind / By day, and were the trouble of my dreams'.[1] He is the created thing that is transformed into something else. These experiences teach him about 'high objects', 'enduring things', and 'grandeur in the beatings of the heart'.[2] Previously discordant notes fall into harmony as the boy gradually coheres as a more deeply thinking and feeling man.

But even this attempt is fragmentary, for the writing of Wordsworth's self, especially during 1798–1800, is scattered among notebooks, letters, and scraps, expressed in false-starts, in jottings in the margins of other poems, in extracts disguised as discrete poems. And the latter class of artefact in particular attests to Wordsworth's perverse resistance to coherence even as he assembles the fragments. We find the fragments juxtaposed and read them to construct a coherent narrative of self. But then again, Wordsworth frequently seems to be daring us to find it because, as David Hume recognized, one cannot clearly distinguish between the now-self and the then-self. For example, in the poem 'Nutting', from the 1800 *Lyrical Ballads*, Wordsworth describes himself as a boy giving way to his inscrutable urge to pull down the branches and boughs in a 'shady nook / Of hazels', an unspoiled spot—indeed a 'virgin scene'—he had discovered and then destroyed.[3] Likely some sort of exercise of adolescent sexuality, this shockingly un-Wordsworthian action and our and the poet's attitude towards it is complicated, as Wordsworth freely admits, by memory:

> and unless I now
> Confound my present feelings with the past,
> Even then, when from the bower I turn'd away,
> Exulting, rich beyond the wealth of kings—
> I felt a sense of pain when I beheld

---

1   *Thirteen-Book Prelude*, 426–28 (p. 117).
2   *Ibid.*, 437, 442 (p. 118).
3   *Lyrical Ballads, and Other Poems, 1797–1800*, ed. by James Butler and Karen Green (Ithaca: Cornell University Press, 1992), 43–44, 19 (pp. 219–20).

The silent trees and the intruding sky.——[1]

'Nutting' was written along with the earliest poetry for *The Prelude*. As he later stated, it was 'intended as part of a poem on my own life, but struck out as not being wanted there'.[2] He was editing his life already and could not let the 1799 *Prelude* rest in peace (that is, in two pieces) because he had himself continued to exist. Wordsworth later remarked that the poem derived from 'the remembrance of feelings I had often had when a boy'.[3] Maybe so. But is the sense of guilt projected by the poet upon his former self? For that matter, is the sense of exultation? Is the past tense a mask for the present? In the poem he is willing to accept that the answer to each of these questions is 'yes'—or at least 'maybe'. In this way, the Goslar notebook and the 'unrememberable being' passage may lead us back to Geoffrey Hartman's wondering question, which is in itself an ineffably provocative answer to the question 'Was it for this?'. Hartman asks, 'Is this indeterminacy the end at which nature aims, this curious and never fully clarified restlessness the ultimate confession of his poetry?'[4] Again, maybe. Or Wordsworth's effort at epic memoir in verse is, as the Goslar notebook shows, is just as phenomenologically astute; Wordsworth, in Goslar, already was grappling with Paul de Man's *aporia*, the unresolvable contradiction of rhetoric, figure, and text—or, more specifically in this case, script.

---

1   *Ibid.*, 46–51 (p. 220).
2   *The Fenwick Notes of William Wordsworth*, ed. Jared Curtis, 2nd edition (Penrith: Humanities-Ebooks, 2007), 62.
3   *Ibid.*
4   *Wordsworth's Poetry 1787–1814* (New Haven: Yale University Press, 1964; repr. Cambridge: Harvard University Press, 1987), 38.

Christopher Simons

Wordsworth in *Geste:* Dissolving the *Ecclesiastical Sketches*

Introduction

With the exception of the sonnet 'Mutability', popular opinion of the *Ecclesiastical Sketches* over the past two centuries might concur with the review in the *Literary Gazette* (30 March 1820), which asserts that 'the chaff is out of all proportion to the grains'.[1] This lecture will suggest that we can read the *Ecclesiastical Sketches* as a narrative and allegorical poem in the vein of a medieval *chanson de geste* (a 'song of great deeds') and early modern equivalents such as Spenser's *Faerie Queene*. The lecture also argues that the interplay in the *Sketches* between national history and personal or autobiographical history reveals tensions over Wordsworth's spiritual beliefs, his poetic creativity, and his self-declared role as the creator of a narrative and national myth for the British church. But as a more general purpose, I hope to demonstrate that the choice grains of this sonnet series are worth winnowing. Out of the 102 sonnets first published as *Ecclesiastical Sketches*, more than a dozen contain excellent poetry, and a few have surprising power.

The greatness of the best of these poems comes from their expression of Wordsworth's deepest and least dogmatic principles, based on love of nature and human life; it comes from returning to the ideas of 1795–1805 and flashes of insight worthy of (that complex expression) 'spots of time'. At the same time, Wordsworth scholars should read the chaff with the grains, as the overall narrative demonstrates the

---

1   Geoffrey Jackson, *Sonnet Series and Itinerary Poems, 1820-1845, by William Wordsworth*, The Cornell Wordsworth (Ithaca and London: Cornell University Press, 2004), 131.

poet struggling to reconcile conflicting beliefs and conflicting aspects of his personality. This struggle contributes to the argument that the sonnet series resembles a *chanson de geste*, in that it is constructing a tradition—in Wordsworth's case, not only a cultural and religious tradition for Britain, but also the tradition of his own self-unity.

The Christian beliefs expressed in *Ecclesiastical Sketches* do not represent an abrupt break with Wordsworth's younger self. As Stephen Gill succinctly puts it:

> [Wordsworth] detested religious cant, mistrusted sectarians who pursued ideological purity, and declined to satisfy those who wanted assurance that the religion of *The Excursion* was four-square with the thirty-nine articles. But by 1822 he had become committed to the Church of England... the necessity of defending it as *the* safeguard against anarchy and social retrogression was a constant in all of his future thinking about politics and national culture.[1]

Although Wordsworth's loyalty to the established church developed gradually, many of the ideas expressed in the *Ecclesiastical Sketches* remain consistent with those of his earliest published work.

The *Ecclesiastical Sketches*, like the *River Duddon* that preceded it, is a narrative in sonnet sequence. While the *Duddon* sonnets follow the topographical structure of Wordsworth's walk along the river, the *Sketches* follow a chronological structure.[2] Yet unlike the *Duddon*, *Ecclesiastical Sketches* is more than a sonnet sequence; it is a stanzaic narrative poem. The stanzaic unit is the sonnet rather than the Spenserian stanza that Wordsworth employed effectively to communicate the gothic mood and romance elements of the *Salisbury Plain* poems.

What is the value of reading *Ecclesiastical Sketches* as a single stanzaic narrative poem? Wordsworth wrote the *Sketches* not as the-

---

1   Stephen Gill, *William Wordsworth: A Life* (Oxford: Clarendon Press, 1989), 344.

2   Part 1 describes the history of Christianity 'From the Introduction of Christianity into Britain, to the Consummation of the Papal Dominion' when Pope Innocent III excommunicated King John. Part 2 narrates from the founding of the Cistercian monasteries 'To the Close of the Troubles in the Reign of Charles I.' Finally, Part 3 recounts church history from the reign of Charles II and 'the Restoration, to the Present Times.'

odicy but ecclesiodicy, a poem justifying the authority of the Church of England as the culmination of a divinely preordained struggle. Wordsworth's history is teleological, that is, representing religion in Britain as progressing from a state of imperfection to perfection, with regrettable errors along the way justified by the present state of affairs. For Wordsworth himself, the poem represents a late attempt at a philosophical history in the vein of *The Recluse*, a demonstration of intellectual and spiritual growth and continuity in his creative self. Reading from this perspective, the poetic genre of *Ecclesiastical Sketches* resembles, more than other more contemporary types of nationalist poetry, the *chanson de geste*, a medieval narrative poem that is on the surface an epic, but has the didactic purpose of constructing or consolidating cultural or national identity.

Part 1: Wordsworth's mis-casting of self

Wordsworth's poetic confidence is strong in the opening poems of the series, when historical fact and legend blur in his description of early Christianity in Britain. The style of sonnets such as 'Conjectures' and 'Trepidation of the Druids' is weak, full of poetic archaisms. Nevertheless these poems have energy. In 'Druidical Excommunication' and 'Uncertainty', Wordsworth returns to the subject matter of *Salisbury Plain* in 1793, even if the symbol of Druid authority has shifted from politics to religion itself. *Salisbury Plain* remained unpublished until *Guilt and Sorrow* in 1842, and *The Prelude* with its Salisbury Plain passage until 1850, but these sonnets show Wordsworth already rooting his historical narrative in a strong autobiographical context.

  The first eight lines of 1.5, 'Uncertainty', although overtly about the impossibility of accurately knowing the historical origins of Christianity in Britain, take us back to Wordsworth's most uncertain years between 1791 and 1794:

> Darkness surrounds us; seeking, we are lost
> On Snowdon's wilds, amid Brigantian coves,
> Or where the solitary Shepherd roves
> Along the Plain of Sarum, by the Ghost

> Of silently departed ages crossed;
> And where the boatman of the Western Isles
> Slackens his course—to mark those holy piles
> Which yet survive on bleak Iona's coast. (1.5, ll.1–8)

Taken out of context, this could be purely autobiographical poetry. As Richard Gravil writes:

> This *tour de force* maps onto the topography of the sacred sites of the tribe a personal poetical history. It tallies Wordsworth's journeys with Jones in Snowdonia, alone on Salisbury Plain, and with Coleridge and Dorothy in search of Burns and Ossian. The Brigantian coves might well include the Leven Estuary, where verses from Gray's *Elegy* were engraved on the headstone of Wordsworth's schoolmaster.[1]

The first line of the sonnet also recalls the uncertainty of crossing of the Alps in *Prelude* Book 6: 'I was lost as in a cloud / Halted without a struggle to break through', and Wordsworth's response to that 'first' 'spot of time' in Book 11, 'Oh! mystery of Man, from what a depth / Proceed thy honours! I am lost, but see / In simple childhood something of the base / On which thy greatness stands…' (*1805 Prelude* 6.529–30, 11.329–32). Wordsworth was himself the 'solitary shepherd' wandering on the 'Plain of Sarum', where he encountered ghosts both living and dead—the Female Vagrant, and the fantasies or hallucinations of ancient Britons and Druidical sacrifice.

However, as Part 1 of *Ecclesiastical Sketches* continues, Wordsworth finds himself without a strong personal context for his narrative. Without this context, his philosophical ideas lose their depth, and he reverts to dogma. These shifts are often abrupt, and obvious to readers who can assess Wordsworth's lifelong philosophical development. For example, the conclusion to 1.4, 'Druidical Excommunication', expresses the idea of 1798–1800 that nature pre-

---

1   Richard Gravil, *Wordsworth's Bardic Vocation, 1787–1842* (Basingstoke: Palgrave Macmillan, 2003), 67. Gravil cites Hutchinson in his note: 'The Brigantes, according to Roman writers, possessed a very large tract of country on the western coast of Britain; but … it is enough for us to observe, they inhabited the district now called Cumberland' William Hutchinson, *History and Antiquities of Cumberland* (Carlisle, 1797), 3.

serves truths which religion can debase:

> ...yon thick woods maintain the primal truth,
> Debased by many a superstitious form... (1.4, ll.12–13)[1]

Yet only four sonnets later, in 'Temptations from Roman Refinements', Wordsworth sounds as puritanical as Malvolio; the 'humanizing graces' of Roman culture are no more than 'soul-subduing vice' and 'instruments of deadliest servitude' (1.8, ll.13, 1, 14). It is perhaps no coincidence that Wordsworth's descriptions of decadent Roman lifestyle, although taken almost verbatim from Samuel Daniel, sound rather like Coleridge's description of Kubla Khan's pleasure dome:

> Fair houses, baths, and banquets delicate,
> And temples flashing, bright as polar ice,
> Their radiance through the woods... (1.8, ll.3–4)[2]

This one example demonstrates a dialectic that appears throughout the *Sketches*, in which Wordsworth's own strain of naturalistic, holistic Christian feeling strives to pierce through his more puritanical instincts.

Wordsworth continues this vacillation throughout Part 1, just as Coleridge attempts to balance the poetically productive pagan or daemonic in *The Ancient Mariner* and 'Kubla Khan' and *Christabel* against more philosophically satisfying, but less instinctive, Christian consolation and oneness. In one of the strongest poems in Part 1 (1.10, 'Struggle of the Britons Against the Barbarians'), Wordsworth takes up the trumpet of Milton and the wreathed horn of Triton that he wielded to such effect in 1802. The sonnet's power depends on the historical fabrication that the post-Roman Druids assimilated Christianity and fought as Christianised Britons against the Saxons:

> Rise!—they *have* risen: of brave Aneurin ask
> How they have scourged old foes, perfidious friends:
> The spirit of Caractacus defends

---

1   For example, consider *Home at Grasmere* and the 'Poems on the Naming of Places'.

2   See Samuel Daniel, *History of England*, 5th ed. (London: 1685, n.d.), 3. Cited in Gravil, *Wordsworth's Bardic Vocation, 1787–1842*, 68.

The Patriots, animates their glorious task:—
Amazement runs before the towering casque
Of Arthur, bearing thro' the stormy field
The Virgin sculptured on his Christian shield:—
Stretched in the sunny light of victory bask
The Host that followed Urien as he strode
O'er heaps of slain;—from Cambrian woods and moss
Druids descend, auxiliars of the Cross;
Bards, nursed on blue Plinlimmon's still abode,
Rush on the fight, to harps preferring swords,
And everlasting deeds to burning words!

The language of this fine sonnet is not as naturalistic as the sonnets of
1802, with the archaic verb-before-noun construction of lines 8–9 and
13, and the cliché of 'strode / O'er heaps of slain'. But lines 10–11
are strong, and the rhyme moss/Cross encapsulates Wordsworth's
early love of the fabric of British churches and monasteries, and the
mutability of their ruin in nature. In another self-referential gesture,
and one of the spectral images of the *Sketches*, Wordsworth returns
to one of his earliest British heroes, Caractacus; he first alluded to
William Mason's dramatic hero in *Descriptive Sketches*, and used
Mason's notes to the play when compiling his 'bibliography of
Druids' for work on *Adventures on Salisbury Plain.*[1]

Line 12, 'Bards, nursed on blue Plinlimmon's still abode,' is one
of the best in the *Sketches:* dense, mellifluous, and carrying the symbolic weight of Wordsworth's 1791, 1793, and 1798 Welsh tours
and the wealth of memory and poetry they produced. Plynlimon, a
mountain in Ceredigion, is the source of both the Severn and the
Wye.[2] Therefore the sonnet draws symbolically on 'Tintern Abbey',
as much as Wordsworth explicitly alludes to his ascent of Snowden
in 'Uncertainty'. It is at least a pleasing coincidence to note that one
of the more vigorous poems in the *Sketches* connects obliquely with

---

1   William Mason, *Caractacus* (York: A. Ward, for R. Horsfield & J. Dodsley,
    London, 1777).. See *Descriptive Sketches* 44; Duncan Wu, *Wordsworth's
    Reading 1770-1799* (Cambridge: Cambridge University Press, 1993), 97–8;
    John R. Nabholtz, "Wordsworth and William Mason," *Review of English Studies*
    15 (1967): 297–302.
2   Jackson, *SSIP*, 241.

Wordsworth's great poem of 1798.

Yet despite the power of this sonnet, Wordsworth cannot continue his narrative without a clear transition—or, we might say, 'conversion'—from legendary history to modern historical evidence. Wordsworth needs to locate a historical figure with which he can identify, and in which he can locate his own unambiguous—and hence legendary—conversion to Christianity. This figure is Edwin, King of Northumbria from 616–32. Edwin was an exile, banished by his predecessor Aethelfrith, and living in a foreign court where his life was in danger. Wordsworth draws on descriptions by Bede and by Sharon Turner. Bede describes Edwin, after an assassination attempt, as 'alone in the open air... affected by a multitude of raging thoughts, not knowing what he should do or whither he should direct his steps'.[1] These phrases have the ring of a melancholy equivalent of the *Prelude*'s 'glad preamble': 'What dwelling shall receive me? In what Vale / Shall be my harbour?' (*1805 Prelude* 1.11–12). Turner, in his *History of the Anglo-Saxons*, describes Edwin as an intellectual warrior-king among barbarians, a description that would have appealed to Wordsworth:

> The vicissitudes of Edwin's life had indued his mind with a contemplative temper, which made him more intellectual than any of the Anglo-Saxon kings that had preceded him, and which fitted him for the reception of Christianity. His progress towards this revolution of mind was gradual... (Turner, 1.344–55) [2]

Wordsworth documents Edwin's conversion over three linked sonnets. Wordsworth may have self-identified with Edwin, yet I believe he also identifies himself with Paulinus, the priest who converts Edwin.[3] In the second sonnet, 1.15, 'Paulinus', Wordsworth follows Bede's physical description of the proselytising monk closely, strangely devoting four-and-a-half lines of the sonnet to it:

> Mark him, of shoulders curved, and stature tall,
> Black hair, and vivid eye, and meagre cheek,

---

1   Ibid., 243.
2   Ibid., 244.
3   A monk who arrived in England in 601, four years after the arrival of St. Augustine of Canterbury.

> His prominent feature like an eagle's beak;
> A Man whose aspect doth at once appal,
> And strike with reverence. (1.15, ll.5–9)

This description seems to fit Wordsworth himself, as well as Paulinus. Wordsworth's nose may not have been aquiline, but it certainly was a 'prominent feature' of his face; in 1822 he was still tall, and had a commanding air about him, even if he had lost the 'convulsive tendency to laughter about the mouth' that Hazlitt recalled from 1798. It may be an example of the oft-mentioned egotistical sublime, but perhaps Wordsworth could bear no other apostle to his own conversion than Wordsworth.

The third sonnet is poetically poor as a whole but contains a few powerful lines that look backwards to 1.10, 'Struggle of the Britons Against the Barbarians', and forward to 'Mutability' in Part 3. After Edwin's conversion, an unnamed priest, one of his counsellors, in full career

> Rides forth, an armed Man, and hurls a spear
> To desecrate the Fane which heretofore
> He served in folly.—Woden falls—and Thor
> Is overturned... (1.17, ll.2–6)

Wordsworth may be following his historical sources closely, but the image of the warrior-priest or bard remains a strong image throughout his poetic career, appearing in such distant poems as 'A Fragment' in *Lyrical Ballads* (1800) ('The Danish Boy') and a late sonnet from the 1837 Italian tour, praising Roman 'Flattery' in contrast to the 'savage passions' of the 'Runic Scald' (4, 'Continued').

Wordsworth's description of the overthrow of Wotan and Thor by a Christian warrior-priest contrasts with the image of a vigorous northern Paganism overcoming the 'insidious arts' of southern, Roman decadence in 1.8, 'Temptations from Roman Refinements' (1.9). It also contrasts with *Prelude* Book 1, in which Wordsworth considered taking for his epic theme

> How vanquish'd Mithridates northward pass'd,
> And, hidden in the cloud of years, became

> That Odin, Father of a Race by whom
> Perish'd the Roman Empire... (*1805 Prelude* 1.186–90)

The Prelude contrasts this unchosen theme with the Anglo-Norman British tale of the 'groves of Chivalry', preferring the Scandinavian epic when 'more sternly mov'd' (*1805 Prelude* 1.186). This northern paganism chimes with Wordsworth's own northern Protestantism and the stricter Calvinism of *The Pedlar* (1803–4), self-educated alike on 'The life and death of Martyrs who sustain'd / Intolerable pangs' and 'Romance of Giants, Chronicle of Fiends' (ll.166–7, 170–1). But by 1822, Wordsworth cannot consciously acknowledge inspiration by the more local of two pagan traditions.

The destruction of Edwin's pagan fane by the unnamed warrior-priest with a strong physical resemblance to Wordsworth contains another negation of Wordsworth's more consistent expressions on nature and mutability throughout his poetry. At the desecration of the pagan altar, Wotan vanishes, 'the God himself is seen no more' (l.8), while

> Temple and Altar sink—to hide their shame
> Amid oblivious weeds. (1.17, ll.9–10)

The 'oblivious weeds' of line 10 allude directly to *The Ruined Cottage*. After hearing the end of the Pedlar's tale, the narrator recounts:

> I bless'd her—in the impotence of grief.
> At length towards the Cottage I returned
> Fondly,—and traced, with interest more mild,
> That secret spirit of humanity
> Which, mid the calm <u>oblivious</u> tendencies
> Of Nature, mid her plants, and <u>weeds</u>, and flowers,
> And silent overgrowings, still survived. (ll.959–65)

In 1798–9, Nature, an oblivious but divinely inspired force, remains indifferent to human suffering, and yet gives evidence of 'The secret spirit of humanity' even as it eradicates it. In contrast, in 1822, Edwin's pagan 'Temple and Altar' assume a Christian anthropomorphism, like Adam and Eve in their nakedness. The 'oblivious weeds' of the sonnet are no longer, like 'the high spear-grass on that wall, / By mist and silent rain-drops silver'd o'er', a compensation for ruin and change 'and all the grief / The passing shews of Being leave behind' (*Ruined Cottage* ll.973–4, 980–1). Instead, they are the fig leaves (as Milton puts it 'not that kind for fruit renowned / But such as to this day to Indians known / In Malabar or Decan' (*PL* 9.1101–3)) that conceal unwelcome or uncomfortable history from a morally rectified present.

The three-sonnet sub-plot of Edwin's conversion may mark the beginning of the disappointments of the poem as a whole, through which Wordsworth gradually converts primitive bardic power into dry Christian authority and the self-satisfaction of pre-ordained history. But Part 1 contains a more shocking example of the dialectic between Christian self-denial and mortification on the one hand, and Wordsworth's delight in nature and 'voluptuous indolence' on the other (1.23, 'Reproof', l.3). Sonnets 21 to 23 show Wordsworth struggling to reconcile two opposite traditions of the theme of reclusiveness, the writer's retreat from society into nature. These three sonnets form anther sub-plot in which the historical narrative grows as thin as in a medieval romance, and the personal allegory shines through. We can look at the first two.

Sonnet 1.21, 'Seclusion', portrays an idealised Anglo-Saxon 'Chieftain' trading his sword for a Bible:

> Lance, shield, and sword relinquished—at his side
> A Bead-roll, in his hand a clasped Book,
> Or staff more harmless than a Shepherd's crook,
> The war-worn Chieftain quits the world—to hide
> His thin <u>autumnal locks</u> where Monks abide
> In cloistered privacy. But not to dwell
> In soft repose he comes. Within his cell,
> <u>Round the decaying trunk of human pride</u>,
> At morn, and eve, and midnight's silent hour,
> Do penitential cogitations cling:
> Like ivy, round some ancient elm, they twine
> In <u>grisly folds</u> and strictures serpentine;
> Yet while they strangle without mercy, bring
> For recompense their own perennial bower.

This is one of the most memorable sonnets in the overall poem, somewhat due to its skill, but more to its strangeness. Here seclusion and reclusiveness are masochistic; the warrior's 'penitential cogitations' 'strangle without mercy'.

The poem's image of nature, while vivid, directly symbolises human physical and spiritual frailty, rather than, as in *The Ruined Cottage*, providing a symbol of the eternal in compensation for this frailty. The ivy strangling the elm circles 'In grisly folds', alluding to Spenser's description of Night in *The Faerie Queene*.[1] The 'strictures serpentine' suggest the 'intertwisted fibres serpentine' of the 'fraternal four', the yew-trees of Borrowdale described in 'That vast eugh-tree, pride of Lorton Vale', and 'Ewtrees' but again, the symbol is reversed: the yew-trees are not 'uninform'd with phantasy, and looks / That threaten the profane', while the serpentine ivy of the sonnet *becomes* profane in its act of strangulation through guilt ('That vast eugh-tree', ll.9–10).

The linked sonnet, 1.22, 'Continued', elaborates a contrasting seclusion, a withdrawal into delight and idleness. Wordsworth writes:

> Methinks that to some vacant Hermitage
> *My* feet would rather turn—to some dry nook
> Scoop'd out of living rock, and near a brook
> Hurl'd down a mountain-cove from stage to stage,
> Yet tempering, for my sight, its bustling rage
> In the soft heaven of a translucent pool;
> Thence creeping under forest arches cool,
> Fit haunt of shapes whose glorious equipage
> Perchance would throng my dreams. A beechen bowl,
> A maple dish, my furniture should be;
> Crisp, yellow leaves my bed; the hooting Owl
> My night-watch: nor should e'er the crested Fowl
> From thorp or vill his matins sound for me,
> Tired of the world and all its industry.

---

1   'And her darke griesly looke them much dismay; / The messenger of death, the ghastly Owle / With drearie shriekes did also her bewray; / And hungry Wolues continually did howle, / At her abhorred face, so filthy and so fowle (i. 5.366–70).'

Apart from scattered eighteenth-century poeticisms ('Thence' / 'Fit haunt' / 'Perchance') and the precious epithet 'crested Fowl' (and the Owl/Fowl rhyme), this is a tremendous sonnet. It belongs more to 1802, a companion piece to 'The world is too much with us'. There is nothing ecclesiastical about this sketch. The 'Hermitage' of the opening line and the 'matins' of the penultimate are a careful linked metaphor—something like Keats' statement to Shelley: 'My imagination is a monastery, and I am its monk' (16 August 1820) (ll.1,13).

This poem is also loaded with the ore of earlier reading and writing. The sonnet looks forward to the poems on the Dissolution of the Monasteries in Part 2 through an allusive connection, since the 'yellow leaves' of line 11 immediately conjure the opening lines of Shakespeare's sonnet 73:

> That time of year thou may'st in me behold
> When <u>yellow leaves</u>, or none, or few, do hang
> Upon those boughs which shake against the cold,
> Bare ruin'd choirs, where late the sweet birds sang.

Shakespeare's ecclesiastical theme in his sonnet, like Wordsworth's, operates only on a metaphorical level.

The dreams Wordsworth has in this shaded bower, of 'shapes' in 'glorious equipage', are not holy visions, but holy visions once removed: dreams of the holy visions of knights in the 'groves of Chivalry' that tempted Wordsworth with a subject for *The Prelude*— either a French *geste* or Arthurian tale, or 'some British theme, some old / Romantic tale, by Milton left unsung' (*1805 Prelude* 1.183, 180–1). They are also the daydreams of chivalric knights he imagines during his walks with Beaupuy along the banks of the Loiret:

> And if a devious Traveller was heard
> Approaching from a distance, as might chance
> …
> It was Angelica thundering through the woods
> Upon her Palfrey, or that gentler Maid,
> Erminia, fugitive as fair as She.
> Sometimes I saw, methought, a pair of Knights
> Joust underneath the trees, that, as in storm,

Did rock above their heads… (*1805 Prelude* 9.450–1, 454–9)

Finally, the wholesome 'beechen bowl' and 'maple dish' that serve as the recluse's only possessions in the poem provide an image of the restorative power of seclusion and nature; they work against the 'useless fragment of a wooden bowl' that remains by the pool by the deserted well in *The Ruined Cottage* (l.525). The restoration of the bowl to wholeness, in the absence of an overt Christian statement, again suggests that the sonnet draws its power from Wordsworth's vein of solace through nature, stretching back to 1798–9. Taken as a whole, this sonnet suggests a reworking of the Bower of Bliss in *Faerie Queene* Book 2:

> It was a chosen plot of fertile land,
> Emongst wide waves set, like a litle nest,
> As if it had by Nature's cunning hand,
> Bene choisely pickèd out from all the rest,
> And laid forth for ensaple of the best:
> No daintie flowre or herbe, that growes on ground,
> No arboret with painted blossomes drest,
> And smelling sweet, but there it might be found
> To bud out faire, and her sweet smels throw all around.
>
> No tree, whose braunches did not bravely spring;
> No braunch, whereon a fine bird did not sit:
> No bird, but did her shrill notes sweetly sing;
> No song but did containe a lovely dit:
> Trees, braunches, birds, and songs were framèd fit,
> For to allure fraile mind to carelesse ease.
> (*FQ* ii. 6.91–105)

Thus this digression, only metaphorically ecclesiastical, demonstrates how the enduring value of the *Ecclesiastical Sketches* lies in all the sonnet-stanzas and moments in which Wordsworth unconsciously breaks off from or subverts the project that occupies him. Wordsworth had mastered this technique of production—narrative poetry of delayed or diminished narrative, or philosophical lyric or epic through ever-delayed engagement with philosophy—over decades in work such as 'The Thorn', *Peter Bell*, *The White Doe*, and the *Prelude* and *Excursion*.

Part 2: Ecclesiastical History as the Autobiography of Belief

But what project is being subverted? Reviewers and critics from 1822 onward have focused on the fact that Wordsworth narrates the divinely ordained history of a national church, without endorsing any of its doctrines. Wordsworth's readers were abundantly aware of this fact, so Wordsworth could hardly have been blind to it. I would argue that the more crucial historical narrative being subverted is Wordsworth's own. Part 2 of the *Sketches* confronts a central moral and aesthetic crisis of the church's history—the break with Rome. The sonnets on the Dissolution of the monasteries seem to show Wordsworth foregrounding this crisis rather than avoiding it; as in Part 1, in the clash of Britons and Saxons, he narrates dark moments of church history as essential to the founding myth. Yet as Slavoj Žižek would argue, this historical crisis is in itself a fantasy—symbolic history that neatly obscures the spectral history which, in this case, really drives the poem.[1]

I will not give a detailed analysis of poems in Part 2 of the *Sketches*; however, I would suggest that a number of poems or stanzas in this section can be read—using the methodology of Barthes' 'existential thematics'—as building towards a more clear idea of what constitutes the spectral or fantasmic history in the poem. The first poem in the series, 'Cistertian Monastery', shows Wordsworth narrating medieval history not as a nineteenth-century poet but as a medieval or early modern one. His idea of nature at the poem's conclusion disputes almost everything he has written for thirty years: 'A gentler life spreads round the holy spires; / Where'er they rise the sylvan waste retires...' (1.1.12–13). This is man not living in harmony with nature, but mastering it; the 'sylvan waste' is the sixteenth-century forest of

---

1   See Slavoj Žižek, *The Fragile Absolute* (London: Verso, 2008), 58: 'One becomes a full member of a community not simply by identifying with its explicit symbolic tradition, but when one also assumes the spectral dimension that sustains this tradition: the undead ghosts that haunt the living, the secret history of traumatic fantasies transmitted 'between the lines' through its lacks and distortions.'

Athens or Arden in Shakespeare, a pre-picturesque landscape. Thus Wordsworth sets himself in history; his rejection of 'rapt Fancy' and the poem's Cistercian motto hints at the wisdom of hindsight, but the last lines of the poem evoke the perspective of the questing knight, braving the wilderness between sanctuaries.

Poems 2–5 and 8 continue this theme, elaborating Wordsworth's enduring, Burkean chivalric values. These sonnets bless the 'flowers of Chivalry' at the courts of Edward III and Henry V, and correspondingly the Catholic chapel as the sanctuary where the 'Knight / And his Retainers of the embattled hall' seek solace during a siege (2.4.7, 2.3.5–6). These few examples reinforce the reading of the *Sketches* as a *geste* narrative, a national myth in which political and religious shifts are explained away or smoothed over in service to the ends of political and religious unity; the 'British church' has always already been what it will become, even if the becoming entailed centuries of civil and religious strife.

But the less obvious and perhaps more interesting point is that, in writing a chivalric *geste*, Wordsworth uses national events to either conceal or allegorise (depending on how overt they appear to the reader) his own symbolic history, which contains and conceals its own crises of spectral history. Poems in Part 2 including 13 ('Monastic Voluptuousness'), 14–16 (the Dissolution poems), 17 ('Saints'), 18 ('The Virgin'), 20 ('Imaginative Regrets') and 29 ('Eminent Reformers') underpin the idea that, as Rylestone and others have suggested, the *Sketches* can be read as 'a portion of *The Recluse*'—that Wordsworth is building a religio-philosophical narrative that, in the end, is as much a narrative of the struggle for poetic self-expression as *The Prelude* and *The Excursion*. Read this way, the 'Reformation' of this section reveals its strong literary and autobiographical context, the same 'existential thematics' that appears in the 'subplot' of Anglo-Saxon conversion and seclusion in Part 1. Wordsworth represents himself in the narrative as a reformer of taste, and allegorically associates the reform of national religion with the reform of poetry. Both reforms, he suggests, require men of character to carry them out, including priests such as John Jewel and Richard Hooker and 'citizens' like Izaac Walton.

Just a few examples will have to suffice. Following the possibility that Wordsworth is not always writing from the historically privileged position of the 1820s, we can see him linking poetic history
and style in the Dissolution subplot. Wordsworth passes through
the history of his own development in four poems, three of which
allude sequentially to the styles of Chaucer, Shakespeare, and Milton.
Sonnet 2.13, 'Monastic Voluptuousness' represents a Prioress and a
Friar much as Chaucer represents them in *The Canterbury Tales*—
even if Wordsworth's satire is more pointed:

> ...round many a Convent's blazing fire
> Unhallowed threads of revelry are spun;
> There Venus sits disguisèd like a Nun,—
> While Bacchus, clothed in semblance of a Friar,
> Pours out his choicest beverage higher and higher
> Sparkling, until it cannot chuse but run
> Over the bowl, whose silver lip hath won
> An instant kiss of masterful desire—
> To stay the precious waste. (2.13.1–9)

Shakespeare could be similarly puritanical, despite his luxuries of
language, and frequently coupled Venus with her more unchaste
associations. But sonnet 2.14, 'Dissolution of the Monasteries',
again alludes to the 'bare ruin'd choirs' of Shakespeare's sonnet 73.
Wordsworth allows nature to return to populate the ruins; the sonnet
bursts with pastoral images of plant and animal life:

> The tapers shall be quenched, the belfries mute,
> And, 'mid their choirs unroofed by selfish rage,
> The warbling wren shall find a leafy cage;
> The gadding bramble hang her purple fruit;
> And the green lizard and the gilded newt
> Lead unmolested lives, and die of age.
> The Owl of evening, and the woodland Fox
> For their abodes the shrines of Waltham chuse...
> (2.14.3–12)

Nineteenth-century ideas are creeping back into the language, with
the 'Owl of evening' now a Wordsworth or Coleridge owl, rather

than the alien symbol of night terror and death as it appears in early modern drama and Spenser. Finally, 2.16, 'Continued', begins with a more Miltonic exultation at the overthrow of papacy in England, before addressing the economic and social impact of the Dissolution on the elderly. With a Miltonic epic simile, the young Noviciates of the monasteries are

> exulting to be free;
> Like ships before whose keels, full long embayed
> In polar ice, propitious winds have made
> Unlook'd for outlet to an open sea,
> Their liquid world, for bold discovery... (2.16.3–7)

By drawing on these images from Catholic, Protestant, and Puritan pillars of English poetry, Wordsworth accomplishes both the goals of the chivalric narrative *geste*, in building national myth out of disparate periods and cultural moments, and the goals of his own creative myth, the reconciliation of ambivalent feelings towards his historical and literary sources.

The most autobiographical examples of this subtext, or autobiographical allegory, or personal symbolic history, come at the end of Part 2. The crises of the English Reformation and civil wars clearly parallel, in their language and ideas, the crises of the French Revolution that Wordsworth experienced firsthand. Sonnet 2.26, 'General Views of the Troubles of the Reformation', describes the Reformation as

> ...a fight
> That shews, ev'n on its better side, the might
> Of proud Self-will, Rapacity, and Lust,
> 'Mid clouds envelop'd of polemic dust,
> Which showers of blood seem rather to incite
> Than to allay.—Anathemas are hurled
> From both sides; veteran thunders (the brute test
> of Truth) are met by fulminations new—
> Tartarean flags are caught at, and unfurled—
> Friends strike at friends—the flying shall pursue—
> And Victory sickens, ignorant where to rest! (2.16.4–14)

Taken out of its historical context, this poem spoke to the generation who could remember 1792–3.

The subsequent sonnet, 'English Reformers in Exile', alludes, in the autobiographical context, both to Wordsworth's travels on the continent in 1792–3 and 1798–9, and the upheavals and rifts they caused in Wordsworth's circles, both in the years following the revolution, and decades later. These eighteenth- and nineteenth-century crises for Wordsworth involved poetics as well as politics; the 'prurient speculations' and 'poisonous weeds' of the infighting among Protestant reformers in exile suggests the gossip and attacks of anti-Jacobinism in the eighteenth century, and accusations of being a political turncoat in the second decade of the nineteenth (2.17.9, 10). Yet Wordsworth's description of the reformers' 'forms' as 'broken staves' associates the sonnet with poetical reform too; the language implies not only the form-breaking of the printing press, but the surrender of creative power in Prospero's broken staff—lines in *The Tempest* to which Wordsworth alludes throughout his poetry. Read autobiographically, this line could suggest either the creative activisim of 1797–8 and the 'experiment' of *Lyrical Ballads*—or the self-described existential crisis of Book 10 of *The Prelude*, with its fears for the loss of creative power in 1793.

Wordsworth's broken stave, however, is made whole again in sonnet 2.29, perhaps one of the best in the poem as a whole. In this stanza of the *geste* narrative, history, autobiography, and philosophy align. The poem ostensibly praises the early modern reformer and thinker Richard Hooker and one of his mentors, John Jewel. But as with King Edwin of Northumbria and the priest who converts him in Part 1 of the *Sketches*, Wordsworth finds a strong personal affinity for Hooker, as a humanist, a lover of poetry, and above all, a peripatetic. Hooker's uncle and mentor was 'Exeter's resident humanist for half a century'.[1] Bishop John Jewel saw Hooker's potential and obtained a place for him at Corpus Christi, Oxford; Hooker 'sometimes journeyed on foot from Oxford to Exeter, on the way visting Jewel' (*DNB*). During the 1570s

---

1   *The Folger Library edition of the works of Richard Hooker*, ed. W. S. Hill, 7 vols. (1977–98), xiii. Cited in *DNB*.

Corpus was a Renaissance foundation, with a humanist cur-
riculum combining classical with Christian wisdom (including
that of the Greek fathers). Hooker's education there was accordingly very wide. Theology was his chief study, but he was well
acquainted with music (he had been a chorister) and poetry,
'all which he had digested and made useful'.... his tutor, John
Rainolds, [was] a moderate and immensely learned puritan, to
whom Hooker submitted some of his later anti-puritan writings
for criticism. (*DNB*)

Wordsworth would have known these details about Hooker from
Izaak Walton's 'Life of Mr. Richard Hooker'.[1]

Wordsworth celebrates Hooker and Jewel with an incident from
Walton's *Lives* that explores none of the churchman's ideas, but
entirely concerns his itinerancy. Wordsworth's quotation from Walton
alludes to his own poverty and itinerancy of 1793 and 1798:

On foot they went, and took Salisbury in their way, purposely
to see the good Bishop, who made Mr. Hooker sit at his own
table... and at the Bishop's parting with him, the Bishop...
forgot to give him money... he sent a Servant in all haste to call
Richard back to him, and at Richard's return, the Bishop said to
him, 'Richard, I sent for you back to lend you a horse which hath
carried me many a mile...' and presently delivered into his hand
a walking-staff with which he professed he had travelled through
many parts of Germany... (*SSIP* 230)

For those in 1822 who knew the biographical context of Wordsworth's
Salisbury Plain poems of 1793–4 (very few people indeed) and his
residence in Goslar in 1798, Wordsworth's choice of quotation would
resonate strongly: a 'youthful' itinerant yet an intellectual and spiritual reformer; a walk across Salisbury plain; the lack of money

---

1   See Izaak Walton, "The Life of Mr. Richard Hooker," in *The Works of Mr.
Richard Hooker*, ed. J. Keble, 7th revised, 1888. Wordsworth expressed his
love for Walton's book as late as 1844, when he wrote to Samuel Crompton:
'You could have scarcely mentioned the influence of my Poems over your mind
in any way so likely to gratify me, as by coupling them with that delightful and
precious book, Walton's Lives. It is singular that this individual Book is the only
one which tempted me to any thing like reading during the last month while I
have been moving from place to place ...' (*LY* 4: 622).

and a horse; and a good walking-stick used in Germany. 'Eminent Reformers', one of the finest poems in the *Sketches*, is not a poem about ecclesiastical reform, but, like an *Excursion* in miniature, a poem about thoughts and feelings roused by a society of intellectual itinerants:

> More sweet than odours caught by him who sails
> Near spicy shores of Araby the blest,
> A thousand times more exquisitely sweet,
> The freight of holy feeling which we meet,
> In thoughtful moments, wafted by the gales
> From fields where good men walk, or bowers wherein they rest.
> (*SSIP* 181, ll.9–14)

Wordsworth looks back on his own itinerant youth, and sees himself as participating in, and shaping, a 'reformation' of poetry and human life in nature, a reformation in which poetic, political, and religious reform play out in the 'fields where good men walk'. The 'walking-staff' of the sort Jewel gives to Hooker does not appear in the sonnet itself, but is a common image in Wordsworth's itinerant poetry from *The Ruined Cottage* and 'The Brothers' to *The Excursion*.

As in the poems or stanzas from Part 1 discussed above, the biographical context of these sonnets presents a number of possible readings, ranging from unconscious, instinctive affinities with certain historical characters and locations; to poetic and biographical associations made deliberately and overtly, but mostly for the benefit of Wordsworth and his closest friends; to the careful construction of a biographical allegory that parallels the public, teleological history of the poem, in a deliberate inversion of other medieval and early modern chivalric narratives and *gestes*, such as *The Song of Roland*, *Orlando Furioso*, and *The Faerie Queene*.

Regardless of which of these the author may have intended, close reading of the *Sketches* reveals a highly *scriptible* text in which authorial intention remains unclear over the poem as a whole, even as the introduction and notes to the poem advocate an unambiguous *lisible* poetic task: the celebration of the Church of England as safeguard of British cultural, artistic, and moral values. Reading the text

through structuralist and poststructuralist approaches allows inter-
pretations that move beyond the dialectic of 'Wordsworth is writing
a poem to support a national church as a bastion of British culture
and a bastion against continental Catholicism, yet at the same time
he expresses affection for aspects of Catholic culture, even "Catholic
envy" for its architecture and monastic culture'.[1] It is worth interro-
gating the dialectic of national vs. personal history; the dialectic of
poetic form (solipsistic sonnet vs. narrative); and the issue of what
constitutes Wordsworth's national myth, if we can accept that he is
writing a sort of chivalric *geste*. Out of these questions, which this
lecture has tried to begin to address, arises the more interesting question: if Wordsworth is writing two founding myths—one national,
one personal—which expose, in their symbolic history, crises such
as the destruction of the Christianised Britons, the Reformation, and
allegorically, the French Revolution, Wordsworth on Salisbury Plain,
etc., then what constitutes what Žižek calls the spectral history, the
deeper national or personal crisis of which the other is a masking
fiction?

An analysis of a few sonnets from Part 3 below will offer some
tentative answers to this question. Yet before this final analysis, I
should acknowledge that even the suggestion that the *Sketches* reveal
as much about Wordsworth's creative development as they do about
church history is not new; comments of this kind date from early
reviews of the volume. Several reviews point to the problem that
Wordsworth makes a poor advocate for the Anglican Church; one (by
a fluent Italian speaker) goes into detail about why his sonnets are not
sonnets (but does not consider the poem as a larger narrative written in stanzaic sonnets). Wordsworth may have felt disappointed that
so few reviewers took his *lisible* text at the face value of its national
project, when so many had done the opposite in reviews of *Lyrical
Ballads*, *Poems, in Two Volumes*, *The White Doe*, and *Peter Bell*—
that is, mistaken narrative simplicity for naïveté.

---

1   See John Davis, 'Catholic Envy: The Visual Culture of Protestant Desire', in *The
Visual Culture of American Religions*, ed. David Morgan and Sally M. Promey
(Berkeley: University of California Press, 2001), 105–28. See also Jon Mee,
*Romanticism, Enthusiasm, and Regulation: Poetics and the Policing of Culture
in the Romantic Period* (Oxford: Oxford University Press, 2003), 214–56.

In the context of the decline in ceremony and ritual documented by Cannadine,[1] the publication of *Ecclesiastical Sketches* in 1822 was not enough to turn the tide of the apathetic religiosity Wordsworth perceived in the second decade of the nineteenth century, even in the light of his improving reputation and sales. Out of the 500 copies of the *Sketches* printed by Longman, only 266 were sold to 1833, and 203 copies remaindered.[2] In contrast, only 30 copies of *The River Duddon*'s print run of 500 were remaindered over the same period (1834), 124 out of 500 copies of *Memorials of a Tour on the Continent*, and only 139 copies out of 1,000 of *Peter Bell* (1819). Wordsworth's four-volume *Miscellaneous Poems* of 1821 sold out their print run of 500 by 1826. In this context, *Ecclesiastical Sketches* sold poorly, even by Wordsworth's standards. Reviews such as that in the *Literary Chronicle*, highlighting the problem in the volume's purpose mentioned above, did not help sales:

> Mr. W.'s object, if indeed he had any other object beyond that of making a volume, is to versify 'certain points in the ecclesiastical history of our country;' and sad work, God knows, he has made of it: all we can gather from this luckless 'century of inventions,' is that Mr. W. is a great admirer of the established church and of priesthood; if the latter, however, have no better advocates, they had better bestir themselves. (*Literary Chronicle* 4 (14 December 1822) 791)

Wordsworth's poetry could not create a taste for religious feeling any more quickly than it could for its own poetics; by 1822 the *Lyrical Ballads* were part of Britain's literary establishment, but the nationalist Victorian future of church and state was in its infancy.

Yet Wordsworthian prophets such as John Wilson helped form this taste. Wilson's dual review of *Ecclesiastical Sketches* and *Memorials of a Tour on the Continent* in *Blackwood's* helped to form the Victorian myth of the poet that, in some aspects, had existed for decades. Wilson's paean supports the argument that the poem is a

---

1   See David Cannadine, "The Context, Performance and Meaning of Ritual: The British Monarchy and the 'Invention of Tradition', C.1820–1977," in The Invention of Tradition, ed. Eric Hobsbawm and Terence Ranger (Cambridge: Cambridge University Press, 1983), 109.

2   William St. Clair, *The Reading Nation in the Romantic Period* (Cambridge, UK; New York: Cambridge University Press, 2004), 663.

narrative with an autobiographical allegory, and pre-Victorian devo-
tees of Wordsworth could read it as such. Wilson uses the trope of
Wordsworth as a devotee of his own religion:

> his poetry is to him religion; and we venture to say, that it has
> been felt to be so by thousands. It would be absolute profanation
> to speak one word against many of his finest breathings; and as
> the author and promulgator of such divine thoughts, Wordsworth,
> beyond all poets, living or dead, is felt to be the object of the
> soul's purest reverence, gratitude, and love.[1]

Yet at the same time Wilson's review participates in the heterogeneous
supernatural language that subverts the dogma of the *Sketches*
and adds to their appeal to the modern reader, who can read in the
text Wordsworth's deliberate and unconscious subverting of his
own polemic. Wilson is more interested in Wordsworth than in
Wordsworth's argument. Here the poetical church father becomes, as
hinted at in 1.5, 'Uncertainty' and 2.27, 'English Reformers in Exile',
the Prospero or Taliesin:

> indeed when the whole series—all its three parts—is perused,
> the effect is magnificent, and great events, and deeds, and minds,
> seem to have been passing processionally before us over the
> floor of an enchanted stage. Mr Wordsworth's mind is familiar
> with all these as with matters of to-day, and therefore he speaks
> of them all as of things known and felt by every man of liberal
> education. He flings a beam of light on some transaction dark in
> antiquity, and it rises up for a moment before us—he raises the
> coffin-lid in some old vault, and we behold the still face of one
> formerly great or wise on earth—he rebuilds, as with a magic
> wand, the holy edifice that for centuries has lain in ruins—monks
> and nuns walk once more in the open sun-light, and all the fading
> or faded pageantries of faith re-appear an vanish in melancholy
> and sublime mutation. (177)

Here we have Wordsworth not as a pious advocate of the British
church, or one of its converts—neither the Anglo-Saxon Edwin nor
his proselytiser Paulinus—but the dramatist-illusionist. The poet is

---

1   *Blackwood's Magazine*, Vol. 12, No. 67 (August 1822), 175.

the master of a raree show of the sort exemplified in *Prelude* Book 7, or he is a Prospero creating a masque of spirits. When he 'flings a beam of light on some transaction dark in antiquity', Wordsworth seems less an antiquary than a Merlin, tampering with dark powers; Wilson's phrase 'transaction dark in antiquity' is a skilful use of poetic juxtaposition to suggest a 'dark transaction' more suited to Faustus. Wordsworth plays the antiquary when 'he raises the coffin-lid in some old vault', but turns magician again—Merlin raising a bridge for Uther Pendragon—when 'he rebuilds, as with a magic wand, the holy edifice that for centuries has lain in ruins'. Wilson's metaphor blends the ruins of the material church in Wordsworth's poems on the Dissolution of the monasteries with the spiritual fabric of the church that Wordsworth is trying to buttress or resurrect.

Although Wordsworth's ecclesiastical poetry drew the attention of the Oxford Movement and made the elderly poet a figurehead for their cause, his poem never achieves the goal of representing the aesthetic beauty of the English church without risking what Wordsworth fears greatly in 1820: the return of the church to its Catholic origins.[1] Wordsworth's faith was by this point too clearly defined, and his character too anti-Catholic, to allow him to indulge in the celebration of material, symbolism, and ritual in a way that Walter Scott, Keats, and later the pre-Raphaelites, Symbolists and Aestheticists could. Yet sonnets in this mould appear throughout the *Ecclesiastical Sketches*. Wordsworth's poems on the Dissolution demonstrate his philosophical and political position as balanced between reverential traditionalism and Protestant reform. He knew it, and so did his reviewers. But a perceptive reviewer like Wilson, for all his effusiveness, detected in the flirtations with fancy, and sonnets such as 'Imaginative Regrets', the charged, even magical, language of Wordsworth attempting to express the symbolic history of his own creativity. Wilson also noted the poem's narrative structure and Wordsworth's particular use of the sonnet to narrative ends.[2]

---

1   See Michael Tomko, 'Superstition, the National Imaginary, and Religious Politics in Wordsworth's *Ecclesiastical Sketches*', *Wordsworth Circle* 39.1–2 (2008): 16–19.

2   'It is obvious, that no one regular connected poem could have been written on so vast a subject. But although each Sonnet, according to the law of that kind

Part 3: Spectral history in the Ecclesiastical Sketches

Part 3 of the *Sketches* offers a number of key sonnets that demonstrate how Wordsworth's religious sensibility can be read as an unconscious mask for autobiography and poetic sensibility, or a conscious allegory, or a more unstable play between the two. In looking at just two examples, I will return to the question posed above, namely, if Wordsworth is writing two founding myths—one national, one personal—which expose as 'symbolic history' the crises of their foundations, then what constitutes what Žižek calls their fantasmic or 'spectral' history, the deeper national or personal crisis of which the others are a masking fiction? In Eric Santner's reading of Freud on the Mosaic myth, the spectral history is a crime which both permits the founding, and must be repressed in memory.[1] Touching on a Freudian reading, I would suggest that the spectral history in the *Sketches* does not depend on the trauma of a violent act (such as the Dissolution, or the Terror of the French Revolution) but a loss; in this case, the dual loss of Wordsworth's mother and father.

The finest poems in Part 3 circumvent or subvert Christian dogma in service of aesthetic conviction or argument. As it is for John Betjeman, the Christian church to Wordsworth is often synonymous with its material fabric: its chapels, spires, and cathedrals.[2] Hewitt details the strong connections between the *Sketches* and the Church Building Act of 1818.[3] But instead of focusing on these, which have

---

of composition, is in itself a whole, yet frequently two or three of the Series are beautifully connected and blended together, so as to read like connected stanzas of one poem' (177).

1   See Eric Santner, "Traumatic Revelations: Freud's Moses and the Origins of Anti-Semitism," in *Sexuation*, ed. Renata Salecl (Durham, NC; London: Duke University Press, 2000); Sigmund Freud, *The Origins of Religion: Totem and Taboo, Moses and Monotheism and Other Works*, ed. Albert Dickson (Harmondsworth: Penguin, 1985).

2   For example, 3.10, 'Places of Worship', 3.16, 'Mutability' and 3.17, 'Old Abbeys'.

3   'I submit that the Prefatory Note encodes reference to an earlier piece of legislation, the Church Building Act of 1818, which Wordsworth sets up as a constructive course of action leading to the renovation of Church and State and which he plays off against the destructive effect he fears Emancipation would produce. Ecclesiastical Sonnets, then, uses a specific political strategy for securing the Church of England, a strategy conditioned by the conservative goals of maintaining a hierarchy and promoting restraint'. See Regina Hewitt,

already received a fair share of critical attention, let us examine
the first of three sonnets on ritual in the Church of England: 3.13,
'Catechizing'. The title sounds dogmatic, but the sonnet provides a
scene worthy of the *Prelude*'s 'spots of time'.

In this sonnet, written in a first-person voice (a rarity in the
Sketches), Wordsworth begins by describing his memory of saying
the catechism in what must be Cockermouth church at Easter. But
the sonnet quickly reveals where the roots of Wordsworth's faith and
convictions lie:

> From little down to least—in due degree,
> Around the Pastor, each in new-wrought vest,
> Each with a vernal posy in his breast,
> We stood, a trembling, earnest Company!
> With low soft murmur, like a distant bee,
> Some spake, by thought-perplexing fears betrayed;
> And some a bold unerring answer made:
> How fluttered then thy anxious heart for me,
> Beloved Mother! Thou whose happy hand
> Had bound the flowers I wore, with faithful tie:
> Sweet flowers! at whose inaudible command
> Her countenance, phantom-like, doth re-appear:
> O lost too early for the frequent tear,
> And ill requited by this heart-felt sigh!

This is unmistakeably a love-sonnet; the final two lines express the
Petrarchan sentiment of distance and loss with the tropes of the 'frequent tear' and 'heart-felt sigh'. This poem is also an early memory,
even by Wordsworth's standards, and marks one of the few appearances of his mother in his poetry, alongside the more philosophically
developed, but less biographically specific, 'Bless'd the infant Babe'
passage of *The Prelude* (*1805 Prelude* 2.237–75).

Despite the presence of the Pastor, the children dressed in white,
and the catechism, this is neither a poem of Christian sentiment nor
Christian argument—as for most of the best sonnets in the overall

'Church Building as Political Strategy in Wordsworth's Ecclesiastical Sonnets,'
Mosaic: A Journal for the Interdisciplinary Study of Literature, 25.3 (January 1,
1992): 31–46, 32.

poem, the church or its history only supply the incident. The poem's key image is the flower, the 'vernal posy' of line 3, a pastoral image that develops through the poem. The company of children murmur the catechism 'like a distant bee', another pastoral image (1.5). (Blake implies a similar mixed metaphor in the 'Holy Thursday' of *Songs of Innocence:* 'The hum of multitudes was there, but multitudes of lambs, / Thousands of little boys and girls raising their innocent hands.')

The sestet reveals that Wordsworth's mother had pinned the flowers to his breast, and the poem's conclusion bestows imaginative power to the flowers, and by Freudian association, to the mother, bringing to mind Ariel's, 'Where the bee sucks, there suck I', a passage as well known to Wordsworth as Prospero's speech mentioned above. The flowers, rather than any Christian God, give the 'inaudible command' that triggers the resurrection not of the son, but of the mother. She appears, 'phantom-like', thus playing the double role of redeemer and Holy Spirit (1.12).

The word 'inaudible' serves as a keyword for the whole sonnet. The silence of the 'vernal posy' aligns with the silence of the mother's phantom in opposition to the murmuring and speaking of the children. The sonnet contains the central question of the national–personal dialectic in *Ecclesiastical Sketches:* to what or to whom does Wordsworth admit spiritual authority? Who gives him his 'inaudible command'? As throughout the *Sketches*, Wordsworth structures the children in the 'earnest Company' of the Easter ceremony as a dialectic. He presents two kinds of children, in their attitude to the call and response of the catechism, without pointing to himself despite the first-person narration:

> With low soft murmur, like a distant bee,
> Some spake, by thought-perplexing fears betrayed;
> And some a bold unerring answer made... (ll.5–7)

Which type of child was Wordsworth? In 1822, the answer is, both. He remains the dweller in uncertainties and 'thought-perplexing fears'. At the same time, in systematizing his earlier philosophical thoughts in the framework of rural piety in his published epic of 1814, and now writing an ecclesiodicy of the English church, he speaks with 'bold unerring answer', a position that bolsters his long-held convictions in support of the *idea* of Anglican dogma, if not the dogma itself—often to the detriment of his poetics. This sonnet is simple and powerful, and owes its spiritual authority to 'the meanest flower that blows'.

This allegorical and dialectical reading of the *Sketches* has revealed, from Part 1, that a personal symbolic history exists in the text, and that in the best sonnets it defers or overrides the religious narrative, and serves Wordsworth's more permanent themes on religious edifice in the natural landscape. There are half a dozen fine examples of this deft avoidance at work, but one poem near the end of Part 3 demonstrates how Wordsworth perhaps used the example of Keats to allow himself aesthetic indulgence in the beauties of the material church, while giving evidence of another dialectic of his struggle in the *Sketches*—the 'Catholic' poetical vs. the puritanical—through an allusion to one of the best known literary examples of ambiguity between Catholicism and Protestantism in English literature.

The sonnet 3.25, 'The Same', is the second of a run of three 'stanzas' on the subject of King's College Chapel in Cambridge. Poetically, this sonnet can't compare with 'Catechizing' or 'Mutability'; it brims with the tropes of Early Modern sonnets that Milton and Wordsworth worked so hard to replace. The first line contains a jarring forced pentameter foot, and two clauses constructed object-subject-verb and verb-subject, diction that gives the sestet its ornate and outmoded feel. But then the rhythms smooth out, and ecstatic language more reminiscent of Shelley and Keats develops. The whole sonnet reads:

> What awful pèrspective! while from our sight
> Their portraiture the lateral windows hide,
> Glimmers their corresponding stone-work, dyed
> With the soft chequerings of a sleepy light.
> Martyr, or King, or sainted Eremite,
> Whoe'er ye be, that thus—yourselves unseen—
> Imbue your prison-bars with solemn sheen,
> Shine on, until ye fade with coming Night!
> But, from the arms of silence—list! O list!

The music bursteth into second life—
The notes luxuriate—every stone is kiss'd
By sound, or ghost of sound, in mazy strife;
Heart-thrilling strains, that cast before the eye
Of the Devout a veil of ecstasy!

This sonnet was composed sometime between 23 November and 6 December 1820, making it the first sonnet of the *Sketches*, as published, to be composed.[1]

Geoffrey Jackson suggests that Wordsworth may have seen Keats' *Eve of St. Agnes*—published in July 1820—'during the two weeks he spent in London following his return from the continental tour, or in Cambridge'.[2] Jackson argues:

> While direct experience would sufficiently account for the description of the effect of light shining through the stained glass… it may be significant that, like WW, Keats uses the word *eremite* (l.227), and dwells on the sound of music (ll.20, 21; 28–31; 258–60; 289–93). WW imagines the figures depicted in the windows to be prisoners between the stone bars, while Keats presents effigies of the dead 'Emprison'd in black, purgatorial rails' (l.15). (*SSIP* 274)

Jackson does not mention that Wordsworth alludes to Shakespeare in this sonnet, whether or not directly or through the influence of Keats' poem. Wordsworth's directive to the reader in line 9, 'list! O list!' leaps out as the plea of the Ghost in a well-known passage from *Hamlet:*

> I am thy father's spirit,
> Doom'd for a certain term to walk the night,
> And for the day confined to fast in fires,
> Till the foul crimes done in my days of nature
> Are burnt and purged away. But that I am forbid
> To tell the secrets of my prison-house,

---

1   An earlier composition, 'A Parsonage in Oxfordshire', was composed on the continent around 14 July 1820, but was relocated before publication to a note on another sonnet, 'Pastoral Character'. It was moved to the 'Miscellaneous Sonnets' in the 1827 collected poems (*SSIP* 127).
2   Jackson, *SSIP*, 274.

> I could a tale unfold whose lightest word
> Would harrow up thy soul…
> But this eternal blazon must not be
> To ears of flesh and blood. <u>List, list, O, list!</u>
> If thou didst ever thy dear father love— (*Hamlet* 1.5)

The 'spectre' of the murdered father in this sonnet on the fabric of the British church points to the real crisis of the poem, which brings together Wordsworth's uncertainties over his creative powers as the philosophical poet of *The Recluse*, and the problems of a long-time cultural borderer creating a myth of a national religion to which he does not, in its specific tenets, adhere. Wordsworth would have known that the appearance of the ghost to Prince Hamlet, and the particulars of his tale, raise one of the most significant problems in Shakespeare's play: the question of whether the puritanical young prince can trust a Catholic ghost. In the words of another tragic hero, 'This supernatural soliciting / Cannot be ill, cannot be good'. In his sonnet, Wordsworth unconsciously identifies himself with the listening Hamlet, as a scholar caught traumatically between ancient tradition and modern sensibility. Yet he is also the speaker, the ghost of old Hamlet, returned to the temporal world to tell a tale that will encourage the nation to shake off its nightly wassail and return to sobriety and national pride. The only problem is that, like the admonitory elder Hamlet—and Shakespeare's rich language that portrays him—Wordsworth's *geste*, his tale of deeds, carries with it the rituals and sensuality of the very sect it disavows.

This is the real spectral history of the *Sketches:* the loss of two parents, and the wandering life that ensued must, the narrative suggests, find recompense in the material fabric of the church—which to Wordsworth, since 1800, has meant his life's work, the philosophical epic. Delivering a national myth and the symbolic history of its origins, Wordsworth throughout the poem questions his place in this myth, and his vocation of poet (rather than warrior or priest), a role too often self-identified as 'recreant soul, that dares to shun the debt / Imposed on human kind' (1.22.10–11). King Edwin, Paulinus, Richard Hooker, and other characters in the poem serve as the heroes of the chivalric narrative, all with their similarities to Wordsworth, but perhaps with the crucial difference of action, or the taking on of decisive public roles in the nation's spiritual history. In 1822, as self-critical as ever, even while just as firmly committed to belief in the power of his own verse, Wordsworth was still making his own myth, as much as his nation's. He could not write, as Sydney, Daniel, Spenser, and Milton could, as a myth-maker who had played a central role in his nation's political and religious landscape. The spectre of Wordsworth's father is once removed as allusion; the spectre of his loving mother is 'ill requited'—by a 'heartfelt sigh' of longing, but also, perhaps, by the poetic life.

Conclusion

In conclusion, the *Ecclesiastical Sketches* shows Wordsworth again at work creating the taste by which he would be read, this time on moral rather than aesthetic grounds. Although they sold poorly, even by Wordsworth's standards, the *Sketches* help lay the foundation— along with the didactic aestheticism of John Ruskin and Matthew Arnold—for late Victorian religiosity and nationalism. Their lack of contemporary popularity suggests they were half a century ahead of their time, in appealing for nationalism and religious feeling at what David Cannadine identifies as a nadir of such sentiment and associated ritual in British culture.

Wordsworth uses the *Ecclesiastical Sketches* to 'convert' himself out of what he worries is a sensual reclusiveness. He is not drastically changing his beliefs, but bringing his religious sense—a combination of feeling and philosophy inextricably linked to his own poetic development—into line with an extrinsic national system. The changes in his thinking that clash on the ears of modern readers comfortable with his earlier work represent the necessary quashing of a few heresies. As the examples in this lecture have hopefully demonstrated, many of these attempts at suppression or extirpation are not successful, as the poetics and images of individual sonnets slip the noose of the larger argument.

On the other hand, any readers who think that the *Sketches* represent a fundamental reordering or revision of the 'Wordsworthian' philosophy of *The Prelude*, the *Ode*, or other early philosophical verse should return to Wordsworth's first extant poem, *Lines on the Bicentenary of Hawkshead School*. Wordsworth writes:

> When Superstition left the golden light
> And fled indignant to the shades of night.
> When pure Religion rear'd the peaceful breast
> And lull'd the warring passions into rest
> …
> Science with joy saw Superstition fly
> Before the lustre of Religion's eye.
> With Rapture she beheld Britannia smile
> Clapp'd her strong wings, and sought the cheerful isle.
> The shades of night no more the soul involve,
> She sheds her beam, and Lo! the shades dissolve.
> No jarring Monks to gloomy cell confin'd
> With mazy rules perplex the weary mind. (ll.29–32, 43–50)

Thus Wordsworth has always been a crusader against dark 'Superstition', clearly associated with the 'jarring Monks' in these lines. Nor does he write as a Deist, or as a young convert to the *philosophes* and the cause of the French Revolution. In *Salisbury Plain* he will oppose 'Superstition' and 'Pride' with the 'herculean mace' of Reason, but here his champion is 'pure Religion', who clears the way for Baconian Science (*Salisbury Plain*, ll.548, 544, 543).

The foundations of Wordsworth's national myth in the *Sketches* are all visible here, 35 years earlier. The British and Saxon warriors give way to Anglo-Norman knights who 'no more in listed fields advance' but give up the war and the joust: 'Quick to the secret grotto they retire' (ll.57, 61). These contrasting images of two types of seclusion, one degenerative and one creative, establish the narrative pattern of the three seclusion sonnets of the *Sketches* (1.21–3).

However, despite what Gerald Newman calls Wordsworth's 'progressive moral and social ideology' and his later Tory devotion to Britain's 'social Reign of Virtue', Wordsworth could rarely, unlike Milton, express his most dogmatic political and religious convictions with poetic power. John Wilson writes correctly, in his rhapsodic review of the *Sketches*, that to Wordsworth 'poetry is… religion', but Wordsworth would probably, and perhaps mistakenly, deny this

(Wilson 175). He struggles to make something new and universal out of the history of the Church of England, but the most vivid and lasting images and symbols of the poem derive their power from the poetic philosophy he had already established by 1805.

Richard Gravil

Wordsworth's Sacred Sites: a Short Tour

1. Preliminary Expectoration

Ideally this morning's talk would encompass several sonnets on King's College Chapel, Staffa and Iona, a full account of the Furness Abbey 'spot of time', and a revisiting of the antiquarian dream on Salisbury Plain. Instead, I shall visit Furness and Swinside very briefly, Asia Minor on a magic carpet; a selection of abbeys viewed as if from a flying balloon; approach the Grande Chartreuse and Long Meg on foot for more leisurely inspection; and come to rest at Rydal Mount, which by the 1840s had itself become a kind of sacred site for curious pilgrims.

Many of those pilgrims were distinguished Americans; but rather more were operatives from the dark Satanic mills, wanting to catch a glimpse of the poet of *Lyrical Ballads* and *The Excursion* — and thronging into the garden of Rydal Mount to do so. In August 1847, Juliet Barker writes, Edward Quillinan reported 50 to 60 'cheap trainers' (it takes a moment to construe that phrase!) exploring the terrace and gardens uninvited, but 'doing no harm'. In the same month Mary Wordsworth noted: 'At this moment, a group of young Tourists are standing before the window ... and William reading a newspaper — and on lifting up his head a profound bow greeted him from each — they look as if come up from the Steamer for the day'.[1]

My selected sacred sites are ones viewed by Wordsworth as set apart by some especial power, connected with divinity, however conceived. Churches and Temples are obviously 'sacred sites', so I must at least mention the three fine and dramatic sonnets devoted to King's

1   Juliet Barker, *Wordsworth: A Life* (Ecco, 2005), 516.

College Chapel in *Ecclesiastical Sketches*, Part 3. The first, 'Tax not the Royal Saint with vain expense' with its wonderful evocation of a space 'scooped into ten thousand cells / Where light and shade repose' and music lingers 'like thoughts', and the second, with its Keatsian luxuriance in the 'mazy strife' of stone and music, both celebrate that 'forzen music' that is architecture, but turn the chapel into a kind of sea shell in which is heard the music of humanity. The third (3: 26) passes from King's College Chapel, via Westminster Abbey, to St Paul's, introducing two of the key themes that arise in Wordsworth's poetry whenever the notion of sacred spaces occurs. First, what happens to those who cross a sacred threshold; and second, what does most to make a building sacred. Philip Larkin famously observed in one of the most popular poems of the twentieth century, that a church is 'a serious house on serious earth / In whose blent air all our compulsions meet', and is a place 'proper to grow wise in, / *If only that so many dead lie round*' ('Church Going'). Wordsworth appears to agree, and St Paul's, it may strike you from Wordsworth's observation that as yet, St Paul's has not accrued its proper fill of 'mementos'—has a little way to go, before, it, like Westminster and Long

Meg, becomes 'satiate with its part / Of grateful England's overflow-
ing Dead'.

In a canny revision to the '1850' version of the Furness Abbey spot
of time, probably made later than most of the poems I shall be referring to, it is quietly implied that the ruined Abbey (which Wordsworth
and his friends visited on some occasions) and the Sunken Kirk at
Swinside shown on the previous page (which they visited on others)
are *equivalent* as places where transcendental experiences *might*
occur (*Prelude* [1850], 2. 100–105). The transcendental moment that
does occur at Furness, and so beautifully, is one that might seem more
appropriate to the man of 38 who wrote *The Tuft of Primroses*, than
to a 12- or 13-year-old indulging himself at the expense of a cautious
but deluded inn-keeper—

>   … And that single wren
> Which one day sang so sweetly in the Nave
> Of the old Church, that, though from recent Showers
> The earth was comfortless, and, touched by faint
> Internal breezes, sobbings of the place
> And respirations, from the roofless walls
> The shuddering ivy dripped large drops, yet still
> So sweetly 'mid the gloom the invisible Bird
> Sang to herself, that there I could have made
> My dwelling-place, and lived for ever there
> To hear such music.... (*1850*, 2. 118b–128a)[1]

—but in Wordsworth's thinking, of course life is structured the way
this narration is structured. This ten-line transcendental moment
is at the still centre of a juvenile maelstrom (115–118a and 128b–
131), which is itself islanded in the passing half-years (95–100
and 131b–137) and the entire narrative of childhood. Such islands
of experience may travel with one, unaltered, through a life whose
days are connected each to each in natural piety. So the road not
taken in 1783 (the road to Furness's binary alternative, the Swinside
stone circle) might have led him even then, to such a vision as he

---

1   Poetry quotations except where noted are from *The Poems of William
Wordsworth: Collected Reading Texts from the Cornell Wordsworth*, ed Jared
Curtis (Penrith: Humanities-Ebooks, 2009), 3 vols. Hereafter, *CWRT*.

experienced a decade later on Salisbury Plain. After all, Wordsworth was at school with William Gilpin's nephew and already knew as a schoolboy much of the druid lore that surfaces in the Salisbury Plain vision he would first tackle in 1794 and would go on refining in all versions of the Salisbury Plain poetry, both full-length verions of *The Prelude*, and numerous poems of the 1820s. That vision, Wordsworth said, gave him confidence, that he had what he needed to become as a poet a power like one of nature's. Stonehenge, antiquarians then believed, was raised as a memorial mausoleum, to British warriors massacred by Saxon treachery. In his vision, Wordsworth composes artfully the polarised conceptions of druidism that he grew up with, on the one hand as the sacrificers of men, conducting their solemn rituals with reference to both 'the living and the dead'; and on the other, as gentle observers of the heavens, moving as if to music— music that in his vision seems to express their entire 'harmony' with nature. I allude to these passages not to examine them now (I have done so elsewhere) but because if we are mindful of nature's music as manifested both in the Furness passage and in the vision on Salisbury Plain, we are likelier to grasp what on earth Wordsworth is getting at in my first port of call, *The Tuft of Primroses*.

2. Monastic Retreats

Anyone still using a one-volume Oxford Wordsworth or Hayden's two-volume Penguin may never have come across this poem, which until it was given a Cornell volume to itself, was known only to the kind of reader who relishes scholarly editions for their notes and appendices (it was consigned to Appendix C in De Selincourt's *Poetical Works*, vol 5). 'The Tuft of Primroses' is a desultory performance made of very disparate passages (including of course one on the eponymous tuft of primroses) but it is important as the only sustained piece of writing ever identified as a component of *The Recluse*, apart from *Home at Grasmere*, which makes its deep preoccupation with reclusiveness and sanctuaries highly significant.

There are hints in *Home at Grasmere* (as there are in the Furness spot and the poem 'On revisiting the Wye') that Wordsworth is

much inclined to retreat, ideally if combined with the sublime energies of intellectual adventure. By the time of *The Tuft of Primroses*
Wordsworth's interest in monasticism has reached its apex, and he
explores it through a series of closely linked meditations on hermi-
tude in general, on St Basil, on the fall of British Abbeys, and on the
Chartreuse, occupying 310 lines of poetry.

If you recognise the questions raised in this passage, but have never
read the *Tuft*, this is because in 1814 the passage was amended for the
Solitary to speak in Book 3 of *The Excursion*:

> What impulse drove the Hermit to his Cell
> And what detain'd him there his whole life long
> Fast anchored in the desart? [...]
>
> Not always from intolerable pangs
> He fled; but in the height of pleasure sigh'd
> For independent happiness, craving peace,
> The central feeling of all happiness,
> Not as a refuge from distress or pain,
> A breathing time, vacation, or a truce,
> But for its absolute self, a life of peace,
> Stability without regret or fear, ('Tuft', 280–2, 285–92)

And

> What other yearning was the master tie
> Of the monastic brotherhood, upon rock
> Aerial or in green secluded vale,
> One after one collected from afar,
> An undissolving fellowship? What but this,
> The universal instinct of repose,
> The longing for confirm'd tranquillity,
> Inward and outward, humble and sublime,
> The life where hope and memory are as one,
> Earth quiet and unchanged, the human soul
> Consistent in self rule, and heaven revealed
> To meditation in that quietness.... (297–308)

It hurts to truncate that passage, because it is one of the most sustained passages of rhythmic meditation in Wordsworth—as clearly imbued with personal imperatives as anything in his work.

There is some doubt when Wordsworth became aware of St Basil. According to the Cornell editor he read the account of Basil in William Cave's, *Apostolici*, 1716 'by May 1808' – when is when he wrote the *Tuft*) from, a copy of which was later in the Rydal Mount Library. But William Cave was an alumnus of St John's, where Wordsworth was a student, and a copy was in the St John's library. Mary Moorman says he might have read Basil's letters in Latin while staying with his brother Christopher in London in 1806 (they weren't translated for another 30 years). Be that as it may, St Basil is celebrated for establishing monastic rules which emphasised the life of community as well as prayer and manual labour, and for practical service to the common man. He founded a community at Arnesi in Pontus (Asia Minor), in AD 358, to which came his widowed mother, his talented sister, Macrina, other women, and eventually his friend, Gregory Nazianzen. One can see, perhaps, why Wordsworth identified with him, and why he identified Grasmere with Basil's 'Pontic solitude'though he is unlikley to have known how topograhically similar the two regions were, as shown in the Pontic Mountains tourist image below, which could be mistaken for part of Silver Howe.

De Selincourt's *Excursion* (PW, V. 484) quotes extensively from Cardinal Newman's translation of St Basil's fascinating Letters to Gregory Nazianzen. Wordsworth seems to have made his own translation, and partly in these terms:

> Come O Friend!
> (Thus did St. Basil fervently break forth,
> Entreated thus the man he held most dear)
> Come Nazianzen to *these happy fields*,
> To this enduring Paradise, these walks
> Of contemplation, piety, and love,
> *Coverts* serene of bless'd mortality. (358–64; my italics)

As Basil tries to seduce Gregory from the disputatious life of Athens to share this 'delicious Pontic solitude', the language suddenly becomes unmistakably redolent of Furness (now twenty-five years back in Wordsworth's experience):

> Unplagu'd, forgetting, and forgotten, here
> Mayst thou possess thy own invisible nest,
> Like one of those small birds that round us chaunt
> In multitudes, their warbling will be thine,
> And freedom to unite thy voice with theirs,
> When they at morn or dewy evening praise
> High heaven in sweet and solemn services. (376–82)

In his reply, however, unimpressed with the offered diet, even if it is in Paradise Regained, Nazianzen at first scorned the invitation, and in Wordsworth's version his reply was full of 'good-humoured ridicule'

> Directed both against the life itself
> And that strong passion for these *fortunate isles*,
> For this *Arcadia* of a golden dream. (my italics)

But in the end, he did come, and the coming is managed in a trope of alighting water fowl that tellingly aligns the passage with 'Home at Grasmere':

> And Amphilochius came, and numbers more,
> Men of all tempers, qualities, estates,

> Came with one spirit, like a troop of fowl
> That, single or in clusters, at a sign
> Given by their leader, settle on the breast
> Of some broad pool, ... (443–48)

Aligned with *Home at Grasmere*, also, is the more famous trope of 'Paradise, and groves elysian, Fortunate Fields'. These, Wordsworth had promised in 'Home at Grasmere'—supposedly six years before he became aware of Basil and Gregory Nazianzen's exchange—shall prove to be 'the simple produce of the common day'. This passage of the 'Tuft' is in fact the first application of that idea, subsequent to the writing of the so-called 'Prospectus' (as the poem I shall end with today is one of the last).

What Basil achieved in Pontus is summarized thus, quite beautifully I think. His mode of life and discipline did not cease when he departed. Rather, its influence, Wordsworth says,

> hung through many an age,
> In bright remembrance, like a shining cloud,
> O'er the vast regions of the western Church;
> *Whence* those communities of holy men
> That spread so far, to shrouded quietness
> Devoted, ...

The lines, with their delicate atmospheric metaphor, make a smooth transition from Asia Minor to Wordsworth's next subject, the decay of remote Abbeys built on 'British lawns', including his first poetic reference to Tintern Abbey (as opposed to the river 'a few miles above Tintern' that he wrote about in 1798):

> Fallen, in a thousand vales, the stately Towers
> And branching windows gorgeously array'd,
> And aisles and roofs magnificent that thrill'd
> With halleluiahs, and the strong-ribb'd vaults
> Are crush'd, and buried under weeds and earth
> The cloistral avenues— (478–83)

Abbeys by Severn, Thames or Tweed are evoked (as Larkin also observed, water is almost inevitably involved in sacred places) and the passage concludes:

> So cleave they to the earth, in monument
> Of Revelation, nor in memory less
> Of nature's pure religion, as in line
> Uninterrupted it hath travelled down
> From the first man who heard a howling storm,
> Or knew a troubled thought or vain desire,

—like those left on the threshold in the sonnet on Westminster—

> Or, ... saddened at a perishable bliss... (497–505)

What, according to Wordsworth, are Abbeys *for*? What they were *intended* for is clear: as 'monuments of revelation'. But the interest lies in the extraordinary balancing passage after the word 'nor': that invocation of 'nature's pure religion' which has travelled down uninterrupted, by some kind of apostolic succession, 'from the first man who heard a howling storm' — and who, perhaps, piled a few stones together to worship or propitiate whatever he heard in that storm. Of this 'pure religion', careless of whether a man is an Anglican, a Catholic, a Druid or a worshipper of Odin, Wordsworth himself in *The Prelude* is overtly a 'priest'.

In 1790, Wordsworth and Robert Jones stopped two nights at the Chartreuse. Wordsworth wrote thirty lines or more on the monastery in *Descriptive Sketches* (1793) showing that it had been important to him at an early date, but passed over the event quite tersely in the *1805 Prelude*. In 1808 he developed a fuller account for the *Tuft of Primroses*, which he then raided for an even longer (but conspicuously weaker) *1850 Prelude* version. In the 'Tuft' version, Nature herself—witnessing how the retreat it is threatened by revolutionary arms—voices a plea that this one temple be left as 'a spot of earth devoted to Eternity'. And Wordsworth introduces an overt variation on the close of the celebration of ruined British abbeys, with much the same proportions between revelation and aspiration. The poet's voice now seconds Nature's. He has no argument with progress, and cannot side with Papal repression against French liberty, but nevertheless:

> "—let it be redeemed
> With all its blameless priesthood—for the sake
> Of Heaven-descended truth; and humbler claim
> Of these majestic floods, my noblest boast;
> These shining cliffs, pure as their home, the sky;
> These forests unapproachable by death,
> That shall endure as long as Man endures
> To think, to hope, to worship, and to feel;
> To struggle,—to be lost within himself
> In trepidation,—from the dim abyss
> To look with bodily eyes, and be consoled."
> ('Tuft', 557—67)

Here again 'Heaven-descended truth' gets three perfunctory words (as did 'monument / Of Revelation') while Nature's truth and the history of human feeling require eight sublime lines. What makes a site sacred? Is it that it associates human construction with nature's power—with sequestered brooks or shining cliffs or forests unapproachable by death? And if so, might such an association act just as powerfully, perhaps more so, when, as at Furness, the human artefact has been re-naturalized? A sacred site memorialises thought, hope, worship and feeling—and it matters little, it seems, whose worship, or of what.[1] The Chartreuse and Stonehenge are both 'embodied dreams' and the plea to spare the one might have been applied equally to the other.

'Spare this house', Wordsworth pleads for the convent—

> if past and present be the wings
> On whose support harmoniously conjoined
> Moves the great Spirit of human knowledge, spare
> This House,

—which plea reminds one, surely, of *Salisbury Plain*'s parallel plea that 'not a trace':

---

1   As le Rochefoucauld wrote in 1784, to his father, 'As to the faith of the English what is it? I have heard a great deal of discussion and have never been able to grasp the conclusion.... Nearly every Englishman holds a different belief: all of them believe in some particular point, peculiar to themselves'. Quoted in David Evans, a Letter to *The Times*, 18/03/2012.

Be left on earth of superstition's reign

Save that eternal pile which frowns on Sarum's plain

And that 'pile', by and by, is joined in the oeuvre by numerous totemic sites, including the 'Sunken Kirk' visited in childhood and commemorated decades later in the Duddon sonnets, and another stone circle known as 'Long Meg and her Daughters'.

3. Long Meg and her Daughters (1821/1836)

A weight of Awe not easy to be borne
Fell suddenly upon my spirit—cast
From the dread bosom of the unknown past,
When first I saw that family forlorn.
Speak Thou, whose massy strength and stature scorn
The power of years—pre-eminent, and placed
Apart, to overlook the circle vast—
Speak, Giant-mother! tell it to the Morn
While she dispels the cumbrous shades of night;
Let the Moon hear, emerging from a cloud;
At whose behest uprose on British ground
That Sisterhood in hieroglyphic round
Forth-shadowing, some have deemed, the infinite
The inviolable God that tames the proud![1]

Remarkably, Wordsworth was fifty when he first visited 'Long Meg' in 1820.[2] As he wrote to Sir George Beaumont on the occasion:

---

1 Quoted from *Wordsworth: Poetical Works*, ed Thomas Hutchinson, rev. Ernest de Selincourt, Oxford Standard Authors edn (Oxford 1936).

2 Inclusion of this sonnet in the poems of the 1833 Scottish Tour is, as Tim Fulford has pointed out in an admirable essay to which I am much indebted, a fiction. It was written in 1821, published in the 1822 *Description of the Scenery of the Lakes in the North of England*, and for a while after 1826 was classified simply as a 'Miscellaneous Sonnet'. It was added to the Tour only in 1836 to complete a sequence which includes five sonnets on Staffa and Iona – three of which Wordsworth recited, hot from composition, to an admiring Ralph Waldo Emerson in 1833. The Iona sonnets of 1833 continue the association of music and architecture in the King's College trio in *Ecclesiastical Sketches*, and they use a common term—'pile'—for both the natural artefact of Fingal's Cave (whose Gaelic name means the musical cave) and the monastic remains on Iona. See Tim Fulford. '"Long Meg" and the Later Wordsworth', *Essays in Criticism* 59:1, 37–57.

> My road brought me suddenly and unexpectedly upon that ancient monument, called by the country people Long Meg and her Daughters. Everybody has heard of it, *and so had I from very early childhood*; but had never seen it before. Next to Stonehenge it is beyond dispute the most noble relic of the kind that this or probably any other country contains. Long Meg is a single block of unhewn stone, eighteen feet high, at a small distance from a vast circle of other stones, some of them of huge size, *though curtailed of their stature, by their own incessant pressure upon it.*[1]

Five thousand years of slow subsidence seems to be imagined here; such as he observes in Duddon sonnet 17 of the so-called 'sunken kirk' at Swinside *not* visited in Book 1 of *The Prelude*—

> that mystic Round of Druid frame,
> Tardily sinking by its proper weight
> Deep into patient Earth, from whose smooth breast it came!

Either Wordsworth thought of stone circles as earth's children, returnng to her bosom rather as 'Lucy' does, or he grasped, counter-intuitively, that the ground surface *rises*. As he points out in a note in the *Guide*,

> It is not improbable that these circles were once numerous, and that many of them may yet endure in a perfect state, under no very deep covering of soil. (*Prose Works*, 2: 195)

The note continues with an anecdote drawn from his Quaker friend Thomas Wilkinson of Yanwath who had excavated:

> a perfect circle of stones, from two to three or four feet high, with a *sanctum sanctorum*,—the whole a complete place of Druidical worship of small dimensions, having the same sort of relation to Stonehenge, Long Meg and her Daughters near the river Eden, and Karl Lofts near Shap ... that a rural chapel bears to a stately church, or to one of our noble cathedrals.

Notably, the image he applies to Long Meg and her Cumbrian

---

1   Letter of 6 January 1821 *The Letters of William and Dorothy Wordsworth: The Later Years 1821-1850*, ed. Ernest de Selincourt, 4 vols., 2nd edn., rev. Alan G. Hill (Oxford, 1978-88), I, 5 .

cousins is the same one he used to describe the relations between the three-part 'Recluse' and all the lesser poems in his oeuvre. It is his favourite mid-life metaphor of integration, or wholeness, and his use of it here relates to his obsession throughout the 1820s with the spiritual 'matter of Britain'.

Wilkinson's discovery was destroyed by the landowner; and informed in part by William Stukeley's observations in *Itinerarium Curiosum*, Wordsworth goes on that 'It is much to be regretted, that the striking relic of antiquity at Shap has been in a great measure destroyed also.'[1]

Compared with the complex vision on Salisbury Plain, this poem is both brief, spare in detail, and surprisingly free both of antiquarian lore and of personal application. It barely concerns itself with some of the circle's major associations. For example he seemingly ignores all of the following. First, the testimony of William Stukely in 1725, followed by Clarke in his *Survey of the Lakes* (1789), and amplified by Thomas Hutchinson, in his *Excursion to the Lakes in Westmoreland and Cumberland*, 1776, that Long Meg is a druidic temple. Second, the legend that the stone circle is a witches coven turned to stone by the wizard and alchemist Michael Scott when he found them holding a Sabbath (Sir Walter Scott deployed the magic books of the 13th century Michael Scott as powerful agents in *The Lay of the Last Minstrel*, where they are released from the wizard's tomb at Melrose Abbey to play their part in the 16th century plot). Many of the circles of Cumbria, were according to William Stukely, attributed by superstitious locals, to 'auld Michael'. The great Alchemist is said to have cast the spell so that nobody attempting to count the stones

---

1   When Stukeley visited Long Meg in 1725, he saw not only the extant stone circles of Long Meg, Little Meg and Glassonby, but a fourth to the South West of which no trace remains. His survey in *Itinerarium Curiosum*, took in Shap and Eamont Bridge (with Mayburgh Henge and Arthur's round table) and is not only the most valuable record of exactly how things stood in this locality a century before Wordsworth's sonnet—but of what was happening to such sites: stones buried by people fearful of their powers; stones blown up or sawn into millstones; stones incorporated at a frightening rate into farms, houses, walls, and roads. Building the township of Shap obliterated most of an astonishing ceremonial avenue, which Stukeley thought would have rivalled Avebury. He judged it to be.1.3 miles long and 75 feet wide, containing some 400 stones, set on each side of the avenue, at intervals of 35 feet.

will arrive at the same number twice. Why? Because to *do so would release the petrified powers of witchcraft*.[1] Third, a further legend of the 1700s, that when the local landowner Colonel Lacy attempting to dynamite the stones so as to improve the use of the land for agriculture, he brought on a thunderstorm of terrifying force attributed by the locals to the druidical powers latent in the stones themselves.

The earliest literary account of the place, was in Camden's *Britannia* (1577–1607). At Little Salkeld, says Camden:

> there bee erected in manner of a circle seventie seaven stones, every one tenne foote high, and a speciall one by it selfe before them at the very entrance, rising fifteene foote in height. This stone the common people thereby dwelling name Long Megge, like as the rest her daughters. And within that ring or circle are heapes of stones, under which, they say, lie covered the bodies of men slaine. And verily, there is reason to thinke that this was a monument of some victory there atchieved, for no man would deem that they were erected in vaine. (*Britannia* (1637) 777)

Notice Camden's assumption here, palatable to Wordsworth one would think, that such a monument must have to do with 'England's grateful dead', and the equally palatable insistence that the name to be used is that bestowed by the 'the common people thereby dwelling'.

Camden's account initiates an odd and rather folksy feature of written accounts of Long Meg. A century later, William Stukeley (1725) observed a circle of 300 ft diameter consisting of 100 stones, though he tended to count stones that were implied by the geometry but had since been removed. Wordsworth, in 1820, estimated the stones at seventy-two in number. Thomas Wilkinson (in his 1824 volume *Tours to the British Mountains*) counted 'seventy-five, but I did not repeat the operation'. Grevel Lindop, in his *Literary Guide to the Lake District*, 1993, says Meg's daughters are 69 boulders. Frank Welsh's *Companion Guide to the Lake District* (1997) speaks of only '59 rather small stones adding the quite recent realization that 'The

---

1   The historical Michael Scott is supposed to have been a Cumbrian Abbot, and to have been offered the Archbishopric of Canterbury by successive Popes in 1223 and 1227. He appears Dante's *Inferno* (canto xx.115-117) in a part of the Eighth Circle of Hell reserved for sorcerers.

carvings on Meg ... are connected with funerary sites' thus confirm-
ing Camden's speculation.[1] With 59 and 69 as the most recent estimates, and 77 and 100 the oldest, and Wordsworth and Wilkinson
in between at 72 and 75, these figures amply confirm the process
of destruction—though one might prefer to conclude that Michael
Scott's spell against anyone making an accurate count has lost none
of its ancient power. (I haven't attempted to count the ones in the fine
antiquarian sketch below, showing the shadow cast by Long Meg, and
the farmer's wall which bisected the site in the eighteenth century.)

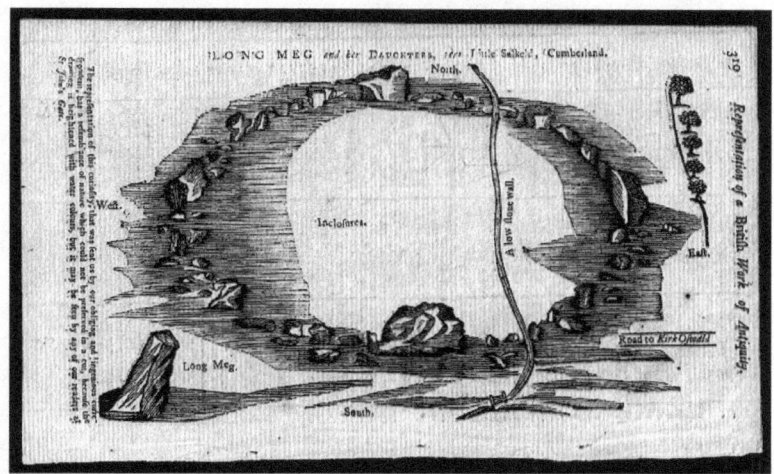

Short though it is, the poem is weighted with cultural implications,
including the family metaphor, so let us look at some of its phrasing,
especially where he made changes over the years. Whatever reason
Wordsworth had for changing his original draft from 'the sisterhood
forlorn ... thy progeny' to 'that family forlorn ... That sisterhood',
both formulae respect the nomenclature bestowed by the country
people of Addingham parish. The dramatic repetition of 'Speak thou'
and 'Speak Giant-mother' is an intensifying repetition introduced in
1836: what it replaces was rather limp: 'When first I saw that sisterhood forlorn / *And her who*'). Instead of the question Meg is now

---

1   'These are quite visible whorls, one of which has associated arched cups, a
type of design common in late Neolithic and early Bronze Age remains'.

asked 'At whose behest uprose on British ground that Sisterhood?'
Wordsworth had originally asked in more rationalist mode (1822):
'When, how and wherefore rose on British ground'. 'At whose
behest' is surely both more haunted and more open-ended?

The phrase 'British ground', however, was there from the start,
relating the poem to other late work that somehow bridges the inter-
val between early and late Wordsworth as he pursues his perennial
concern with nationhood. Inevitably, of course, British (in 'British
ground') signifies Welsh. All of what might be termed Wordsworth's
megalithic portal poems embrace wonderingly a pre-Saxon world to
which we have no archival access, the records having been extin-
guished by tribal prejudice, scandalously endorsed by Bede (as
Wordsworth complains in *Ecclesiastical Sketches*). In fact, of 23
uses of the word 'British' I can find in Wordsworth's poetry, only
7 do *not* clearly have that precise historical inflection. Think, *inter
alia*, of 'the Cairn / Of some old British Chief' imagined on one of
the islands of Rydal; of 'our British Hill', referring to Skiddaw in
'Pelion and Ossa'); of the ancient 'British Harp' in *The Excursion*;
or of Wordsworth seeing from the top of Black Comb the amplest
view 'that British ground commands'; or asking whether the waters
at Devil's Bridge, can have 'a British source'; or remarking that
'Her course was for the British strand' in the Arthurian poem 'The
Egyptian Maid', and invoking 'our British ancestors' in the headnote
to 'Humanity' (1829), which usage of 'ancestors' quietly challenges
the now debunked notion of displacement.

Wordsworth had been foraging in antiquarian lore for a long time to
prepare his Ecclesiastical and Duddon sonnets as 'The dread bosom
of the unknown past' reminds us. The tone of Long Meg is shared
with Sonnet 5 in *Ecclesiastical Sketches*, a tour-de-force which not
only tallies the sacred sites of 'British ground', from Stonehenge
to Iona, via Snowdon and Cumbria, but folds the lost annals of the
Celtic church into the conjectural ones of Druidism. It makes British
pre-history into a *native stream* whose exact sources, unlike those of
the Duddon ('I seek the birth-place of a native Stream') can *not* be
found: no one's researches, he says at its close

>   To an unquestionable Source have led;

> Enough—if eyes that sought the fountain-head,
> In vain, upon the growing Rill may gaze.

Why, one might ask, are Meg's imagined auditors the Moon and Sun? Because *light* is of course of the essence of stone circles and because Stukeley (correctly) divined a solsticial purpose at Stonehenge. Long Meg herself, a piece of sandstone transported from the banks of the River Eden, points to the setting sun on the shortest day of the year, when her shadow falls, also, over one of the portal stones. The circle is said to be made up primarily of glacial erratics of a fairly common sort, but with four larger quartz crystal stones, so placed that viewed from their opposite numbers, they point to sunrise and sunset in midwinter and midsummer.

And finally, what of that 'Hieroglyphic round'? Wordsworth originally wrote 'That wondrous monument in mystic round'; echoing his own Duddon sonnet on Swinside. But hieroglyphs do belong to more or less the right period for this circle. They were invented between the second and third millennium BC, and are in most cases, certainly in Asia Minor (Anatolia) logographic – i.e. they represent a Word. In this case, one might say, the *Logos*. The builders of Long Meg are quietly represented as in tune with Stukeley's idea that Druids were as Wordsworth said 'auxiliars of the cross' (*Ecc*

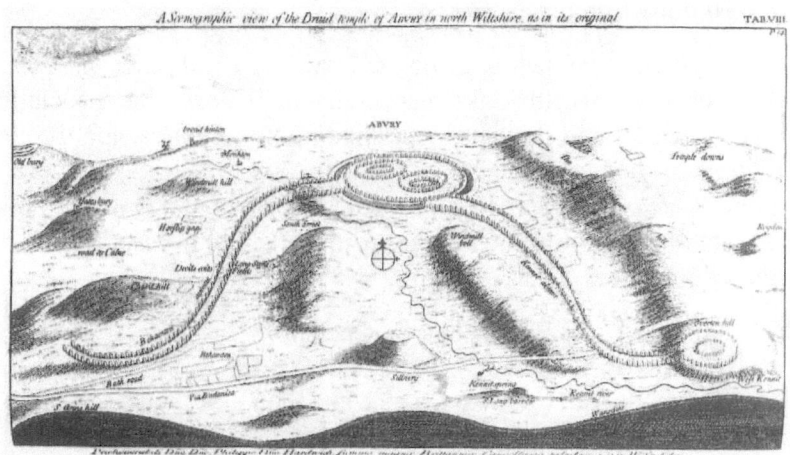

Sketches, sonnet 10). Stukeley argued, and demonstrated in his wonderful sketch, that the great structure at Avebury was a 'hieroglyph'.

Its layout signified, Stukeley came to believe, not only Deity, but indeed the Trinity, as numerous associated drawings in his Avebury volume make sufficiently clear. Wordsworth's 'some have deemed', in the penultimate line of his sonnet, expresses due caution concerning Stukeley's theodicy:

> Forth-shadowing, some have deemed, the infinite
> The inviolable God that tames the proud

but the same fascination with architectural hieroglyphs (and with comparative religion) is found in these lines on the Chartreuse:

> "O leave in quiet this embodied dream,
> This substance by which mortal men have clothed,
> Humanly cloth'd the ghostliness of things ..." (Tuft, 540

and in the strange homage to St Paul's cathedral in *Ecclesiastical Sketches*, 3: 26:

> that younger Pile, whose sky-like dome
> Hath typified by reach of daring art
> Infinity's embrace.

Plus ça change, he seems to be saying, *plus c'est le même chose*. Wherever Wordsworth looks, especially in Britain, the association between natural and divine is inscribed upon the landscape through millennia of human shaping.

For *Ecclesiastical Sketches* he wrote a curious sestet which never found itself an appropriate octave, so the fragment exists as a poem *editorially* entitled 'Druid Temple';

> And thus a Structure potent to enchain
> The eye of Wonder rose in this fair Isle;
> Not built with calculations nice and vain
> But in mysterious Nature's boldest style,

> Yet orderly as some basaltic Pile
> That steadfastly repels the fretful main. (*CWRT*, 3. 413)

The six lines (which can only refer to Stonehenge, as no other stone circle would suggest the geology of Fingal's Cave) *seem* to counterpoint, in one vision of spiritual continuity, Stonehenge and Long Meg, the wonders of King's College Chapel and even the 'nice calculations' of St Paul's. They do, though, hint Wordsworthianly at some degenerative principle taking one from nature's steadfast architecture to the vanities of Sir Christopher Wren. If, by the way, Staffa's Cave did not evoke verse as impressive as the lines on Long Meg this may be because he visited Long Meg alone and on foot and not on a steamboat with a 'motley crowd', as in the wonderfully grumpy 26th sonnet of the Scottish Tour:

> We saw, but surely, in the motley crowd,
> Not One of us has felt, the far-famed sight;
> How could we feel it? each the other's blight.

4. Rydal Mount

My final sacred site is that Victorian place of pilgrimage, Rydal Mount. Much of Wordsworth's late composition, disappointing though modern readers have found it, is a deliberate exploration of the idea that through the exercise of imagination, paradise and groves elysian, can be, and are, as *Home at Grasmere* promised, 'the simple produce of the common day'. In such a mind-set, the garden spring is a small sister of the great family of floods, distantly related to the Ganges, and the mound in front of Rydal Mount can easily become conflated with Beersheba, home of Jacob in the 28th chapter of Genesis, and even the refuge of the prophet Elijah in the first Book of Kings.

When Wordsworth was threatened with expulsion from Rydal Mount, what such expulsion threw into relief was not the marketable features—a beautiful home, with its magnificent view of Windermere, and a much-improved garden—but the meaning of a feature few visitors to Rydal Mount ever notice: a 'pellucid Spring'

> Who with the comforts of my daily meal,
> Hast blended, thro' the space of twice seven years,
> Beverage as choice as ever Hermit prized,
> That Persian Kings might envy; ... (*CWRT*, 2: 294)

To this spring Wordsworth devotes sustained descriptive attention in the poem known to the household as the 'Lines on Nab Well', and to editors, less poetically, as 'Composed when the probability existed of our being obliged to quit Rydal Mount as a Residence'.

Adoration of watery elements, the poem implies, is a universal, as appropriate to a British spring as it is to the Ganges. The indispensable Henry Crabb Robinson recorded in his diary that the lines on Nab Well were meant to introduce a lengthy portion of *The Recluse* offering 'a poetical view of water as an element in the composition of our globe'. It would, one may conjecture, have dealt with the relation between springs and ritual, whether in India, as specifically mentioned in this very multicultural poem, or at the druidical sites described by Stukeley (there is a spring just north of Long Meg, for instance, and another at the entrance to Mayburgh Henge), or at riverside chapels, like St Ninian's on the Eden, or the ancient wells associated with the Cumbrian missions of Saint Patrick, St Ninian and St Kentigern.

But water in another manifestation, vapour, is the theme of a slightly earlier poem which also makes of Rydal Mount a sacred site. The 'Ode Composed on an evening of extraordinary Splendour and Beauty' was, Wordsworth says in the *Fenwick Notes*, 'Felt, and in a great measure composed, upon the little mount in front of our abode at Rydal.'[1] Wordsworth's note on the poem points out that the atmospheric effect it describes is not uncommon, and can be produced either by watery vapours or by sunny haze.

Wordsworth also acknowledges that the angelic frisson in 'wings at my shoulder seem to play' was suggested by Washington Allston's very dull painting of Jacob's ladder which Wordsworth saw in London in December 1817. It is hard to believe, however, that Wordsworth

---

1   *The Fenwick Notes of William Wordsworth*, ed. Jared Curtis, 2nd edn, revised and corrected (Penrith: Humanities-Ebooks, 2007), 148. The first version of the poem lacked the third stanza with its explicit allusion to the 'bright steps' of Jacob's ladder.

did not also have in mind an earlier treatment of 'Jacob's Dream' by
Aert de Gelder, whose painting (in the Dulwich Museum) Allston
acknowledged as his own inspiration.[1]. It is hard, also, not to regret
that despite his friendship with Crabb Robinson, source of much of

1   For Allston and Gelder see http://www.ntprints.com/image/348477/jacobs-dream-
     exh-1819-by-washington-allston-1779-1843   and   http://www.bbc.co.uk/arts/
     yourpaintings/paintings/jacobs-dream-200007 respectively.

our knowledge of William Blake, Wordsworth is unlikely to have known of Blake's very different treatment (previous page). The Gelder seems to me much the most Wordsworthian of these three treatments, and is certainly the most naturalistic; but Allston claimed that he was breaking new ground in his treatment of the theme. Indeed his claims would serve to describe Blake's vision: 'instead of two or three angels I have introduced a vast multitude: and instead of a ladder or narrow steps I have endeavoured to give the idea of unmeasurable flights of steps, with platform above platform, rising and extending into space immeasurable'.

Despite its biblical foundation, the process of vision recorded in Wordsworth's poem is not unlike the habitual cast of Wordsworth's imagination. Reviewing *The Excursion*, William Hazlitt fastened on the Wanderer's great speech about the history of religious feeling, or as Hazlitt puts it, 'tracing the fictions of Eastern mythology to *the immediate intercourse of the imagination with Nature*'. In a famous passage of that speech (*Excursion*, 4: 847–56; *CWRT*, 2. 415) Wordsworth travels to ancient Greece on his magic carpet:

> —In that fair clime, the lonely Herdsman, stretch'd
> On the soft grass through half a summer's day,
> With music lulled his indolent repose.
> And in some fit of weariness, if he,
> When his own breath was silent, chanced to hear
> A distant strain, far sweeter than the sounds
> Which his poor skill could make, his fancy fetch'd
> Even from the blazing chariot of the sun,
> A beardless youth, who touched a golden lute,
> And filled the illumined groves with ravishment.

The Wanderer treats this theme of Hellenic mythopoeia, sensitively and respectfully—so much so that this passage of the poem undoubtedly inspired the rampant Hellenism of the next generation of Romantics—but he treats it very much as one might expect a son of the Kirk to do, that is from the outside, and with the air of one who makes a *qualitative* distinction between the imagination of a Greek herdsman and the religious belief of a practising Calvinist.

Wordsworth, whose poetry on Nab Well shows him capable of having become, if he had so wished, a distinguished and liberal-minded anthropologist, does *not*, it seems to me, make that reservation when he treats the belief systems of the past.

What ratifies the daily libation drawn from Rydal spring is 'a primary law of our human nature' manifested alike in the votive shrines of ancient Britons with their genii loci, the missionary Celts with their baptismal springs, and the worship of Vishnu. What matters is not the doctrinal content of religion, but the sense of the infinite; the capacity to be lost simultaneously within oneself and in something greater than oneself, of which Stonehenge or Glen Almain or the Cave of Staffa or St Herbert's Island or even the Chartreuse, or one day even St Paul's, may all be the adequate symbol. So where the Wanderer in 1814 is *commenting* on Hellenic mythopoeia, as part of a teleological ascent towards revelation, Wordsworth in his evening ode (and indeed in the 'Nab Well' poem of 1825) is *practising* it.

So, to the poem, with its vision of Jacob's ladder:

> Had this effulgence disappeared
> With flying haste, I might have sent,
> Among the speechless clouds, a look
> Of blank astonishment;
> But 'tis endued with power to stay,
> And solemnize one closing day,
> That frail Mortality may see—
> What is? ah no—but what *can* beI (*PW*, 4: 10, ll. 1–8)

Characteristically, when he published this poem, Wordsworth advised any reader not yet familiar with *Intimations of Immortality* to rectify that ignorance promptly. *Intimations* is indeed echoed from the outset, with its 'Time was when field and watry cove' motif, to the close with its overt intimations of immortality. The whole poem appears to cast doubt upon the premise of *Intimations*, that

> nothing can bring back the hour
> Of splendour in the grass, of glory in the flower;

There is an inversion in train, in that this poem's concern is less with *whence* than with *whither*; on future not past 'glory.' But being by Wordsworth, the confidence is hedged about. The sense of loss is insistent; the sense of possibility conditional. What is revealed is not 'What is', but 'what *can* be'; the glorious light is 'at this moment' only, even in the last stanza.

What is most impressive in the poem (as in other poems of this decade) is its almost Keatsian tactility or sensation. The poet's fleshly eyes are excited by the

> ... beamy radiance that imbues
> Whate'er it strikes with gem-like hues!
> In vision exquisitely clear
> Herds graze along the mountain-side;
> And glistening antlers are descried;
> And gilded flocks appear. (27–32)

But being by Wordsworth, the poem has his characteristically troubling undertones, underpresences, undertows. The third stanza's declaration that 'From worlds unquicken'd by the Sun / A portion of the gift is won' reminds one of how in the *Extempore Effusion* the sense of heaven is muted by the expression 'How fast has brother followed brother, / From sunshine to the sunless land!'—a way of picturing heaven that while logically exact, makes it sound deeply uninviting. Or of the strange (suspiciously Plotinian) idea in *Intimations* that our heavenly origins and destiny have power to make 'Our noisy years seem moments in the being / Of the eternal Silence'. One expects more loyalty from poets to 'our noisy years'.

As the vision lingers, the poet tentatively invokes, or half-revokes, the loss 'deplored' in 'Intimations':

> Oh, let Thy grace remind me of the light,
> Full early lost, and fruitlessly deplored;
> Which, at this moment, on my waking sight
> Appears to shine, by miracle restored; (73–76)

But the next lines enact a dramatic reversal as a spasm of ecstasy is instantly admonished in symbolic chastisement:

> My Soul, though yet confined to earth

> Rejoices in a second birth!
> —'Tis past—the visionary splendor fades;
> And night approaches with her shades.

Yet for a moment the mound in the garden of Rydal Mount has become a new Mount Pisgah from which for a moment could be *beheld* the promised land; a land to which (not unamusingly in stanza 3) 'ye drooping old men' are invited to look forward. In the heady metaphysics of 1798 Wordsworth had represented himself as one who 'must think, do all I can' (*CWRT*, 1: 335), that budding twigs enjoy the breezy air. Here the sceptical tug is stronger. The older poet *cannot* quite think, do all he can, that celestial ladders appear in the sky. But the young man's terrestrial conceit is father of the man's celestial one.

Is there a common thread connecting these various sacred sites, these thresholds of spirit? To rewind this journey, we have glimpsed a ladder to heaven, arising from Rydal Mount's own 'little mount' and recognised as the 'simple produce' of Cumbria's all-too-natural vapours; a spring whose waters bind Wordsworth into the community of water-worshippers in all climes and periods; a petrific 'giant mother', speaking of the instinct for eternity and the reverence for natural cycles among the neolithic peoples who first etched the Cumbran landscape with symbols of 'infinity's embrace'; those 'aisles and roofs magnificent' of monastic foundations, now fallen 'in a thousand vales' and folded back into the forest groves that perhaps inspired them and that 'shall endure as long as Man endures'; the nest-like dwellings of Pontus and Furness, and the ten-thousand cells of Cambridge's great chapel where 'music dwells ... like thoughts'; and a premature childhood glimpse of the contemplative life inspired by the music of a wren. Perhaps the common element is simply Wordsworth's mysterious 'natural piety', that which binds the poet's days 'each to each'—a reverence for whatever affective imperatives arise from 'the primary laws of our human nature', and whatever forms of worship and architecture those imperatives may engender. But what imperatives, and what laws?

Kimiyo Ogawa

Embodying Disinterest: William Godwin and William Hazlitt

What did 'disinterestedness' mean in the Romantic era? Wordsworth, Coleridge, Godwin, Hunt, Wollstonecraft, Hazlitt and Keats—to name just a few—wrote about the concept, yet disagreed as to its meaning. On the face of it, 'disinterestedness' means impartial, unselfish, without self-interest—what Keats would call 'negative capability'. Godwin's two novels, *St Leon* (1799) and *Fleetwood* (1805), however, attest that 'disinterestedness' is not a passive expression of natural benevolence, but a quality to be striven for because of the many human contingencies— passion, pride, envy—that conflict with it (Grayling 151). The tenuous control Godwin's protagonists have over such feelings demonstrates a waning of his commitment to the mechanistic psychology and philo-sophical necessarianism of *An Enquiry Concerning Political Justice* (1793), a book that Wordsworth had thought 'promised to abstract the hopes of man / Out of his feelings' (*The Prelude* X. 807–8). Godwin's novels also register his growing interest in selfhood as transitory, con-flicted, haunted. In this essay, I aim to show that a reading of Godwin's two novels in the light of Hazlitt's *Essay Concerning the Principles of Human Action* (1805) reveals similarities in phraseology and a depiction of human subjectivity that suggest a close mutual influence.

Hazlitt and Godwin

When Hazlitt and Godwin first met in summer 1794, Hazlitt was 16 and Godwin 38.[1] Considering Godwin's age, it's understandable

---

1   The online database *William Godwin's Diary*, http://godwindiary.bodleian.ox.ac. uk/index2.html lists Godwin's seven encounters with the Hazlitt family in 1794, although none of these identifies William Hazlitt. The entry for 17 September, 'Hazlit junr' was, however, very likely Wiliam Hazlitt.

that he should be portrayed as mentor to this inexperienced, ambitious young writer. Duncan Wu and William St Clair have characterised their relationship thus, with scant consideration of a possible exchange of ideas and, especially, of Hazlitt's contribution to Godwin's thinking (Wu 102–3; St Clair 224–5). Some of Godwin's works reveal curious echoes of Hazlitt's thinking on disinterestedness and the precarious nature of selfhood. Godwin had explored philosophical questions such as 'Is mind passive or active against passions?' or 'Is there such a thing as free-will?' in *Political Justice*, but his concern for mind in relation to bodily experiences becomes more prominent in *St Leon* and *Fleetwood*. As Pamela Clemit points out, *St Leon* foregrounds individual experience, as if in writing these novels he was testing *Political Justice*'s hypothesis that progressive understanding will achieve a rational regulation of the physiological or 'embodied' nature of man (Clemit xix).

In *St Leon* the protagonist, Reginald St Leon, is habituated to think highly of honour, ambition and luxury. He gambles away his fortune sacrificing domestic happiness with his wife, Marguerite, and their children. When he meets a mysterious stranger, and is asked if he could be entrusted with the secrets of the Elixir of Life and the Philosopher's Stone, he accepts. The mental effects of possessing these superhuman powers become the novel's principal subject. The plot of *Fleetwood* turns on the marital life of Casimir Fleetwood and his beautiful and blameless wife, Mary. As in *St Leon* there is a contrast between the affective realm of shared happiness, represented by Mary, and the isolated and alienating experiences of her husband. Fleetwood's nephew, Gifford, tries to dupe him into accusing his wife of adultery, hoping that a divorce will bring Fleetwood's property to him. As will be evident from these plot outlines, Godwin's post-Calvinist faith in rational self-control is viewed critically in both novels. Despite their emotional capacity to feel for others, his protagonists repeatedly fail to regulate their passions and selfish desires appropriately. This is at odds with the unassailable rationalism for which Godwin had argued in *Political Justice*: 'I stand upon the foundation of right. This is a title, which brute force may refuse to acknowledge, but which all the force in the world cannot annihilate'.[1] All the force, one might agree, except human emotion—which cannot be so coerced.

So, are we dealing with *two* Godwins—the sternly rationalist philosopher of *Political Justice*, and the novelist Godwin as a man of feeling? In *St Leon* and *Fleetwood*, he highlights the challenges that humanity faces in striving to become 'disinterested' even though this inevitably compromises his optimistic belief in the perfectibility of man. From 1799 Godwin's diary shows that Hazlitt began to visit frequently (there were at least fourteen meetings in that year alone)[2]. After 1804, when Hazlitt was at work on his *Essay on the Principles of Human Action*, he became familiar with the entire family, which, at this time, included Godwin's and Mary Wollstonecraft's daughter Mary (there were 16 meetings in 1804, 34 in 1805).[3] Given their mutual interest in the topic, it is likely that Hazlitt talked to Godwin about his belief that disinterestedness must arise 'without respect of persons' (Howe 1: 15). In that Godwin and Hazlitt both came from dissenting backgrounds—Calvinist, Unitarian—it is perhaps not surprising that they presented philosophical ideas in a similar manner. Their fathers were dissenting ministers, and they themselves went to Dissenting schools. Obviously Godwin's evolving idea of disinterestedness was not influenced by Hazlitt alone, but I would like to suggest that there was a confluence of ideas between them, despite their difference in age.

Disinterestedness and Self

Resemblances between Godwin and Hazlitt appear most notably in their vocabulary. Their ways of illustrating thought processes are more physiological, more dynamic, than earlier philosophers such as Locke and Hume. In *Political Justice*, Godwin begins his inquiry into the human mind by saying, 'Let us proceed to consider what is

---

1   William Godwin, *An Enquiry Concerning Political Justice*, In *Political and Philosophical Writings of William Godwin*, vol.3 (London: Pickering & Chatto, 1993), 420. Subsequent quotations will be cited as *PJ* in parentheses with page numbers.

2   The online database *William Godwin's Diary* lists sixteen possible encounters with William Hazlitt in 1799, on two of which they apparently did not meet.

3   The online database *William Godwin's Diary*.

the nature of those thoughts by which the limbs and organs of our body are set in motion' (*PJ* 177). Similarly, in his *Essay*, Hazlitt suggests that the mystery of mental processes, or thoughts, can never be revealed without acknowledging their material relation to the organs of the brain and nervous system, consequently dismissing a purely meta-physical explanation. He adds that mind cannot be likened to a tranquil room in which ideas or sense impressions are stocked up; according to Hazlitt, mind can never be a 'safe and dry gallery' far removed from the 'turbulence of the senses' and bodily passions (Howe 1: 69–70). Interestingly, the image of 'turbulence' had also been added to the 'calmness' of mind in *St Leon*. Godwin says, 'the turbulence of a scene of high play alone had power to distract my attention from the storm within'.[1] The words 'turbulence', 'storm within' and 'distract' indicate how Godwin was now revisiting and confronting his earlier theories of imperturbable and rational 'disinterest'.

It has often been pointed out that Godwin's philosophy was indebted to David Hartley, and Hazlitt to Hartley *and* Helvetius, and that their theories were grounded on mechanical association. Hartley's *Observations on Man* (1749) explained the associative processes of memory in terms of the physiology of the brain and vibrations of the nerves. Helvetius, taking Locke's empirical ground of knowledge in sensation to an extreme, argued that sensation and bodily response are the sources of human learning and action (Burwick 138). As David Bromwich has suggested, Hazlitt may have read Wordsworth's play *The Borderers* (1796–7) before starting to write his *Essay on the Principles of Human Action* and was struck by the lines evoking the fickle and transitory nature of selfhood. It is said that Hazlitt quoted these lines of the play from memory (Bromwich 21): 'Action is transitory', Wordsworth had written, ''Tis done, and in the after vacancy / We wonder at ourselves like men betrayed'.[2] The self who carried out a violent act, and the 'modified' self who

---

1   William Godwin, *St Leon*, in *Collected novels and memoirs of William Godwin*, vol.4, ed. Pamela Clemit (London: W. Pickering, 1992), 55. Subsequent quotations will be cited as *SL* in parentheses with page numbers.

2   William Wordsworth, *The Borderers*, ed. Robert Osborn (Ithaca and London: Cornell UP, 1982), 214–15.

now consequently reflects and suffers, are apparently discontinuous even while superficially appertaining to the same person.

'We wonder at ourselves', as if contemplating a stranger. To overcome this paradox, Hazlitt tried to demonstrate the materiality of consciousness by claiming that 'every idea, or perception is communicated to all the parts of the brain' (Howe 1: 53). By relying on materialist theory and vocabulary, or on the connotative mode of association, both Hazlitt and Godwin could fall back on the reductive idea that the physiological system of the brain and senses determined human action—an idea that inevitably invokes mind as mechanism. According to A. C. Grayling, Hazlitt's theory of 'gusto' could offer a more dynamic, vital solution to this kind of materialist impasse. Grayling quotes Hazlitt from 'On Egotism':

> The greater a man is, the less he necessarily thinks of himself, for his knowledge enlarges with his attainments. In himself he feels that he is nothing, a point, a speck in the universe, except as his mind reflects that universe, and as he enters into the infinite variety of the truth, beauty, and power contained in it. (Howe 12: 164)

Thinking less of oneself is important for Hazlitt as a condition for the expression of 'gusto' or 'entering into'. This trait is not just manifest in Shakespeare's plays, Titian's paintings, or Keats's idea of 'negative capability'; it can also be a state actively to be striven for. Hazlitt almost suggests that, with experience and knowledge, one can realize oneself as a 'speck' in the universe and thereby, perhaps, enter other existences and grasp their essence. As John Kinnaird has argued, '... the best, most original and least perishable part of Hazlitt's theory of 'distinteresteness'... [is] his sense of self as always in some mode or degree intersubjective' (Kinnaird 56). However, this generates a baffling philosophical conundrum. Is this 'speck' an embodied being with material corporeal existence, or a disembodied element like Ianthe in Shelley's *Queen Mab*?

Godwin shares the same ambivalence about the embodiedness or disembodiedness of self. He claims it is possible to be virtuous by 'divesting ... selfish and personal considerations' (*PJ* 195), without indicating how an embodied being can 'divest' itself of its physical

nature. Godwin's 'disinterested benevolence' depends upon humanity's capacity for rational thought, and this is homologous with
Hazlitt's rejection of self as a mere passive 'receiver' of external pressures. Hazlitt posits self as an active 'transmitter' or 'reactor' who
employs inner resources to modify external pressures or influences—
but this process is still attached or in close proximity to the physical
body. As Hazlitt said in the preface to his Abridgement of Abraham
Tucker's *Light of Nature Pursued* (1807) '…the fact is, that our ideas
of certain things are interwoven into the finer texture of the mind, in
a certain order and connection, as closely as the things themselves
are joined in nature' (xxvii). Likewise, although Godwin's *Enquirer*
essay 'On Awakening the Mind' claims that 'Man is a social being,
and cannot be separated'—suggesting that sympathy for others is
an inherent capacity (Flanders 537)—in his novels he gives more
emphasis to educative influences than innate traits.

Self as Moral Agent

Godwin's literary experiments in his novels may have been aimed
at extricating the agency of 'self' from the physical body. For him
human behaviour was the accumulation of experiential imprints on
the body, as he suggests at one point in *St Leon* with the phrase: '…
what I had perceived pressed upon my mind' (*SL* 98). Accordingly,
personality formation in both novels is described in terms of education given and passions stirred by external stimuli. St Leon is a
descendant of 'one of the most ancient and honourable families of
the kingdom of France' (*SL* 14), and his mother is obsessed with edu-
cating him suitably for a person of that birth. The first circumstance
that impacts on St Leon's youthful mind is the splendid scene of the
meeting between Francis the First and Henry the Eighth (*SL* 15); relevant here is his attraction to the 'splendour of dress' worn upon this
occasion (*SL* 16) and to the 'variety of garments' (*SL* 16)—in other
words, the '*vestments*' on display at the encounter. The riveting scene
continues with 'the beauty of armour, the caparisons of the steeds,
the mettle of the animals themselves, and the ardour and grace of
the combatants' (*SL* 16–17). The narrative is immersed in subjective

experience or, in Godwin's phrase, the 'sensorium' (*PJ* 185). Next comes St Leon's 'military passion' (*SL* 24) awakened in the battle of Pavia. After the battle, St Leon's pent-up passions find outlet in the 'indulgences of the table' (*SL* 33), namely, gambling, and Godwin depicts St Leon's mind as gushing with passion and 'turbulence' (*SL* 55). His irrational gambling and irresponsibly 'splendid and luxurious' living (*SL* 37) were both thoroughly un-Godwinian aspects of behaviour – but they had arisen, crucially, by what had 'pressed upon his mind'.

In *Fleetwood*, environment's role in shaping behaviour is given even more weight. As often in literature of the time an idyllic upbringing close to nature is contrasted with an urban setting for less salubrious behaviour. In early life Fleetwood could experience 'a disinterested joy in human relief and human happiness, independently of the question whether [he] had been concerned in producing it'.[1] As an old man he recollects that in a rural environment, 'The general sympathy which animated [his] charitable deeds was pure; it flowed from a celestial source, and maintained its crystal current, as unmingled with the vulgar stream of personal passions…. (*FW* 23). This scene of pristine origin reminds us of Hazlitt's account that 'a sense of self-interest with this very being, with the motions of our blood, and with life itself' is 'the work of time, the gradual result of habit' (Howe 1: 5). Accordingly, when Fleetwood leaves his Merionethshire home for Oxford University, and is separated from his father, he becomes 'vicious by the operation of a populous and crowded residence . . . , unwarned by experience against the rocks that awaited him' (*FW* 46). The key word here is 'operation', pinpointing how for Godwin environment (here 'populous and crowded') shapes behaviour.

Both *St Leon* and *Fleetwood* show the tenuous link between past experiences and impressions, and what the self faces in the present moment—as the character in Wordsworth's *Borderers* was shocked into realising. Hazlitt argues likewise that self as a continuous entity is an illusion. Transposing the wondering retrospection of

---

1   William Godwin, *Fleetwood*, in *Collected Novels and Memoirs of William Godwin*, vol.5 (London: W. Pickering, 1992), 23. Subsequent quotations will be cited as *FW* in parentheses with page numbers.

The Borderers into a future prospect, Hazlitt's *Essay* argues that 'I neither am, nor can possibly be affected at present by what I am to feel hereafter, I am not to any moral or practical purpose the *same* being' (Howe 1: 10–11). So, at one moment St Leon rebuffs domestic affections, and at another values them: 'Marguerite, the generous Marguerite, stood, with a soul almost indifferent, between the opposite ideas of riches and poverty. Not so her husband. I had been formed, by every accident of my life, to the love of splendor', he says (*SL* 74). He experiences 'dejection and despair,' sees the 'barrier that divides innocence from guilt' (*SL* 77) but is at other times poignantly aware that the 'human face and the human heart, reciprocations of kindness and love, and all the nameless sympathies of our nature,—these are the only objects worth being attached to' (*SL* 84). Again, when he is endowed with superhuman power, he becomes 'in a considerable degree alienated from domestic sentiments and pleasures' (*SL* 177). Fleetwood shows the same kind of inward oscillation between believing in his wife's virtue, and conflicting moods of doubt. After Gifford has manipulated Mary so that she appears to Fleetwood to be guilty of adultery, Fleetwood goes through a long period of suffering. He describes his experience thus: 'it was a strange war that was continually going on in my bosom.... My whole existence was tempestuous' (*FW* 212). Godwin's experiment on these protagonists shows that, rather than being able to 'redirect' thought or inclination and thereby keep trains of association rationally in check, they both constantly face the danger of being assailed and overpowered by stimuli which are internal and self-generated. The contrast with Hartley's measured, mechanical associationism could not be clearer.

This brings us to the philosophical impasse both Godwin and Hazlitt may have reached, which was to reject the 'mechanical' tendency of human action. Hazlitt argued that '[t]here appears to be ... little propriety in making the mechanical tendency to our own good the foundation of human actions' (Howe 1: 85). They distinguish between the concepts of 'mechanical' and 'voluntary' to make a point that human action is not all automatic: 'Our mechanical, and voluntary motives are not therefore the same, and it is absurd to attempt to reduce them under the same law'.[1] St Leon actually calls his state 'mechanical' (*SL* 76) when he loses his fortune; in that 'mechanical' state, his spirits languish—lacking in 'the powers, of a human body' while his 'soul had not force enough to give motion to the organs of speech, or scarcely to raise a finger' (*SL* 75-6). That 'soul force' is precisely what distinguishes Hazlitt's and Godwin's developing concepts of mind from mere 'mechanical principle' (the very existence of 'soul' or 'spirit' had long been at issue for materialist thinkers).

Neither Hazlitt nor Godwin is a proponent of the mechanical theory of human action. They wished somehow to salvage a voluntary power that they believed existed in-between the nervous system and the brain's abstract ideas. In his *Essay*, Hazlitt consigns this role to imaginative power—or what he calls an act of 'willing': 'The reason why a child first distinctly wills or pursues his own good is not because it is his, but because it is good' (Howe 1: 12). A classic example may be that St Leon, after losing his fortune, tries to escape his 'mechanical' state by escaping to the mountains. He says, 'This was a refinement beyond me, and serves to evince the superiority which Marguerite's virtue and force of mind still retained over mine. The virtue I had so recently adopted was a strenuous effort' (*SL* 88).

One setback, however, is that inconsistent or discontinuous selfhood does not give any guarantee that 'strenuous effort' after virtue will have the intended outcome in the feelings of a future self. As Hazlitt had put it: 'I neither am, nor can possibly be affected at present by what I am to feel hereafter, I am not to any moral or practical purpose the *same* being'. This paradox is also shown in *St Leon* when the protagonist discovers that the future has proved different from the Romantic prospect he had anticipated:

> Fool that I was, I had imagined that, when endowed with the bequests of the stranger, no further evil could approach me! I had, in my visionary mood, created castles and palaces, and expatiated in the most distant futurity! (*SL* 148)

One could argue that the reunion of Fleetwood and his wife, after

---

1   William Hazlitt, Preface to *An Abridgement of the Light of Nature Pursued by Abraham Tucker*, p. xxviii.

their circumstances are explained at the end of the novel, may suggest Godwin's attempt to restore a sympathetic relationship. However, Fleetwood's guilt will not be denied. Feelings of jealousy and rancour have left deep marks on his mind, and, as he says, '[i]t seemed as if, now that what the vulgar mind would call the obstacles to our reunion were removed, we were more certainly divided than ever' (*FW* 334–35). Visionary moods and the self-generated mental 'marks' of jealousy show us how far Godwin's new understanding of a discontinuous, 'imaginative' self had carried him from *Political Justice*.

Conclusion

In the years following the publication of *Political Justice*, Godwin and Hazlitt were both in pursuit of a humanizing mission—they were both well aware of the associationist theory in which 'self' was transformed into a mechanical entity, and both tried to restore the roles of a vital and morally responsible self. Both Hazlitt and Godwin use words such as 'endeavour' or 'strenuous,' revealing their awareness that one cannot easily overcome the mechanical inclination of associationism. But even when the protagonists fail in this humanizing mission, it is somehow warranted by a lawful necessity. For example, whenever Godwin depicts the formation of St Leon's ignoble habits, the protagonist is often portrayed as being passively 'led into' these vices (*SL* 37). Godwin's problematic relation to the determinism of his early Calvinist education may help to explain this. Of course, there are characters who are guilt-free moral agents, such as the marchese Filosanto (in Pisa) in *St Leon* and Ruffigney and McNeil in *Fleetwood* but these resemble the uncomplicated idealized characters of Rousseau. In contrast, Godwin's conflicted protagonists, whose moral pursuits are often betrayed by their passions, may not win the sympathy of their relations, friends, or us readers, but, at least, Godwin may have thought, they present a more real picture of transient beings 'wondering at themselves'.

Bibliography

Bromwich, David. 'Disinterested Imagining and Impersonal Feeling.' In Natarajan et al., ed., *Metaphysical Hazlitt.*

Burwick, Frederick. 'Schelling and Hazlitt on Disinterestedness and Freedom.' In Natarajan et al., ed., *Metaphysical Hazlitt.*

Clemit, Pamela. Introduction to William Godwin's *St Leon*. Oxford and New York: Oxford University Press, 1994.

Flanders, Wallace Austin. 'Godwin and Gothicism: *St Leon*' in *Texas Studies in Literature and Language: A Journal of the Humanities*, 8.4, (1967).

Grayling, A. C. '"A Nature Towards One Another": Hazlitt and the inherent disinterestedness of moral agency.' In Natarajan et al., ed., *Metaphysical Hazlitt.*

Godwin, William. *An Enquiry Concerning Political Justice*, In *Political and Philosophical Writings of William Godwin*. Vol.3. London: Pickering & Chatto, 1993.

——. *St Leon.* Ed. Pamela Clemit. London: William Pickering, 1992.

——. *Fleetwood.* In *Collected Novels and Memoirs of William Godwin.* Vol.5. London: W. Pickering, 1992.

Hazlitt, William. Preface to *An Abridgement of the Light of Nature Pursued by Abraham Tucker, Esq.* London: J. Johnson, 1807.

——. *The Complete Works of William Hazlitt In Twenty-One Volumes.* Ed. P. P. Howe. London and Toronto: J. M. Dent and Sons Ltd., 1930.

Kinnaird, John. *William Hazlitt: Critic of Power.* New York: Columbia University Press, 1978.

Natarajan, Uttara, Tom Paulin and Duncan Wu, ed. *Metaphysical Hazlitt: Bicentenary Essays*. London & New York: Routledge, 2005.

St Clair, William. *The Godwins and the Shelleys: The Biography of a*

Family. London and Boston: Faber and Faber, 1989.

Wordsworth, William. *The Borderers*. Ed. Robert Osborn. Ithaca and London: Cornell University Press, 1982.

——, *The Prelude*. In *William Wordsworth*. Ed. Stephen Gill. Oxford 21st-Century Authors. Oxford: Oxford University Press, 2010.

Wu, Duncan. *William Hazlitt: The First Modern Man*. Oxford: Oxford University Press, 2008.

Richard Lansdown

Coralline Geohistory in James Montgomery's *Pelican Island*

'The first branch of natural science to become genuinely historical', Stephen Toulmin and June Goodfield wrote in *The Discovery of
Time*, 'was geology.' In the early nineteenth century, between the eras
of Cuvier and Darwin, biology arose to accompany geology, and 'the
intellectual claims of the modern, extended time-scale were finally
established by the resultant interweaving of geological considerations with evolutionary ones.'[1]

Another doyen of the history of geology, Martin Rudwick, reminds
us of two key features of that discovery—or two misunderstand-
ings of it, to be precise. First: that 'religious and scientific practices
and knowledge *interacted*' during the interweaving Toulmin and
Goodfield describe. 'Rather than being the enemy of progress in the
sciences of the earth,' Christianity in fact 'fostered the extension of
historicity to the previously uncharted vastnesses of pre-human time',
as a product and a result of its own fascination with Biblical history,
Biblical origins, and Biblical accounts of the creation.[2] Second: that
'it was...the human *imagination* that needed to be stretched, even
among savants, before talk of vast amounts of time could begin to
seem anything more than vacuous and scientifically irresponsible
hand-waving.' (Rudwick, 124–5.) This was a matter of what he calls
'human constructions: not unconstrained by the natural evidence
available at a given period, but certainly using that evidence in a representation that has many other inputs besides the fossil bones and

1   Stephen Toulmin and June Goodfield, *The Discovery of Time* (London:
     Hutchinson, 1965), 141, 143.
2   Martin J. S. Rudwick, *Bursting the Limits of Time: The Reconstruction of
     Geohistory in the Age of Revolution* (Chicago: University of Chicago Press,
     2005), 6, 643; my italics.

shells themselves.'[1] Religious people and imaginative people played their roles in the discovery of time, and it is the work of one particular religious imaginist I want to discuss here: the sub- or proto-evolutionary epic, *Pelican Island*, published by the direct contemporary of Wordsworth, James Montgomery, in 1827. (A poem 'worth ten *Excursions*', in Ralph Waldo Emerson's view.)[2] Above all, *Pelican Island* takes its origin in *coral*: a zoological interweaver whose biological activity has a posthumous geological result.

Without rehearsing the debate between the 'Vulcanists' (for whom volcanic forces were the chief engine of geological change) and the 'Neptunists' (for whom changes in sea level performed the same role), it is clear that the sea played a massive role in the confluence of geology and biology just described. But the sea in the late eighteenth century was an element that empirical observation could hardly penetrate at all. Objects could be dropped into it and hauled back up again; a person could dive a few fathoms with his eyes open; creatures of all sorts came up in fishermen's nets; but there was no way the sea could systematically be explored beneath its surface: so the imagination had a peculiarly rich field once the greatest ocean in the world was opened up to exploration in the mid-eighteenth century.

Two individuals—one writing at the beginning of the period, the other writing near its end—give us a sense of the obscurity of Pacific Neptunism in the first half of the nineteenth century. François Péron was every inch a product of revolutionary Napoleonism: a self-made (indeed, *soi-disant*) polymath from the provinces who talked his way onto the luckless Baudin expedition to Australia in 1802 and, by a series of accidents and desertions, became in effect its chief scientist. John Williams, hero and martyr of the London Missionary Society, was every inch Péron's antithesis: the product of the British religious revival that had emerged in response to the Enlightenment whose principles the Frenchman served, and stolidly, almost painfully, devout, right up to his murder at the hands of indigenes on a beach at Eromanga in 1839. Thirty years and an immense ideological gulf

---

1   Martin J. S. Rudwick, *Scenes from Deep Time: Early Pictorial Representations of the Prehistoric World* (Chicago: University of Chicago Press, 1992), 223.
2   Ralph Waldo Emerson, *Journals, 1820–1872*, Vol. 2 (Boston: Houghton Mifflin, 1909), 235.

divided these two travellers in the Pacific, but they possessed essentially the same imaginative restrictions on their capacity to burst the limits of time.

As part of his account of the Baudin expedition, Péron included a volume of 'dissertations on various subjects', including one 'On Some Phenomena of the Zoology of the Southern Regions, which can be Applied to the Physical History of the Earth and of the Human Species'. 'One of the finest results of modern geological research, and also one of the most uncontestable,' he asserted, 'is the certainty that the level of the sea was once much higher than it is now.' The evidence for this conclusion was twofold: petrified seashells found on elevated pieces of ground, and 'Zoophytes observed at great heights above the present level of the sea; madreporic islands and archipelagoes.' Volcanos are the only things that make land rise, Péron was sure; but they could not possibly have raised all this coralline rock above the sea — and, besides, they always left evidence of their activity, and none was to be seen in the antipodes. Thus in his 'General Results' Péron concluded: 'We discovered living zoophytes sowing the seas with fresh dangers, multiplying reefs, increasing the size of islands and archipelagoes, cluttering roadsteads and ports and raising up new calcareous mountains everywhere.'[1]

For Williams, 'modern geological research' would have counted mostly as what he called 'prying researches after knowledge'. 'The great object for which all knowledge should be sought, and for which it ought to be employed,' he wrote in his discussion of coral formations,

> is to illustrate the wisdom or goodness of the great and beneficent Creator. And if we come to the study of natural phenomena, with minds unchilled by scepticism or infidelity, we shall be led to sublime religious contemplations; and whether we examine the little coral insect of the ocean, or gaze upon the gigantic beast of the forest ... we shall be led to exclaim: 'How manifold, O God, are thy works! in wisdom thou hast made them all.'[2]

---

1   François Péron, *Voyage of Discovery to the Southern Lands*, 2nd edn. (1824), Vol. 3, trans. Christine Cornell (Adelaide: Friends of the State Library of South Australia, 2007), 34, 47.
2   John Williams, *A Narrative of Missionary Enterprises in the South Sea Islands*

In a sense, Williams was nearer to the mark than Péron, who thought that coral reefs were built 'from the floor of the ocean right up to its surface' (Péron, 41). Coral, in his view, needed to find a suitable spot, a suitable platform, and having found it, 'innumerable myriads of these wonderful little animals work with incredible diligence until they reach the surface of the water, above which they cannot build.' (Williams, 8.) Their diligence was worthy of the Victorian seal of approval, but coral could not have built the islands, in Williams' view: they simply did not have the time. According to current scientific estimates of growth, 'eighteen thousand years would be required to produce the island visited by Captain Beechy, thirty thousand for the rocks of Rurutu, and fifty to sixty thousand for those of Mangaia; and only that portion of them which appears above water!' This 'amazing length of time', since it was inconsistent with Biblical history, must be inconsistent with nature; and so, 'After all…that I have seen, and thought, and read upon the subject, my impression is, that the islands remain much in the same state as the deluge left them, and that every subsequent alteration has been partial in its character, and exceedingly limited in its extent.' (Williams, 9–10.)

So it was that Péron managed to exaggerate coral activity in the Pacific region, and Williams managed to underestimate it. The first spoke about the 'prodigious antiquity' of coral activity, but could account for coral islands only in terms of prodigious dynamism; the second spoke about 'incredible diligence', but strictly curtailed the amount of antiquity he would afford it. But both were striving to account, imaginatively as well as rationally, for the manifestations they witnessed in the Pacific: in particular, coral rock above the surface of the water.

There was something about innumerable myriads of wonderful little animals working with incredible diligence until they reached the surface of the sea that English writers would not willingly let die. Thus in 1828 Granville Penn sought to explain the geological world in a set of conversations two children are imagined to have with their—very well informed—mother. 'I think I remember

(London: John Snow, 1840), 7.

seeing it remarked in some book of voyages,' the daughter of the house observes, 'that Otaheité, and all the islands of the South Seas, have been raised from the sea by insects; now, I cannot help thinking this, if true, to be very extraordinary.' In her explanation her mother cites Cook, Forster, and Flinders, and points out, *inter alia*, that coral atolls are built 'with their backs to the sea, as if the coral animalcules were aware of the properties of the arch.' Such a thing, she added, 'cannot be explained otherwise than by the operation of intelligence and design.'[1] A year later Andrew Ure, reconciling the whole field of study 'at once to modern science and sacred history', theorized that 'the numerous volcanic chimnies which ... rise through the vast Pacific, are remnants of the general convulsion which raged at the deluge, ending in the submersion of some primeval continent, corresponding probably in area to the surface of that ocean.'[2] Again: it is easy to smile at this; but 'volcanic chimnies' is by no means the worst expression to use of those tectonic vents that are the sources of all the non-continental islands of the Pacific, high and low.

Andrew Ure imagined a disappearing Pacific continent. Two years later John MacCullough imagined a rising one. By common consent, he wrote, it was understood that coral atolls and islets were 'crowding the whole of the sea, under a rapid increase'. Was it not likely, therefore, that they were 'destined to become the seats of vegetation, and the habitations of man, and perhaps, at length, to form a continent in the Pacific Ocean'? Like Penn's, MacCullough's vision was one of intelligent design. As islands rose, the seawater trapped in their atolls would surely become diluted by rain, until it ceased to be salt at all, thus opening the way for animal life. Was this not a case of 'foresight and contrivance'?[3] Even as late as 1838, Gideon Mantell was indulging himself, Jules Verne-style: 'From the depths of the ocean they

---

1   Granville Penn, *Conversations on Geology* (London: Samuel Maunder, 1828), 147, 152, 157.

2   Andrew Ure, *A New System of Geology, in which the Great Revolutions of the Earth and Animated Nature, Are Reconciled at Once to Modern Science and Sacred History* (London: Longman, Rees, Orme, Brown, and Green, 1829), 467.

3   John MacCullough, *A System of Geology, with a Theory of the Earth, and an Explanation of its Connexion, with the Sacred Records* (London: Longman, Rees, Orme, Brown, and Green, 1831), 338, 341–2.

elevate those immense reefs that may hereafter form a communication between the inhabitants of the temperate zones.'[1] Twenty-five
years later, Louis Agassiz still clung to the idea of a purposeful theodicy. Like coal, coral humiliated our sense of time:

> Leaving aside ... all historical chronology, how far back can we
> trace our own geological period, and the Species belonging to
> it? By what means can we determine its duration? Within what
> limits, by what standard, may it be measured? Shall hundreds, or
> thousands, or hundreds of thousands, or millions of years be the
> unit from which we start?[2]

Agassiz was prepared to give corals the time John Williams denied
them. But the ubiquity and stability of coral species only made a
pious conclusion more inevitable. 'These little beings' had a primary
role to play in Creation: 'to make a masonry solid, compact, time-
defying, such a masonry as was needed by the great Architect, who
meant that these smallest creatures of His hand should help to build
His islands and His continents.' (Agassiz, 200.) This was an imaginative pattern that many found simply too attractive, and too harmonious, to deny.

But Agassiz had begun to burst the limits of time, and speculate
in terms of millions of years. That was the most important lesson
Charles Lyell, James Dana, and Charles Darwin drew from coral.
'When we admit the increase of coral limestone to be slow,' Lyell
pointed out, 'we are merely speaking with relation to periods of
human observation'. 'Natural chronometers', with their roots in deep
time, would be needed to grasp the prodigious antiquity at which
Péron had only waved his hand.[3] Dana estimated coral growth at a
thousand years per five feet; it was a scale of this temporal magni-
tude that led him to conclude: 'In this direction ... we find the grand-
est teaching of coral formations.'[4] Darwin treated the antiquity and

---

1   Gideon Mantell, *The Wonders of Geology* (London: Rolfe and Fletcher, 1838),
    472.
2   Louis Agassiz, *Methods of Study of Natural History* (Boston: Ticknor and Fields,
    1863), 151.
3   Charles Lyell, *Principles of Geology*, Vol. 2 (London: John Murray, 1832), 287,
    288.
4   James D. Dana, *Corals and Coral Islands* (London: Sampson, Low, Marston,

the rate of growth of coral reefs with the peculiar Olympian grave insouciance that marks his entire project. For him such reefs, 'young' or 'old' (whatever those words might mean), belonged only to 'the present geological æra'. Accordingly, coralline growth is *never* slow, 'when referred either to the standard of the average oscillations of level in the earth's crust, or to the more precise but less important one of a cycle of years.'[1]

How much of this context the philanthropist, newspaper editor, and man Gideon Mantell (491) described as 'one of the most amiable and elegant of our modern poets', James Montgomery, knew in detail is hard to say. (Lyell, Darwin, Dana, and Agassiz, of course, he could not have known when *Pelican Island* was published in 1827.) He read explorers' accounts from the Pacific, and his biographers recorded a conversation that suggests he was well abreast of the 'construction' of coralline geohistory in his era. 'Seeing that coral islands are still constantly in progress of formation and enlargement,' he told John Holland, 'a time might arrive when these would coalesce, and a new continent appear where now only spreads a vast expanse of ocean with its insular spots'. Montgomery's indestructible philanthropy — and his imaginative instinct — envisaged this new world in evangelical terms: 'a continent peopled with human beings blessed with the gospel, basking beneath the meridian blaze of a sun more glorious than ours, and reflecting back to the moon, looking down in loveliness on the scene, a light thirteen degrees broader and brighter than that which the earth at present imparts.'[2]

Around 1818 Montgomery read Matthew Flinders' *Voyage to Terra Australis*, four years after its publication, and was struck by the circumnavigator's account of Kangaroo Island, off present-day South Australia. Flinders' visit to Kangaroo Island was clearly a memorable episode for him. Its isolation is reminiscent in certain respects

---

Low and Searle, 1872), 253, 318.
1   Charles Darwin, *The Structure and Distribution of Coral Reefs* (London: Smith, Elder, 1842), 79.
2   John Holland and James Everett, *Memoirs of the Life and Writings of James Montgomery*, 6 vols. (London: Longman, Brown, Green, and Longmans, 1855), 4:249.

of Darwin's encounter with the Galapagos thirty years later. Like Galapagos, Kangaroo Island presented few *species*, but immense numbers of *individuals*: in particular of kangaroos and seals. Another animal present in huge numbers was the pelican, on islets in Nepean Bay:

> Flocks of old birds were sitting upon the beaches of the lagoon, and it appeared that the islands were their breeding places; not only so, but from the number of skeletons and bones there scattered, it should seem that they had for ages been selected for the closing scene of their existence. Certainly none more likely to be free from disturbance of every kind could have been chosen, than these islets in a hidden lagoon of an uninhabited island, situate upon an unknown coast near the antipodes of Europe; nor can anything be more consonant to the feelings, if pelicans have any, than quietly to resign their breath, whilst surrounded by their progeny, and in the same spot where they first drew it. Alas, for the pelicans! Their golden age is past; but it has much exceeded in duration that of man.[1]

In Flinders' account we can clearly see someone trying to burst the limits of time, by contrasting—and by those means comparing—the history of a pelican rookery with the history of civilization.

But there is no reef-building coral on Kangaroo Island; it is located in temperate waters between the Great Australian Bight and Bass Strait, off Spencer Gulf. So Flinders cannot have been Montgomery's only inspiration. Basil Hall's account of his voyage to the far East was published in the year Montgomery read Flinders; and Montgomery read that, too, reprinting this passage from Hall's book alongside Flinders in his preface to *Pelican Island*:

> The examination of a coral reef during the different stages of the one tide, is particularly interesting. When the tide has left it for some time it becomes dry, and appears to be compact rock, exceedingly hard and ragged; but as the tide rises, and the waves begin to wash over it, the coral worms protrude themselves from holes which were before invisible. These animals are of a great

---

1   Matthew Flinders, *Voyage to Terra Australis*, 2 vols. (London: G. and W. Nichol, 1814), 1:183–4.

variety of shapes and sizes, and in such prodigious numbers,
that, in a short time, the whole surface of the rock appears to
be alive and in motion…. When the coral is broken, about high
water mark, it is solid hard stone, but if any part of it be detached
at a spot where the tide reaches every day, it is found to be full
of worms of different lengths and colours, some being as fine as
a thread and several feet long, of a bright yellow, and sometimes
of a blue colour: others resemble snails, and some are not unlike
lobsters in shape, but soft, and not above two inches long.[1]

That this magic living stone might inspire a poet is reasonable enough;
but what has Basil Hall's tropical reef to do with Matthew Flinders'
temperate island? The answer, I take it, is that Flinders' pelicans were
doing what coral does: *hatch new generations of themselves on the
remains of the old.* For ages unknown to man the pelicans of South
Australia had replicated themselves, like coral, and resigned their
breath in the spot where they first drew it. Taken together, therefore,
Flinders and Hall planted a seed in Montgomery's religiously imaginative mind.

But it took time for that seed to sprout. In March 1827 Montgomery
told John Holland that the idea for the poem 'has been floating in
my mind several years'—at least since 1818 when he came across
Flinders' pelicans, 'unseen as they were unsung by man.' 'Impressed
as I was with the subject,' he went on,

> I thought it would do very well for the foundation of a mission-
> ary speech, and serve to illustrate the manner in which the hea-
> then on the adjacent islands had been born, grown up, and per-
> ished as ignorant of God, and of all that is good, as we were
> ignorant of them, and of their neighbours the pelicans. (Holland
> and Everett, 4:198)

Then, in September 1826, travelling home to Sheffield from
Scarborough, he witnessed a flood at the Wharfedale village of Thorp
Arch, and had a moment of inspiration:

> only a few more prominent points of ground were seen, like

---

1   Basil Hall, *Account of a Voyage of Discovery to the West Coast of Corea, and
the Great Loo-Choo Island* (London: John Murray, 1818), 107–8.

> green islands amidst the lake. By some involuntary association
> of ideas, I was powerfully reminded of the Pelican Island. In a
> moment the radical thought of which I had been so long in quest
> rushed into my mind; and I saw the whole plan of my poem
> from beginning to end. I immediately began the subject in blank
> verse; and by the time we reached Ferrybridge, I had composed
> a number of lines, which I wrote down with my pencil in the inn
> there.... (Holland and Everett, 4:199)

The equation is evident: summits of hills in a flooded plain (even in
far-off Yorkshire) suggest coral islands in a vast ocean. The result-
ing poem was eventually published in 1827, and was more optimistic
than the original idea for a missionary speech. In *Pelican Island* we
see the coral reef become one of those primeval Pacific continents the
geohistorians had dreamt of; but this time man is left at the end of the
poem, instinctively aware that a beneficent deity is supervising his
existence, and bowing, like an antipodal Adam, to his creator.

Pelican Island did not meet with universal approval in the scientific community. 'It is not...within the sphere of science to criticise
the poet', Dana suggested; but,

> more error in the same compass could scarcely be found than in
> the part of Montgomery's 'Pelican Island' relating to coral for-
> mations. The poetry of this excellent author is good, but the facts
> nearly all errors—if literature allows of such an incongruity.

'The poet oversteps his license, and besides degrades his subject,'
Dana bluntly concluded (19), 'when downright false to nature.'

But there are more inputs to the construction of geohistory than
purely scientific ones—or purely religious ones, come to that.
'There is no authentic history of the world from the Creation to the
Deluge, besides that which is found in the first chapters of Genesis',
Montgomery had written in his preface to *The World Before the Flood*
in 1815.[1] But his later imaginative construction prefigured the geo-
historical interweavings of its era in a more ambivalent way. *Pelican
Island* is told by one of the ultimate omniscient narrators in English
literature: a radically disembodied roaming point of vision that starts

---

1   James Montgomery, *The World Before the Flood* (London: Longman, Hurst,
     Rees, Orme, and Brown, 1815), vii.

the poem saying, 'Methought I lived through ages, and beheld / Their generations pass so swiftly by me, / That years were moments in their flight, and hours / The scenes of crowded centuries reveal'd; / While Time, Life, Death the world's great actors, wrought / New and amazing changes:—these I sing.'[1] The poem's first canto essentially rehearses Genesis, moving from 'The sun, the stars, / The moon … / The planets seeking rest and finding none' (7), through a pair of Vulcanist and Neptunist catastrophes (a 'war of mountains' and a 'wild whirl of foaming surges'), via a rainbow and a dove to a post-diluvian world apparently without life. The first to announce itself is the nautilus, followed by the flying fish, the dolphin, and the whale (13–14). 'In the free element beneath me', the narrator says in Canto Two,

> swam,
> Flounder'd, and dived, in play, in chase, in battle,
> Fishes of every colour, form, and kind,
> (Strange forms, resplendent colours, kinds unnumber'd,)
> Which language cannot paint, and mariner
> Hath never seen; from dread Leviathan
> To insect-millions peopling every wave;
> And nameless tribes, half-plant, half-animal,
> Rooted and slumbering through a dream of life.
> The livelier inmates to the surface sprang,
> To taste the freshness of heaven's breath, and feel
> That light is pleasant, and the sunbeam warm.
> Most in the middle region sought their prey,
> Safety, or pastime; solitary some,
> And some in pairs affectionately join'd;
> Others in shoals immense, like floating islands,
> Led by mysterious instinct through that waste
> And trackless region, though on every side
> Assaulted by voracious enemies,
> —Whales, sharks, and monsters, arm'd in front or jaw,
> With swords, saws, spiral horns, or hooked fangs.
> While ravening Death of slaughter ne'er grew weary,

---

1   James Montgomery, *Pelican Island and Other Poems*, 2nd edn. (London: Longman, Hurst, Rees, Orme, and Brown, 1828), 1.

Life multiplied the immortal meal as fast.
War, reckless, universal war, prevail'd;
All were devourers, all in turn devour'd;
Yet every unit in the uncounted sum
Of victims had its share of bliss, its pang,
And but a pang, of dissolution; each
Was happy till its moment came, and then
Its first, last suffering, unforeseen, unfear'd,
Closed, with one struggle, pain and life for ever. (17-19)

Here is a Darwinian intimation of the survival of the fittest and of the indefeasible adaptation to that struggle. It is brutal, but not cruel: the pangs here are only those of dissolution, unforeseen and unfeared; and death is only a stoical unravelling of pain and life. But it cannot help blending the language of affect with the language of apathy: fish (or the livelier ones among them, anyway) appreciate fresh air and sunshine; individuals are driven by instinct by also by affection; prey species are 'voracious' but those predated upon enjoy their 'share of bliss'. The discussion is as anthropomorphic in some respects as it is scientifically neutral in others, but its summary statement is of a marine environment bleakly unredeemed by any sense of purpose:

They roam'd, they fed, they slept, they died, and left
Race after race, to roam feed, sleep, then die,
And leave their like through countless generations;
—Incessant change of actors, none of scene,
Through all that boundless theatre of strife! (20)

But a boundless theatre of strife is not the last word on the world; the scene does change, however slowly. In 'thrice a thousand years'—half the age Archbishop Ussher ascribed to the Earth—Montgomery's narrator witnesses 'ocean's bed, as from the hand / Of its Creator, hollow'd and prepared / For his unfathomable counsels there,/To work slow miracles of power divine, / From century to century' (23). These slow miracles are worked by coral, and they are the corollary of the 'empty', 'purposeless' marine realm Montgomery had just described. This time the deaths of trillions of individuals leave behind them not the 'universal war' of the survival of the fittest, but a monument in stone:

Enlongated like worms, they writhed and shrunk
Their tortuous bodies to grotesque dimensions;
Compress'd like wedges, radiated like stars,
Branching like sea-weed, whirl'd in dazzling rings;
Subtle and variable as flickering flames,
Sight could not trace their evanescent changes,
Nor comprehend their motions, till minute
And curious observation caught the clew
To this live labyrinth,—where every one,
By instinct taught, perform'd its little task;
—To build its dwelling and its sepulchre. (26)

'Millions of millions thus, from age to age,' Montgomery goes on,

With simplest skill, and toil unweariable,
No moment and no movement unimproved,
Laid line on line, on terrace terrace spread,
To swell the heightening, brightening gradual mound,
By marvellous structure climbing tow'rds the day.
Each wrought alone, yet all together wrought,
Unconscious, not unworthy, instruments,
By which a hand invisible was rearing
A new creation in the secret deep.
Omnipotence wrought in them, with them, by them;
Hence what Omnipotence alone could do
Worms did. I saw the living pile ascend,
The mausoleum of its architects,
Stilly dying upwards as their labours closed:
Slime the material, but the slime was turn'd
To adamant, by their petrific touch;
Frail were their frames, ephemeral their lives,
Their masonry imperishable. All
Life's needful functions, food, exertion, rest,
By nice economy of Providence
Were overruled to carry on the process,
Which out of water brought forth solid rock. (27–8)

Here the Biblical and the proto-Darwinian visions interweave at
will. Darwin's faith in instinct and stupidity—in the capacity of 'toil

unweariable' among countless individuals to wear out the rock of mortality and keep the species alive by mutation, so that in actual truth the individual and the variety are indivisible—magically elides with the Biblical language of Omnipotence, Providence, and miraculous transfiguration ('Which out of water brought forth solid rock'). The coral reef becomes an objective correlative for human existence, where simple skill and toil are put to higher purposes, economies, and processes, and where ephemeral lives leave imperishable masonry behind them. The Darwinian and the Biblical theodicies reveal a common gene here: *of course* it is the lowliest of the low, in countless numbers, which have the greatest effect in the end, rather than the charismatic personalities of the animal kingdom. *Of course* the meek shall inherit the earth, in just the same way as Darwin watched humble earthworms bury a slab of granite in his garden at Down House. If they could do that in twenty years, what could they not achieve, given time? What valleys might they not fill, or mountains bring low? For both Darwin and the Bible, such things were inevitable, whether they were the will of Yahweh or of evolution.

But Montgomery would not rest satisfied with an analogy as complacent and anthropocentric as that between coral reef and human community. 'Compared with this amazing edifice,/Raised by the weakest creatures in existence,' he asks, 'What are the works of intellectual man?'

> Towers, temples, palaces, and sepulchres;
> Ideal images in sculptured forms, or in domes expanded,
> Fancies through every maze of beauty shown;
> Pride, gratitude, affection turn'd to marble,
> In honour of the living or the dead;
> What are they?—fine-wrought miniatures of art,
> Too exquisite to bear the weight of dew,
> Which every morn lets fall in pearls upon them,
> Till all their pomp sinks down in mouldering relics,
> Yet in their ruin lovelier than their prime!
> —Dust in the balance, atoms in the gale,
> Compared with these achievements of the deep,
> Were all the monuments of olden time,

In days when there were giants on the earth... (30–31)

Compared to them, 'Great Babylon was like a wreath of sand,/Left by one tide and cancell'd by the next', and Egypt's 'pyramids would be mere pinnacles,/Her giant statues, wrought from rocks of granite,/But puny ornaments for such a pile/As this stupendous mound of catacombs/Fill'd with dry mummies of the builder-worms.' (31–32.) The perspective is enamoured with science and with providence; but it is mostly enamoured with *time*, and with what time *does*—and no work of literature, not even Shakespeare's plays, is as intent on what time does as the Bible. In the Old Testament time is fate, the medium of destiny, the spinner of cycles of crime and punishment, rise and fall. All that Darwin did, in one perspective, was exchange divine omnipotence for blind force.

In 1841 an essay of Montgomery's written some years earlier was published in the minute book of the Sheffield and Attercliffe Auxiliary of the Tract Society. The source may sound painfully provincial, but there is nothing parochial about its author's moral imagination:

> An earthquake may suddenly engulf the pyramids of Ghizza, and leave the sand of the desert where they stood as blank as the tide would have left it on the sea-shore. A hammer in the hand of an idiot may break in pieces the Apollo Belvidere, or the Venus de Medici, which are scarcely less worshipped as miracles of art in our day, than they were by idolaters of old as the representatives of deities.

'Looking abroad over the whole world after the lapse of nearly six thousand years,' Montgomery concluded, 'what have we of the past but the words in which its history is recorded? What besides a few mouldering a brittle ruins which time in insensibly touching down to dust?'[1] It was a Biblical perspective in the hands of Montgomery the missionary; it was a secular one in the hands of Péron the anthropologist; it was an imaginative perspective the vision of either. 'Thus, while man', Péron wrote (3:47), '—who proclaims himself king of the natural world—laboriously constructs on the earth's surface those

---

1   Samuel Ellis, *Life, Times, and Character of James Montgomery* (London: Jackson, Walford, and Hodder, 1864), 50, 51.

frail buildings which the effect of time must soon bring down, feeble little worms (whose existence he was but lately ignorant of and still disdains) create in the depth of the ocean more and more of these prodigious monuments, whose strength defies the ages and is such that even the imagination declines to conceive of....'

It was James Hutton who said, 'time is not made to flow in vain; nor does there ever appear the exertion superfluous to power, or the manifestation of design, not calculated in wisdom to effect some general end.' (Quoted in Toulmin and Goodfield, 156.) It is, if one may say so, a sort of Whiggish interpretation of geohistory, that the nineteenth century began to replace with a sometimes scarcely renovated version something far older: a cyclical vision of contending forces, neither achieving final victory over the other. 'Whatever destroying tendencies, then, exist on earth,' William Knight wrote, 'these renovating powers compensate for them.... No marks of a degradation acting through a prolonged series of ages are exposed to our observation, without being met by constant renewal. *The one arises out of the other*.'[1] For Agassiz, too (176), 'destruction and construction go hand in hand, and the materials broken or worn away from one part of the Reef help to build it up elsewhere.' This was a theodicy Darwin himself (at least in his early days) was prepared to walk towards, in his infinitely methodical but also visionary way:

> These coral islands stand, and are victorious: for here another power, as antagonist to the former, takes part in the contest. The organic forces separate the atoms of carbonate of lime one by one from the foaming breakers, and unite them into a symmetrical structure. Let the hurricane tear up its thousand huge fragments; yet what will this tell against the accumulated labour of myriads of architects at work night and day, month after month? Thus do we see the soft and gelatinous body of a polypus ... conquering the great mechanical power of the waves of an ocean, which neither the art of man, nor the inanimate works of nature could successfully resist.

---

1   William Knight, *Facts and Observations towards Forming a New Theory of the Earth* (London: Longman, Rees, Orme, Brown, and Green, 1818), 258; my italics.

James Montgomery could not see atoms of calcium carbonate being woven and unwoven by coral polyps and the action of the waves. But he could see the Pacific in a flooded Yorkshire valley—and come to similar conclusions.

Alexandra Paterson

'The Atmosphere of Human Thought': Atmospheric Science in Shelley's *Prometheus Unbound*

In his lecture 'On the Atmosphere' in *A System of Familiar Philosophy*, Adam Walker figures the air as a 'vast laboratory, in which nature brings about an immense analysis; solutions, precipitations, and combinations.'[1] Walker, whose updated edition of his famous work was published in 1802, gave lectures at Percy Bysshe Shelley's boarding school that 'fascinated' the young poet and, according to Richard Holmes, 'vastly enlarged [Shelley's] field for practical experiments, devices and fantastic speculation.'[2] *Prometheus Unbound* itself is a work in which Shelley experiments with poetic and dramatic forms, and which he describes in a letter of 1819 to Thomas Love Peacock as 'a drama, with characters & mechanism of a kind yet unattempted.'[3] It is appropriate, then, that so much of the drama's action should take place in the wide, ambiguous, and often chaotic air: Walker's 'vast laboratory.'

The influence of both contemporary and early modern science in *Prometheus Unbound* has long been acknowledged: Shelley's extensive and varied scientific references in *Prometheus Unbound* were first laid out relatively exhaustively by Carl Grabo in 1930, and other critics have expanded on this work since.[4] Yet, while Walker is fre-

1   Adam Walker, 'On the Atmosphere' in *A System of Familiar Philosophy: In Twelve Lectures*, 2 vols (London: 1802), I, 225–306 (225) in *Hathi Trust Digital Library* <http://www.hathitrust.org/> [accessed 7 April 2013].
2   Richard Holmes, *Shelley: The Pursuit* (New York: Dutton, 1975), 16.
3   Percy Bysshe Shelley, *The Letters of Percy Bysshe Shelley*, ed. by Frederick L. Jones, 2 vols (Oxford: Clarendon Press,1964), II, 94.
4   Carl Grabo, *A Newton Among Poets: Shelley's Use of Science in* Prometheus Unbound (Chapel Hill: University of North Carolina Press, 1930); Earl Wasserman's seminal work, *Shelley's* Prometheus Unbound: *A Critical Reading* (Baltimore: Johns Hopkins University Press, 1965), for instance, considers the

quently mentioned by critics, he has not been the subject of a great deal of attention until recently, as the focus has tended towards more contemporary scientists, such as Davy and Herschel, whose work in many instances overturns earlier theories held by Walker. Sharon Ruston is a notable exception, and she demonstrates the resemblance between the Shelley's concern with 'electricity and light' in *Prometheus Unbound* and Walker's 'one principle', drawing a parallel between Walker's conception of 'fire' and Shelley's of love.[1] Ruston also argues convincingly for a reconsideration of scientists like Walker who 'did not make major discoveries,' but who 'were important scientists in their own right during their lifetimes' and had an influence on Shelley that is evident in his engagement with their work in his poetry.[2] In keeping with this, then, I consider in particular Walker's lecture 'On the Atmosphere' in relation to the ambiguous and airy space in which much of the action of *Prometheus Unbound* plays out. Shelley's figuring of the atmosphere in terms of water and the ocean repeats Walker's own language and suggests that he is conducting his own poetic, rather than scientific, experiment, mixing air and water to discover the best means for human thought to travel—and be received—on a global scale. In the 'Ode to the West Wind' Shelley famously calls upon the wind to '[d]rive [his] dead thoughts over the universe' and to '[s]catter ... [his] words among mankind.'[3] But while the ode offers the possibility of poetic thought being dispersed by the wind, *Prometheus Unbound* considers the implications of the auricular properties of the air itself to spread ideas of revolution. And although it is Asia, the immortal lover of Prometheus, who effects the revolutionary change in the atmosphere as the tyrant Jupiter falls in the third act of the play, the blurred boundaries between the Earth's atmosphere and the 'atmosphere of human thought' suggest the significance of elemental changes for the human mind as well.

influence of contemporary science in conjunction with earlier scientific thinking.

1   Sharon Ruston, *Shelley and Vitality* (New York: Palgrave, 2005), 128–29.

2   Sharon Ruston, 'Shelley's Links to the Midlands' Enlightenment: James Lind and Adam Walker', *British Journal for Eighteenth-Century Studies*, 30.2 (2007), 227–242 (227).

3   Percy Bysshe Shelley, 'Ode to the West Wind' in *The Poems of Shelley*, ed. by Jack Donovan and others, 3 vols (London: Longman, 1989–2011), III (2011), 200–11 (63–67).

Walker devotes a significant portion of his lecture to the relation-ship between air and water, opening with a simile that describes '[t]he atmosphere' as 'a thin fluid that surrounds our globe on all sides, like an immense ocean' (225). Shelley's figurative language suggests an equal preoccupation with the relationship between air and water. In Act II, Asia compares Panthea's eyes to the 'deep blue, boundless Heaven,' lending depth to the sky when the phrase 'deep blue' might describe the sea with equal precision.[1] Panthea herself ties the comparison together when she refers to the 'deep ocean' a few scenes later (2.4.29).

These similes and metaphors highlight the interchangeability between air and water, but what is of particular interest to Walker—and, I will argue, to Shelley—is the effect of the mixing of the two elements. Walker contends that 'air is contained in a dissolved state in the pores of water' and sets out to prove that the opposite is also true, describing experiments that test his hypothesis that the air is a 'dissolver of water; and that the two fluids mutually imbibe and enter into combination with each other' (233–34). He concludes that water is, indeed, '[a]bsorbed, soaked up, dissolved in the air' (234). That he frequently uses the word 'dissolve' to describe the process is particularly pertinent here for it is a word that Shelley also uses to describe atmospheres—both literal and figurative—in *Prometheus Unbound*. When, in the second act, Panthea describes to Asia the sexual encounter with Prometheus that she has dreamt, it is in terms of an 'all-dissolving' 'atmosphere'—Prometheus's love—which 'mingle[s]' with Panthea's blood until, like a dew-drop in the morn-ing sun, she is 'absorbed'—another word Walker uses in his account (2.1.75–82).

What we do not quite see here is the mutuality that Walker high-lights; Panthea plays a relatively passive role while Prometheus, whose atmosphere is 'all-dissolving', absorbs *her* and not the other way around. It is important to note, however, that this occurs before the crucial revolutionary moment of the play. With the fall of Jupiter

---

1   Percy Bysshe Shelley, *Prometheus Unbound* in *The Poems of Shelley*, ed. by Kelvin Everest and Geoffrey Matthews, 3 vols (London: Longman, 1989–2011), II (1989), 456–649 (2.1.114).

comes a change in the elements, and it is only in the lead up to this that Asia, in her own particular embodiment of love, does inspire a mutual dissolving of water and atmosphere. Rather than act as a solvent herself, she 'enkindles' the air, providing heat to the elements around her which then dissolve into each other. Walker emphasizes that heat is often 'the medium by which air and water chemically unite' and that rather than dissolving any other element on its own it 'increases the solvent qualities of fluid' (235). This can be evidenced by analogy, for of course 'the greater quantity of salt, sugar, tea, &c. ... may be dissolved in hot than in cold water' (235).

Fire, of course, is the element that generates this heat, and it was Walker's belief that *'light is the true essence of all inflammability,'* a point he italicizes for emphasis, and which Shelley takes up with verve (268). For Shelley, however, it is love, expressed by light, that holds the *'essence of all inflammability,'* as Ruston has previously noted (*Shelley and Vitality,* 129). In *Prometheus Unbound* Asia embodies both love and light, and this is made clear in Panthea's recollection of the story of Asia's birth, where

> love, like the atmosphere
> Of the sun's fire filling the living world,
> Burst from thee, and illuminated Earth and Heaven
> (2.5.26–28)

In the crucial lead up to the fall of Jupiter, however, Asia transforms into light, in a process that recalls her birth, as the light begins to burst through her again with such bright 'radiance' that Panthea can 'feel' it but 'dare[s] not look on' her (2.5.14–16). And where fire was only a simile for the love of Asia's birth, here it is represented physically as the spirits in the surrounding air articulate their observations to Asia, telling her what they see:

> thy lips enkindle
> With their love the breath between them;
> And thy smiles before they dwindle
> Make the cold air fire (2.5.48–51)

Panthea has already noted that '[s]ome good change / Is working in the elements' that surround Asia as a result of her transformation and the cold air turning to fire may be part of this 'good change' (2.5.18–19). Cold has been a feature of Jupiter's reign, and we see in the image of the air alighting, of turning 'the cold air fire,' a radical climax to the transformation that had really begun a few scenes earlier, as Asia began to effect springtime in her vale (2.1.6). But the heat suggested by the 'enkindling' of Asia's breath has another vital function: it allows the love it carries to travel. As Walker points out, warm air that has been exhaled rises away from the mouth so that one is constantly inhaling new air. In fact, the combination of colder air that is yet to be inhaled with warmer, exhaled air causes, Walker argues, 'two currents of air ... moving in opposite directions' (291). As Asia enkindles her breath with love, her exhalations carry it against the tide of the cold air associated with Jupiter's tyranny as it begins to spread its message of harmony.

I have so far discussed the changes wrought in the air at this revolutionary moment without mentioning the unifying of air and water that I began with, but this very unifying is directly associated with the movement of the music of the spirits in the air that begins at the same time as Asia 'enkindles' that air with love. As Asia transforms into light, she and Panthea hear 'sounds i' the air which speak the love / Of all articulate beings' (2.5.35–36), and as these sounds become one with the air and spread down towards the earth, Asia is carried along with them: 'My soul is an enchanted Boat,' she says,

> Which, like a sleeping swan, doth float
> Upon the silver waves of thy sweet singing;
>   [...]
> Whilst all the winds with melody are ringing.
>   It seems to float ever, forever,
>   Upon that many-winding river,
>   Between mountains, woods, abysses,
>   A paradise of wildernesses!
> Till, like one in slumber bound,
> Borne to the ocean, I float down, around,
> Into a sea profound, of ever-spreading sound. (2.5.72–84)

What is remarkable about this passage is that it consistently subverts the reader's expectations of the surrounding air as it dramatizes its transformation. The metaphor of the 'enchanted boat' is first used to describe a journey through the air, and just when the metaphorical boat seems to fit its surroundings by travelling along a 'river' the image is destabilized again as it is '[b]orne to the Ocean,' which turns out to be, in fact, 'a Sea ... of ever-spreading sound' and not a body of water at all. Air, sea, and sound are all one, and the music Asia travels on forms not only her mode of conveyance, but the destination as well, and 'ever-spreading,' the sound fills the world like an atmosphere. Air and water are united in being totally subsumed by sound, while at the same time being vital to its movement. Walker writes that '[t]he air is ... the most proper medium for conveying auricular intelligence from one creature to another' (297–98), but water is also 'an excellent conductor of sound' (299). Here, in their combined state, their reach is immeasurable, and this sets the scene for global communication.

Mary Favret has noted that during the romantic period weather came to be increasingly thought of in global terms: she reminds us that Luke Howard's *Climate of London* is more globally-attuned than the title alone suggests, and also recalls Howard's insistence on Latin terminology for his pioneering categorizations of cloud modifications precisely to enable the exchange of ideas on a global scale.[1] Shelley himself had long been attracted to the possibilities of airborne communication—and in particular that of communication via *heated* air through the medium of hot air balloons, which held vast revolutionary potential for him. During his stay at Lynmouth in 1812 a young Shelley, with the help of his first wife Harriet and friend Miss Hitchener, constructed a number of 'fire balloons' carrying copies of his *Declaration of Rights* and set them sailing through the air above the Bristol Channel (Holmes, 149). At the revolutionary moment of *Prometheus Unbound*, however, the messages conveyed through the heated air are not arguments articulated linguistically, but rather senses to be felt.

---

1   Mary Favret, *War at a Distance: Romanticism and the Making of Modern Wartime* (Princeton: Princeton University Press, 2010), 135.

Favret argues that one can find 'in the clouds and winds of romantic literature elements of a global system of communication, bearing if not news then pulses of feeling, currents from abroad' (120). It is 'pulses of feeling' that spread through the air in *Prometheus Unbound*. The notes of love are not only heard; they are also felt by Panthea, who asks Asia, 'Hearest thou not sounds i' the air which speak the love / Of all articulate beings? Feelest thou not / The inanimate winds enamoured with thee?' (2.5.35–37). The placement of these lines suggests that Asia should be able to feel the sound, rather than the movement, of the winds. After all, wind can only be physically felt when it is in motion, and these winds are 'inanimate.' Similarly, in Act IV, Ione does not hear the re-entrance of Demogorgon ('a mighty Power .... rising out of Earth, and from the sky ... and from within the air' (4.510–12)). Instead, she feels 'a sense of words upon mine ear' (4.517). In his essay 'On Love' Shelley conceives of a sympathetic love that can be felt in the movement of the natural world:

> Hence in solitude ... we love the flowers, the grass, and the waters, and the sky. In the motion of the very leaves of spring, in the blue air, there is then found a secret correspondence with our heart. There is eloquence in the tongueless wind, and a melody in the flowing brooks and the rustling of the reeds beside them, which by their inconceivable relation to something within the soul, awaken the spirits to a dance of breathless rapture, and bring tears of mysterious tenderness to the eyes.[1]

The composition date of the essay is unknown but its themes suggest that there is a continuation of Shelley's ideas about sympathetic love between the essay and *Prometheus Unbound*.[2] While in the essay the 'motion' of the natural world causes the sound of 'a melody in the flowing brooks and the rustling of the reeds,' in *Prometheus Unbound*

---

1   Percy Bysshe Shelley, 'On Love' in *Shelley's Prose, or The Trumpet of a Prophecy*, ed. by David Lee Clark (Albuquerque: University of New Mexico Press, 1954), 169–70 (170).

2   David Lee Clark notes that '"On Love" has been dated 'anywhere from 1815 to 1819' and makes a case for the earlier end of the spectrum (*Shelley's Prose*, 169). Others, including Donald H. Reiman and Neil Fraistat, have placed the composition date closer to the time of the composition of *Prometheus Unbound* at 1818–19 (*Shelley's Poetry and Prose*, ed. by Reiman and Fraistat (New York: Norton, 2002), 503).

the emphasis between sound and physical motion has shifted, so that sound is not only produced by movement, but is also felt *as* a kind of physical motion.

This close relationship between the physical and the auricular properties of air in *Prometheus Unbound* suggests the influence of Walker's conception of 'sympathy of sound' in the development of Shelley's thought about sympathetic love (301). Walker, describing the effect of sound waves on the cochlea, emphasizes the physicality of hearing, writing that '[t]he waves of the air are propagated up the meatus auditorius, and give a mechanical stroke, or impression, to the auditory nerves; so that hearing may be said to be a species of feeling' (304). Sound waves have another physical function too, which Walker calls 'the sympathy of sound.' Sound waves elicited by any object that can make noise, he argues, can cause a sympathetic repetition in another object near enough to catch the waves it produces. He uses the example of 'the wild and wonderful harmony of the Eolian harp' and describes the process by which air currents and waves produced by the movement of the strings combine to create harmonies of sound (301–302). In the fourth act of the drama, after the fall of Jupiter, a chorus of spirits and hours joins together to celebrate the newfound harmony of the post-revolutionary world in song. When the chorus exits, taking its song with it, Panthea and Ione notice a new sound arising, which Panthea identifies as 'the deep music of the rolling world / Kindling within the strings of the waved air / Aeolian modulations' (4.186–88). Here, the air itself is figured as a stringed instrument which harmonizes sympathetically with the earth, taking its cue from 'the rolling world' rather than producing its own music. Walker's scientific sympathy—an echo, more or less—produced by sound waves is here turned into something else entirely; it is an emotional sympathy that transcends the category of echo as it enhances the beauty of the sound with its harmony.

If messages of revolution become 'pulses of feeling,' 'senses,' rather than words upon an ear, what does this mean for the human thought that populates the air of the drama? The spirits of human thought, who appear in the first and final acts of the play, describe themselves in the first act as '[g]entle guides and guardians ... / Of

Heaven-oppressed mortality' who 'breathe [...] / The atmosphere of human thought' (1.673–76). When they return in Act IV to 'join the throng / Of the dance and the song' they are changed in much the same way as the earth's atmosphere has been. They unite with the Chorus of Hours in a way that recalls the uniting of air and water as they compare themselves to 'flying-fish' (4.86) 'mix[ing]' (4.88) with the birds in the sky. In Act I they also use images of birds and fish to describe themselves '[a]s the birds within the wind, / As the fish within the wave,' but the two images appear as catalogue items that are distinct from one another (1.683–84). In Act IV the word 'mix' deliberately unites the images as, concurrently, the spirits unite with the hours in dance and song, '[a]s the flying-fish leap / From the Indian deep, / And mix with the sea birds half asleep' (4.86–88). The mixing of sea and air in the metaphor also carries over in the spirits' description of the change that has come over the human mind, which they used to travel through like birds or clouds, and is now both 'an Ocean / Of clear emotion' and '[a] Heaven of serene and mighty motion' (4.95–98).

The description of the human mind that so clearly mirrors earlier descriptions of the surrounding atmosphere strongly suggests the possibility for a human thought as mobile as the love that Asia spreads throughout the atmosphere—although what this entails, and whether it allows for a variety of human thought to be dispersed or only that of, say, a poet-prophet, is not clear. What I would like to suggest is that Shelley is here experimenting with notions of the widespread reception of ideas—a move he continues to make in his 'Ode to the West Wind'—and Walker's science contributes to the hypothesis of the existence of an atmosphere which could allow his thoughts and ideas to spread, to be felt in sympathetic 'pulses of feeling,' all at a global scale. In his preface to the drama he famously writes that many of his images come from 'the operations of the human mind' (473), but in figuring for the human mind an atmosphere much like the earth's, he also conceives of a future of human thought which is taken from the operations of the air.

Deirdre Coleman

Keats, India, and the Vale of Soul-Making

I started this new project on Romantic India and Indian Romantics with Coleridge because of course he read everything and took copious notes, either into his notebooks or in the shape of marginalia; and like so many of his contemporaries, he was tremendously interested in the writings and translations of Sir William Jones and other Orientalists in the Hastings circle in Calcutta in the 1780s. Throughout the 1780s, the Orientalists made large claims for the Sanskrit language and for all aspects of Eastern thought and culture. For instance, Jones was in no doubt as to the superiority of Sanskrit to Greek and Latin, writing that it was 'more perfect than the *Greek*, more copious than the *Latin*, and more exquisitely refined than either'.[1] Such was the 'wonderful structure' and beauty of this ancient language that he and others believed that the influence of their translations would penetrate as deeply as did the revival of Greek literature in the fifteenth century, heralding a revivification of English poetry through what Jones described as a wholly 'new set of images and similitudes', symbols, and mystical allegories.[2] The classical world's jaded Pantheon would be refreshed by a splendid new array of mythological stories—a strange and colourful new Indian pantheon of gods and goddesses, such as Brahma, Vishnu, Lakshmi, many of whom were (he claimed) the forerunners of the later classical deities.

At one point Coleridge was so enthused by all of this that he sketched out some Hindu-style 'Hymns to the Sun, the Moon, and the Elements', modelled on Jones's work (*CN*, 1:174). He was also

---

1   'The third anniversary discourse, on the Hindus, delivered to the Asiatic Society, 2 February, 1786'; *Sir William Jones: selected poetical and prose works*, ed. Michael Franklin (Cardiff: University of Wales Press, 1995), 355–67 (361).

2   'An essay on the poetry of the eastern nations' (1772); Franklin, *Sir William Jones*, 319–36 (336).

very taken with Thomas Maurice's *History of Hindostan* (2 vols, 1795–8) which contained the striking image of Veeshnu slumbering on a bed of serpents for 'an Astronomical Period of a thousand Ages'.

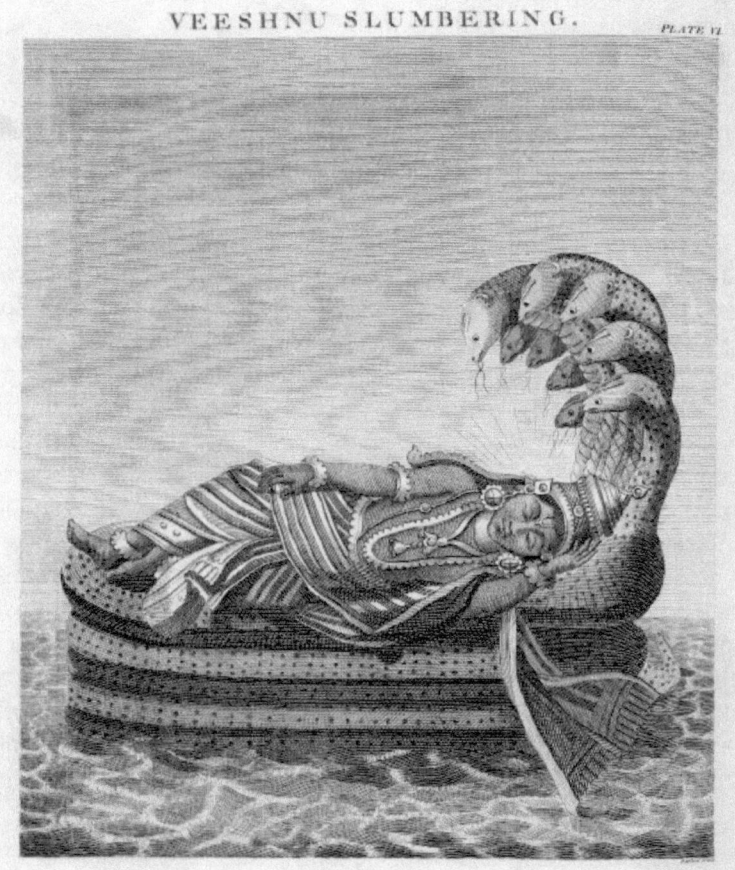

VEESHNU SLUMBERING.

PLATE VI

VEESHNU reposing during a CALPA, an Astronomical Period of a thousand Ages, upon the Serpent ANANTA; copied from a sculptured Rock in the Ganges.

To Charles Wilkins Esq. who first explored the Mine of Sanscreet Literature, this Plate, an humble Tribute of sincere respect for Talents & Virtue united is gratefully inscribed by —

Image: courtesy of Baillieu library, University of Melbourne

Many believe that this image inspired the famous letter to John Thelwall in October 1797, in which the poet launches into a strange dreamlike evocation of the Brahmanic code. While sometimes (he tells Thelwall) he pushes his intellect to great spiritual heights, at other times he adopts 'the Brahman Creed':

> It is better to sit than to stand, it is better to lie than to sit, it is better to sleep than to wake—but Death is the best of all!—I should much wish, like the Indian Vishna, to float about along an infinite ocean cradled in the flower of the Lotos, & wake once in a million years for a few minutes—just to know I was going to sleep a million years more. (*CL*, I:349)

John Drew, in his important *India and the Romantic Imagination* (1987) has observed that these descriptions of Vishnu and the floating lotus correspond with imagery in Charles Wilkins's translation of the *Gita* in 1785.[1] To this end, I have recently argued that the domes and pleasure gardens of India have been overlooked in readings of the geopolitical landscape of *Kubla Khan*.[2] Although I don't have many followers—most folk who talk about Coleridge's orientalism in *Kubla Khan* are much more interested in China, Mongolia, or Tartary—Livingston Lowes was right to argue for the influence on Coleridge of some of the earlier travellers to India, especially Francois Bernier and his *Travels in the Mogul Empire* (1670). Lowes focuses on Bernier's account of travelling over the mountains into the valley of Cashmere, but Bernier also reveals the very Eastern character of pantheism. A perception of divine unity, or the presence of God in all things, is the hallmark of his Eastern–inspired philosophy:

> all this World is nothing but a kind of Dream and a meer Illusion . . . all this multiplicity and diversity of things that appear to us, is nothing but one and the same thing, which is *God himself.*[3]

---

1   John Drew, *India and the Romantic Imagination* (Delhi: Oxford University Press, 1987), 193. For more on Coleridge and Hinduism, see Natalie Tal Harries 'The One Life Within Us and Abroad' in *Coleridge, Romanticism and the Orient: Cultural Negotiations,* eds. D. Vallins, Kaz Oishi and Seamus Perry (London: Bloomsbury, 2013), 131–44.

2   See Coleman, 'The "dark tide of time": Coleridge and William Hodges' India', in *Coleridge, Romanticism and the Orient*, 39–54.

3   Bernier, quoted in Ros Ballaster, *Fabulous Orients: Fictions of the East in*

There was also the drama and high visibility of Edmund Burke's protracted assault on Warren Hastings in London, plus the fact that Coleridge had lost two brothers in India, the eldest child John (who he never knew) and Frank who was only two years older than him (Frank is famous for crumbling the poet's cheese and provoking a murderous attack). Coleridge was himself destined for India, as can be seen in his family's repeated attempts to enlist him in the military, with a certain General Goddard assigned to the job after Coleridge's father died in 1781.[1] Finally, there is the likely influence of the Indian paintings and writings of William Hodges, a figure well known in the antipodes as one of the principal artists on Cook's second voyage. As the great Australian art historian Bernard Smith has demonstrated, Coleridge was steeped in the lore of this particular voyage because his mathematics master at Christ's Hospital, William Wales, was Cook's astronomer on the *Resolution*.[2] Wales took Hodges under his wing on that voyage, and Smith argues that the younger man's drawings of what Coleridge would call the 'tremendities of nature'— whirlwind-waterspouts and icebergs—very likely featured in Wales's accounts of the voyage. Later, in the early 1780s, Hodges was in India under the patronage of Hastings, travelling around Bengal like an embedded artist/journalist as the East India Company conducted their wars. Hodges's visual record of India was circulating in London when Coleridge was Wales's pupil and after he left school. From 1785 until 1794, between which years Coleridge's two brothers died, Hodges exhibited twenty-five oil paintings at the Royal Academy, including the highly picturesque and romantic Diploma piece, *The Ghauts at Benares* and a striking painting of the Taj Mahal, now in New Delhi. During the impeachment and trial of Warren Hastings, Hodges also published a book, *Travels in India* in 1793 (borrowed by Joseph Cottle from the Bristol Library in 1796). So there is much to connect Hodges's paintings and his *Travels in India* with *Kubla*

England, 1662–1785 (Oxford University Press, 2005), 266.
1   See James Engell, ed. Coleridge: The Early Family Letters (Oxford: Clarendon Press, 1994), p. 73.
2   Bernard Smith, 'Coleridge's Ancient Mariner and Cook's Second Voyage', in Imagining the Pacific in the wake of the Cook Voyages (Carlton, Vic.: Melbourne University Press, 1992), 146.

Khan: the dreamy, nostalgic evocation of a Miltonic garden of Eden, the false paradise, inter-generational strife, territorial conquest, war, and the decline and fall of empire: 'And 'mid this tumult Kubla heard from far/Ancestral voices prophesying war!' (*PW*, vol 1, part 1, 513).

But it wasn't long before Coleridge's deep ambivalence towards pantheism and pantheistic idealism got the better of any enthusiasm he had felt for composing Hindu-style hymns in the mid-1790s. As a Christian he was also increasingly unsettled by Jones's claims about the great antiquity of India's sacred texts, and the implications for biblical authority of the so-called Hindu chronology which posited the existence of a very old, 'almost primaeval language', an ancestral ur-language from which all the principal languages of Asia and Europe were derived.[1]

As early as the end of the 1790s, Coleridge's ambivalence towards ideas of the 'One Life' killed off any enthusiasm he felt for writing Hindu-style 'Hymns' to the 'Elements'. Then, much later in life, in what we now call his *Opus Maximum*, Coleridge would demonize Indian pantheism as the 'true oriental Deity', no more than 'a painted Atheism': a 'Universal God—*all-God* an Oceanic God, Man, Beast and Plant being mere & merely wavelets & wrinkles on the surface of the Depth'.[2]

While we have a whole-of-career story to develop about Coleridge, what sort of case can be mounted for John Keats, whose life was so short and whose reading is much less well documented? There were points when I thought I was being totally daft, and of course all the experts in the field were against me. Keats struck Marilyn Butler as 'not normally much of an orientalist',[3] certainly when you compared him to Shelley and Byron, and the poet barely figures in John Drew's book. Indeed, of all the Romantic poets, it is argued that Keats's orientalism is 'primarily a question of style, an

---

1   Drew, *India and the Romantic Imagination*, 52.
2   *Opus Maximum*, ed. T. McFarland (2002), 229. For a fuller account of Coleridge's later disenchantment, see my 'The "dark tide of time"'.
3   Butler, 'Orientalism', 438. In a recent study of eastern religion in Romantic writing, Keats only appears in very general terms; see Mark S. Lussier's *Romantic Dharma: the emergence of Buddhism into nineteenth-century Europe* (New York, 2011).

imperial heraldry'.[1] The generally received view of his literary and intellectual development is that the only writers who mattered to him were English ones, principally Shakespeare, Spenser, Chatterton, and Milton, an impression reinforced by the brief list of books left behind after his death,[2] in which there are no titles associated with Indian or other Eastern literature. Amidst all this doubting, I stuck to my hunch, doggedly pursuing hints and sometimes more than hints, such as Barry Cornwall's description of the consumptive Keats as a metaphorical sati, consumed from within by a burning creative fire. In this very odd passage which invokes the horrible gynophobic practice of widow-burning, Cornwall refers to 'the wear and wasting which an ardent, ambitious, and restless intellect makes in the 'human form divine'. Sadly (he reflects), 'the flame burning within would shortly consume the outward shell'. So far this is all standard Romantic fare, but then he continues: Keats's

> spirit was like burning oil in a vessel of some precious and costly wood, which when the flame has consumed its nutriment, will then burn that which contained it . . . Unlike the pyre that consumes the devoted widow of the Hindoo husband, where we may see the fire but not the victim, in him we saw the fire and the victim too. He, however, was a self–devoted martyr to intellect, and not to a senseless and brutal custom; and if literature had its army of martyrs, as Religion gloriously has, his name would not be forgotten in its calends.[3]

That Keats's contemporaries saw the poet and his work as coloured by the East can be seen in the distinctly Orientalist discourse which greeted his poetry, frequently described as excessive, unmanly, luxurious, and degenerate. In 1826, for instance, *Blackwood's Edinburgh*

---

1   Nigel Leask, *British Romantic writers and the East: Anxieties of Empire* (Cambirdge University Press, 2004), 125; see also Tim Fulford, 'Romanticism and colonialism: races, places, peoples, 1800–30', *Romanticism and colonialism: Writing and Empire, 1780-1830* (Cambridge University Press, 2005), 35–47 (45).

2   'List of Keats's books', in Hyder E. Rollins, ed. *The Keats circle: letters and papers and more letters and poems of the Keats circle*, 2 vols (Cambridge, MA, 1965), 1:253–60.

3   Quoted in Alan Bewell, *Romanticism and Colonial Disease* (Johns Hopkins University Press, 2003), 192.

magazine accused his work of outhunting Leigh Hunt 'in a species of emasculated pruriency, that [. . .] looks as if it were the product of some imaginative Eunuch's muse within the melancholy inspiration of the Haram'.[1]

Others too have brought Keats and India into the same frame. The American poet William Logan wrote a poem entitled 'Keats in India', published in his collection *Vain Empires* (1998). This poem, which received the prestigious John Masefield Memorial Award from the Poetry Society of America, is a blank-verse monologue which imagines a posthumous life for Keats in India in 1848. Inspired by Keats's consideration of a career as an Indiaman' surgeon, voyaging to and from India, the poem captures the illusory effects generated by India's decayed grandeur, including passages reminiscent of Hodges's *Travels in India*, with its preoccupation with the decline and fall of empire. Of the city of Lucknow, Keats says (in Logan's words):

> We rode like princes into India's mirage,
> but as we rode, the vision thinned and wavered.
> The distant, starry color of the buildings,
> serene Italian marble in the sun,
> up close was whitewash, peeling, fly-blown. . . .
> You come at last to the conclusion,
> the city of your dreams is but a fraud.[2]

Formative Influences

The task of tracing the resonances and affinities of Indian philosophy in Keats's writings is similar to the task Stuart Sperry took on a few decades ago, when he set out to chart Keats's intellectual affinities with Voltaire, for the young poet seems to have held 'no fixed philosophical position'.[3] But while there may not have been any single major philosophical influence, Sperry put his faith in Keats's poetical temperament—one which was open to speculations and impres-

---

1   *Blackwood's Edinburgh Magazine*, 19 (January–June 1826): xxvi.
2   William Logan, 'Keats in India, 1848', *Vain Empires* (Penguin Poets, 1998), 70.
3   Stuart M. Sperry, 'Keats's skepticism and Voltaire', *Keats–Shelley Journal* 12 (1963): 75–93.

sions from a number of sources. Furthermore, Keats's ideas about the progress of mankind—what he termed 'the general and gregarious advance of intellect'—incorporated wide views of world history and global linkages.[1] As one recent Orientalist has put it: 'The acknowledged antiquity of the civilization of the Hindus, their ancient literature, and the mystery attached to writings locked up in a dead language, excited the imagination of all who took an interest in the history of human progress'.[2] Developed amongst, and reinforcing Keats's many assertions of the advance of human intellect, lie his key aesthetic concepts—the 'vale of Soul-making', 'negative capability', and its closely related paradox of 'diligent indolence'. All these ideas were touched by his understanding of Indian thought—an understanding which developed from his schooldays onwards and was strengthened by the circle of writers in which he later moved.

As is well known, Charles Cowden Clarke, in his recollections of Keats as a schoolboy, recorded that Lemprière's *Classical dictionary* was one of the poet's three favourite books.[3] It is not often noted that Lemprière ranged outside the Western tradition, including an entry on India. Under the letter 'I' in Lemprière's *Classical dictionary* Keats would have read:

> India, the most celebrated and opulent of all the countries of Asia, bounded on one side by the Indus, from which it derives its name . . . It has always been reckoned famous for the riches it contains; and so persuaded were the ancients of its wealth, that they supposed its very sands were gold. It contained 9000 different nations, and 5000 remarkable cities, according to geographers. Bacchus was the first who conquered it.[4]

The reference to the wine-god as the East's first conqueror is

---

1 Letter to the George Keatses (14 Feb–3 May 1819); *Letters*, 2:102. Letter to J. H. Reynolds (3 May 1818); *Letters*, 1:281.

2 T. E. Colebrooke, quoted in P. J. Marshall, 'The empire of the officials', *Romantic Representations of British India*, ed. M. J. Franklin (London & New York: Routledge, 2006), 47.

3 Charles and Mary Cowden Clarke, *Recollections of writers* (London, 1878), 123–24.

4 John Lemprière, *Bibliotheca classica; or, a classical dictionary* (London, 1792), no pagination.

notable because Bacchus is an important and recurring figure in
Keats's work, spanning the worlds of Greek and Indian mythology.
According to myth, Bacchus spent many years travelling in the east,
and from ancient times onwards was often depicted in the moment
of his triumphal return from India, laden with the spoils of conquest.
Furthermore, learned orientalists argued that there was a 'simili-
tude' between Bacchus and the Hindu divinity Iswara. Alexander
Hamilton, in his review of J. D. Paterson's 'On the Origins of the
Hindu Religion' (1808), argued that the two gods shared the same
phallic cult: 'the same obscenities, the same bloody rites, and the
same emblem of the generative power'.[1] Iswara's chief emblem was
'the phallus', and his rites consisted in its worship: with the phallus
'wrapped in a tiger's skin, and mounted on a sacred bull . . . [Iswara]
is followed by a mixed crowd of males and female votaries, whose
wild dances and frantic revels accompany his steps, or announce his
presence'.[2] Ian Jack has rightly argued for the importance to Keats of
the sacrificial or religious procession, both of which come together
in the Indian maid's description of Bacchus's triumphant return from
the East in her roundelay in Book IV of Endymion (published 1818):

> And as I sat, over the light blue hills
> There came a noise of revellers: the rills
> Into the wide stream came of purple hue—
> 'Twas Bacchus and his crew!
> The earnest trumpet spake, and silver thrills
> From kissing cymbals made a merry din—
> 'Twas Bacchus and his kin!
> Like to a moving vintage down they came
> Crown'd with green leaves, and faces all on flame:
> All madly dancing through the pleasant valley,
> To scare thee, Melancholy![3]

1   See J. D. Paterson, 'On the Origins of the Hindu Religion', *Asiatic Researches*,
    vol.8 (London, 1808): 50–51.
2   Alexander Hamilton, review of J. D. Paterson, *Edinburgh Review*, 15 (April
    1808): 38.
3   *The Poems of John Keats*, ed. Jack Stillinger (Cambridge, MA, 1978), 198. See
    Grant F. Scott, ed. *Joseph Severn: Letters and Memoirs* (Aldershot: Ashgate,
    2005), 662–3; (62). For Keats and Bacchus, see Ian Jack's excellent *Keats and
    the Mirror of Art* (Oxford at the Clarendon Press, 1967).

We know from Joseph Severn that Keats was much struck by Titian's 'Bacchus and Ariadne' (1520–23) when he saw it in London in 1817, just as he was beginning to compose *Endymion*. That Keats was aware of the learned discourse around Indian and Greek 'similitudes' can be seen in a passage where one of the followers describes the homage paid to the young Bacchus by all other gods, including a somewhat begrudging, father-like Brahma:

> Great Brahma from his mystic heaven groans,
> And all his priesthood moans;
> Before young Bacchus' eye-wink turning pale.[1]

From the 'mad' and 'wild minstrelsy' of *Endymion* would arise the Bacchic frenzy and abandon of 'Ode on a Grecian Urn': 'What men or gods are these? What maidens loth?/What mad pursuit? What struggle to escape?/What pipes and timbrels? What wild ecstasy?'[2] Bacchus's mythic journey through the East appears yet again in 'Ode to a nightingale': 'Away! away! for I will fly to thee,/Not charioted by Bacchus and his pards,/But on the viewless wings of Poesy.[3] The importance of Bacchus at this time for Keats and his circle can be seen in William Hazlitt's *Lectures on the English poets* (1818), where the somewhat paltry Bacchus of John Dryden's 'Ode in Honour of St Cecilia's Day' is roundly berated. Hazlitt's own vision of Bacchus was, like Keats's, a majestic one—of the wine-god (and I quote Hazlitt here) 'returning from the conquest of India, with satyrs and wild beasts, that he had tamed, following in his train; crowned with vine leaves, and riding in a chariot drawn by leopards—such as we have seen him painted by Titian or Rubens'.[4]

As Marilyn Butler has shown, the enthusiasm of Keats's circle for ancient, especially Greek, mythology went hand in hand with a renewed interest in the writings of an earlier generation of 'infidel anthropologists' such as Sir William Hamilton, Richard Payne Knight, and Erasmus Darwin. Butler argues that, faced with the contraction

---

1   Stillinger, *Poems of John Keats*, 200.
2   Stillinger, *Poems of John Keats*,, 372.
3   Keats, 'Ode to a nightingale'; Stillinger, *Poems of John Keats*, 369–72 (l.31–33).
4   William Hazlitt, *Complete works*, ed. P. P. Howe, 21 vols (London, 1930-34), 5:81.

of intellectual life during the long years of war, these Enlightenment thinkers provided a counter-politics amidst the conservative gloom, drawing the second-generation Romantics towards a 'free and humanistic paganism', a cheerful creed which included republicanism, guilt-free sexuality, a jovial interest in priapus and phallus worship, and the pursuit of ideal love, or nympholepsy.[1] Did India and Hinduism offer a similar counter-politics to the younger generation of Romantics? There are many ideal nymphs in Keats, including the Indian maid of *Endymion* who, in a neat piece of East–West syncretism, turns out to be one and the same as the moon-goddess Cynthia. In terms of the Indian maid's avatars, there were several striking examples for Keats to model her on, such as Robert Southey's heroine, Kailyal, from *The Curse of Kehama* (1810), a poem Keats certainly knew for he alludes to it in *Isabella, or the pot of basil* (1818) where Isabella's vision of the dead Lorenzo is described as 'like a lance,/Waking an Indian from his cloudy hall/ With cruel pierce, and bringing him again/Sense of the gnawing fire at heart and brain'.[2] There was also the Indian priestess Luxima from Sydney Owenson's novel, *The Missionary* (1811), a work steeped in William Jones's orientalism and syncretism. Shelley was obsessed with Owenson's Indian tale, describing it as a 'divine' and 'beautiful thing' and urging all his friends to read it. His own 'veiled maid' in *Alastor, or The Spirit of Solitude*, published in 1816, is modelled on Owenson's priestess. 1816 is also the year in which Keats first met Shelley so it is very likely that he read *The Missionary* at Shelley's prompting, and that this fed into the poetical, mystical, and sensual shape of his conceptual voyaging in *Endymion*.[3]

Despite the centrality and prominence of classical allusions

---

1   Marilyn Butler, *Peacock Displayed: a satirist in his context* (London: Routledge, 1979), 109.

2   Stillinger, *Poems of John Keats*, 255. Kehama's curse on Ladurad contains the lines: 'Thou shalt live in thy pain,/While Kehama shall reign,/With a fire in thy heart/And a fire in thy brain', *The Curse of Kehama* (London: Longman, 1810), 19.

3   For Shelley's championing of *The Missionary* and Jones's influence on Owenson, see Michael J. Franklin, '"Passion's Empire": Sydney Owenson's "Indian Venture," Phoenicianism, Orientalism, and Binarism', *Studies in Romanticism*, vol45, no2 (Summer 2006), 181–97.

in Keats's work—his reputation (as one contemporary put it) for 'the power of putting a spirit of life and novelty into the Heathen Mythology'[1]—Keats sometimes signalled a readiness for other, new sensations—for a new and different cosmology beyond a pagan 'creed outworn'. His Preface to *Endymion* signals the prospect of change: 'I hope I have not in too late a day touched the beautiful mythology of Greece, and dulled its brightness: for I wish to try once more, before I bid it farewel'.[2] Further evidence (as I hope to show shortly) will support my argument that he was fascinated by Hinduism's challenge to the originality and antiquity of Europe's Greco-Roman inheritance.

But to return to Lemprière as a formative influence. Lemprière also included entries on the Ganges and the 'Indian philosophers' known as Brachmanes. This last entry is quite long, describing the derivation of the name 'Brachmanes' from Brahma, 'one of the three beings whom God, according to their theology, created, and with whose assistance he formed the world'. Lemprière continues: 'According to modern authors, Brahma is the parent of all mankind, and he produced as many worlds as there are parts in the body, which they reckoned fourteen. They believed that there were seven seas, of water, milk, curds, butter, salt, sugar, and wine, each blessed with its particular paradise'.[3] Keats was also given as a school prize C. H. Kauffman's *Dictionary of Merchandize* (1803), a book brimful of descriptions of exotic commodities, many with medicinal properties.[4] Of the many spices, food-stuffs and dyes associated with India and Ceylon, there were entries on cardamon, cloves, coconut, Colombo root, frankincense, gamboge, ginger, indigo, and turmeric, all of which entries described in rich detail the tastes, smells, and uses of these products. In Kauffman the young Keats would also have read

---

1   Unsigned, '*The Quarterly review—Mr. Keats*', *The Examiner* (11 October 1818), 649.
2   John Keats, 'Preface', *Endymion: a poetic romance* in Stillinger, *Poems of John Keats*, 103.
3   Lemprière, *Bibliotheca classica*, no pagination.
4   [Kauffman, C. H.] *The dictionary of merchandize, and nomenclature in all languages: for the use of counting-houses: containing, the History, Places of Growth, Culture, Use, and Marks of Excellency, of such natural productions, as form Articles of Commerce. By a Merchant* (London: Printed for the Author, 1803). I thank Nicholas Roe for bringing this book to my attention.

about the manufacture of seductive narcotics such as opium, and the dangers of deep-sea pearl-fishing off the coast of Ceylon.

It is very likely that he read Volney's *The Ruins* as well, an English edition of which was published in Paris in 1802. Not only are there many evocative descriptions of the ruined cities of the kingdoms of Egypt and Syria, there are many sections as well on Indian religions, on Brahminism, and on Zoroastrianism. This book also has some eye-catching sentences on the spices and precious stones of Ceylon, the shawls of Cashmere, the diamonds of Golconda, the amber of Maldivia, the musk of Thibet, the aloes of Cochin, and the apes and peacocks of the continent of India.[1]

Of his other reading, Clarke tells us that Keats (and I quote Clarke here) 'exhausted the school library, which consisted principally of abridgments of all the voyages and travels of any note; Mavor's collection, also his "Universal History"'.[2] William Fordyce Mavor was a compiler of educational books, principally marketed for schools, 'written with an eye to youthful innocence and female delicacy'.[3] In these pocket-size multi-volume sets, Keats would have discovered in volumes 11 and 12 of the *Universal history* histories of Hindostan; of the mogul Empire; parts of Tartary; and of China, as well as an up-to-date history of India. In this last section there was a digest of most of what was popularly known about Calcutta and the Asiatic Society, the latter described as 'a noble monument of science in a distant country' instituted by 'the late admirable Sir William Jones'.[4] Mavor also provided an abstract of the 'genuine principles of the Hindoo religion' which inculcates 'the most sublime notions—though its rites are debased with idolatry and superstition':

> These principles teach, that the universe is governed by one supreme and intelligent Ruler, whose divine essence pervades

1   See C. F. Volney, *The Ruins, or, A survey of the revolutions of empires* (1791; S. Shaw: Albany, 1822), 37.
2   Clarke, *Recollections of writers*, 123.
3   William Mavor, 'Prefatory remarks', *Historical account of the most celebrated voyages, travels, and discoveries, from the time of Columbus to the present period*, 25 vols (London, 1796–97; 1801).
4   William Mavor, *Universal history, ancient and modern; comprehending a general view of the transactions of every nation, kingdom, and empire in the world, from the earliest records of time*, 25 vols (London, 1802–05), 11:280.

the whole circle of nature, gives motion to the luminaries of the sky, and vivifies the animal creation; that the soul, after death, re-ascends to the immortal spirit of God, and that the body returns to dust; that he who distinguishes himself in this world by pious and charitable actions, shall attain immortality; but that he who destroys the purity of his own soul, shall dwell, for a certain time, with evil spirits in the regions which utter darkness involves, and that, after he has received the punishment due to his crimes, his spirit shall be sent back to this world, to inhabit the bodies of beasts [. . .]. In the Vedas, one God only is acknowledged, who is called Brahma, or the Great One. He is declared to be a being without shape, whose essence is incomprehensible, and who must therefore be worshipped through symbolical representations of his divine attributes. The triple divinity of Vishnu, Brahma, and Shiva, which are expressed by the mystical word OM, are said to be emblems of the creative, preservative, and destructive powers of the Almighty.[1]

Furthermore, in Mavor's extensive 25-volume set of the *Most celebrated voyages*, there was John Holwell's account of the infamous 'Black-Hole of Calcutta' (vol 20), and George Forster's 'Travels in the northern part of India, Kashmire, Afghanistan, and Persia, and into Russia by the Caspian Sea, performed in the years 1782, 83, and 84' (vol 24). Finally, as John Whale reminds us in his essay on William Hazlitt's 'The Indian jugglers', the London in which Keats grew up in the early nineteenth century enjoyed frequent visits by troupes of Indian fakirs, snake-charmers, sword-swallowers and jugglers.[2]

The Vale of Soul-making

That Keats saw life as a mystic drama can be seen in his famous journal letter of February–May, 1819. Here, in pursuit of a religion which would not affront his 'reason and humanity', Keats repudiates the gloomy and 'straightened' Christian teaching of life as a 'vale of tears'. The creed he groped towards in his letters during this time was

---

1   Mavor, Universal history, 11:289–90.
2   See John Whale, 'Indian jugglers: Hazlitt, Romantic orientalism and the difference of view', *Romanticism and colonialism*, 206–20 (208).

the 'vale of Soul-making', a conception which invoked as part of its definition other world religions, including the 'Hindoos' and 'their Vishnu':

> Seriously I think it probable that this System of Soul-making—may have been the Parent of all the more palpable and personal Schemes of Redemption, among the Zoroastrians the Christians and the Hindoos. For as one part of the human species must have their carved Jupiter; so another part must have the palpable and named Mediator and saviour, their Christ their Oromanes and their Vishnu.[1]

The 'carved Jupiter' takes us straight to Keats's earliest lesson in syncretism and comparative religion, provided by one of his favourite school books, Andrew Tooke's *The Pantheon* (1798).[2] In the book's opening entry on Jupiter, *'the father and king of Gods and men'*, we read that 'there is not one *Jupiter*, but many, who are sprung from different families [. . .] *Varro* reckoned up three hundred *Jupiters*; and others reckon almost an innumerable company of them; for, there was hardly any nation which did not worship a *Jupiter* of their own, and suppose him to be born among themselves'.[3] The other instructors in comparative religion were the Frenchmen Volney (a likely influence) and Voltaire (an undisputed influence). On the list of Keats's books drawn up after his death we find three books of Voltaire's, including his *Dictionnaire philosophique* (Paris, 1816), *Siecle de Louis XIV*, and *Essai sur les moeurs* (Paris, 1804–5). It is likely that Keats first read Voltaire at school under the guidance of Clarke, who was not just Keats's mentor but a Voltaire enthusiast as well. As is well known, Voltaire was an admirer of India as an ancient civilization to which the Greeks had travelled for instruction, quipping that his contemporaries in Europe only travelled there to enrich themselves and to kill each other in the process. Hinduism, along with other world religions, was also of course central to Voltaire's comparative mythology

---

1   Letter to the George Keatses (14 Feb–3 May 1819); *Letters*, 2:101–103.
2   Clarke, *Recollections of writers*, 123–24.
3   Andrew Tooke, *The pantheon, representing the fabulous histories of the heathen gods, and most illustrious heroes; in a short, plain, and familiar method, by way of dialogue*, 13th ed. (London, 1798), 10, 12.

and anti-Christian polemic.

To conclude this section: unlike Coleridge whose Christian apologetics led to a rejection of the Hindu chronology and Voltaire's 'levities', Keats was a self-professed deist who, 'straining at particles of light in the midst of a great darkness', was searching for an alternative, more cheerful belief system.[1] In rejecting certain Christian doctrines such as eternal punishment as inhuman and repellent, Keats resembled his friends William Hazlitt and the radical journalist Leigh Hunt. Like William Jones he might have argued: 'I am no Hindu, but I hold the doctrine of the Hindus concerning a future state to be incomparably more rational, pious, and more likely to deter men from vice, than the horrid opinions inculcated by Christians on punishments *without end*'.[2]

Leigh Hunt's Examiner and British Empire in India

On the liberal side of politics, attuned to matters of empire, and keen to do some good in the world, Keats sometimes felt trapped between his muse and a more active engagement in political life.[3] For instance, at the same time that he was developing his creed of the 'vale of Soul–making', he was seriously considering a career as an Indiaman's surgeon, voyaging 'to and from India for a few years'.[4] It may have been Dr George Darling who suggested this, as he had himself been a surgeon on an Indiaman. To find out more about this option, Keats had two acquaintances at the East India House in London—Charles Lamb and Thomas Love Peacock—and it seems that he visited there because of the appearance in his poem, *The Cap and Bells*, or *The Jealousies: A Fairy Tale* (1819) of Emperor Elfinan's 'Man-Tiger-Organ', 'A play-thing of the Emperor's choice . . . prettiest of his

---

1   Letter to the George Keatses (14 Feb–3 May 1819); *Letters*, 2:80.
2   Quoted in M. J. Franklin, *Orientalist Jones: Sir William Jones, Poet, Lawyer, and, Lawyer, 1746–1794 (Oxford: OUP: 2011)*, 253.
3   Keats's determination to take an active role in political life can be seen intermittently throughout his letters; see *Letters*, 1:267, 293, 386–87. For his awareness of empire, see his comments on Richard Carlisle's trial; *Letters*, 2:194.
4   See Keats's letter to Sarah Jeffrey (31 May 1819); *Letters*, 2:113. See also a month later to Dilke: 'my mind [h]as been at work all over the world to find out what to do [. . .] South America or Surgeon to an I[n]diaman—which last I think will be my fate'; *Letters*, 2:114.

toys', Keats writes. This 'Man-Tiger-Organ', better known as Tippoo Sultan's automaton tiger (see below), is still in London, on display in the Victoria and Albert Museum.

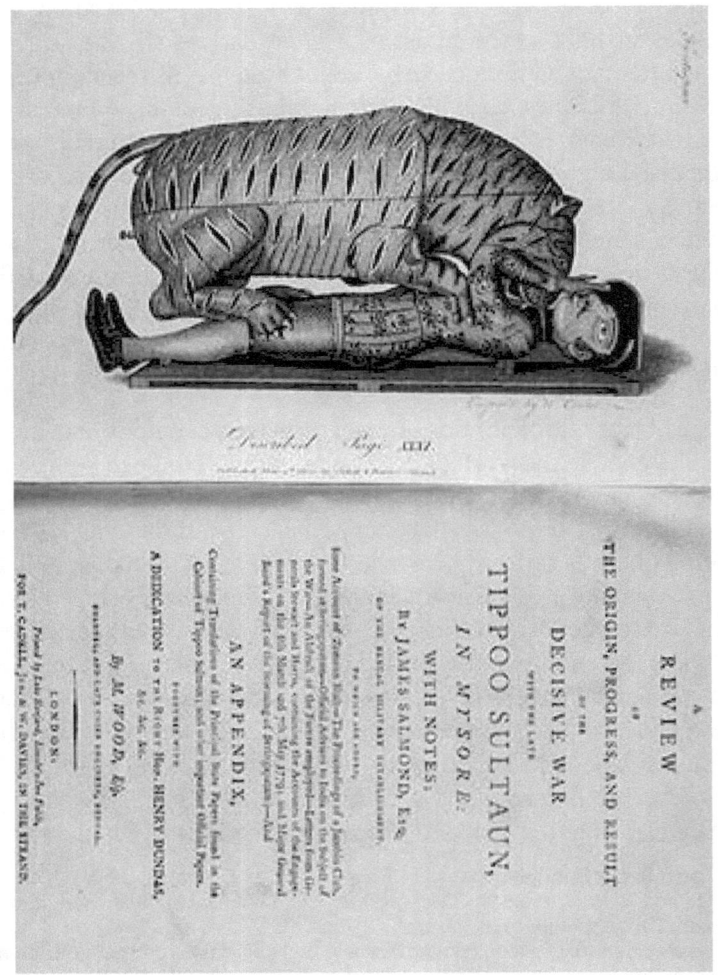

Travelling as a surgeon on an East Indiaman was hardly a top priority, though, described instead as one of 'two Poisons', the other being 'a fevrous life alone with Poetry' (*Letters*, 2:113). But why did

India present itself as the setting for a more active role and, more particularly, as an alternative to the poetical life? One answer might be Leigh Hunt's editorial interweaving of notices of Keats's poetry with his ongoing coverage of Britain's crimes in India.

The subject of British rule in India had begun to take a higher profile in the public press with the passing of an amendment to the India Act in 1813, giving Christian missionaries the green light to pursue their proselytizing agenda. Leigh Hunt's *The Examiner*, assiduously read by Keats, began to cover the East quite intensively from 1815, the year in which Ceylon was ceded to Britain, but Hunt had long been a diligent observer and critic of British crimes in India, in particular the East India Company's systematic warfare in Bengal. In 1808 Hunt declared that he would look on the 'loss of India without a sigh'. The tyranny exerted by Britain over the Indians—'grinding Nabobs into gold-dust', burning their cities and oppressing their wives and children—had ensured the natives' hatred, and all to 'enrich a few lazy individuals, who return to this country, with yellow death in their countenances [. . .]. The sun of India sucks up our seas to return us nothing but a few turbid and unprofitable showers'.[1]

As an opponent of dogmatism of all kinds, Hunt ran a regular feature in *The Examiner* on 'Superstition—its civil and political consequences'. Keen to promote his own cheery view of a benevolent God, and horrified (like William Jones and Keats) by the Christian notion of eternal punishment, he was vehemently opposed to the evangelization which had been unleashed on India. Happily, few converts had been found, a situation which would remain (he joked) as long as the British missionary kept on threatening the Hindoos that, if they 'do not come over to his humaner opinions, they will be tortured to all eternity!'[2] That God 'is pleased with a diversity of religions' is an opinion for which Hindus had much better grounds than 'believing in such a thing as eternal punishment'. Hunt's positive feelings towards the Hindus only magnified Britain's offenses against them. In *The Examiner* he wrote that they 'are by

---

1   'Necessity of peace to our Indian possessions' (27 March 1808); *The selected writings of Leigh Hunt*, eds. Greg Kucich and Jeffrey N. Cox, 6 vols (London, 2003), 1:46–48.
2   Leigh Hunt, *The Examiner* (18 October 1818), 657.

nature one of the gentlest and kindest people on the face of the earth, and literally would not hurt a worm; for they believe in the metempsychosis. They think it barbarous even to eat meat'.[1]

Fearless in putting forward his own radical views, Hunt was particularly concerned at the secrecy which surrounded Britain's mission in India. In the lead article of *The Examiner* for September 20, 1818 he declared that the Anglo-Indian press was 'in the lowest state of slavery', muzzled under the direct control of government. The upshot of this was that

> the people in England seldom even think of India. [. . .] India only presents itself occasionally to their minds, as a great distant place with strange beasts and trees in it, where Brahmins meditate and Musselmen keep seraglios,—where white people in regimentals are always fighting for some cause or other with the dark natives in vests and turbans,—and from which sallow elderly gentlemen are every now and then coming away to enjoy the large fortunes which they have acquired,—which they cannot do for the bile.

It was part of Hunt's soul-searching on British imperialism to raise the topic of India (and Ceylon) in his newspaper. He also took a wide, European perspective on Britain's imperial activities. For instance, in his leader of 20 September, 1818, Hunt argued that complaints about Bonaparte's behaviour were completely hypocritical when 'we have been encroaching, and conquering, and usurping in India', and 'with less excuse' than Bonaparte in Europe. To such hypocrisy, illogicality must be added: 'Either our encroaching and conquering system in India, under the plea of bettering the natives, is a bad and unjustifiable one [. . .] or the same proceedings on the part of Bonaparte with regard to Spain and some other countries, where the Inquisition and slavery were to be rooted out, is good and justifiable.'[2] This leader is then followed directly by what would become a series of letters entitled 'Indian atrocities' addressed to the Editor by ex-Lieutenant George Strachan who, as a young cadet aged 18 in 1800, was involved in the Cotiote war which ended with the 'entire extirpation

---

1   Leigh Hunt, 'Superstition – its civil and political consequences', *The Examiner* (18 October 1818), 657.
2   Leigh Hunt, 'India', *The Examiner* (20 September 1818), 593–94 (594).

of both the prince and the people known as Nairs, on the coast of Malabar'.[1] The warlike Nairs perished in the cause of their oppressed sovereign, and Strachan spares no details in describing the massacres of them carried out by British forces.

A week later, in the issue of September 27, 1818, Hunt published on his front page (see next page) a second instalment of 'Indian atrocities'. Strachan's second letter led off with a quotation from Shakespeare—'I, from the Orient to the drooping West, making the winds my post horse, thus do ride.—I speak of sudden deaths, of treasons, murders, plots, conspiracies'.[2] The regular mixing of politics and poetry was standard fare for *The Examiner*. Keats himself had been introduced under the heading, 'Young Poets', a few years earlier, and since that time notices and reviews of his work had appeared intermittently. What is remarkable about this particular issue, with its front-page feature, 'Indian Atrocities', is that Hunt appends to his left-hand column the following sarcastic note: 'We congratulate, most *sincerely*, our young friend JOHN KEATS on the involuntary homage that, we understand, has been paid to his undoubted genius, in an article full of grovelling abuse'.[3] Hunt is referring, of course, to the notorious attack on his friend in the 'half-witted, half-hearted' *Quarterly review*.[4] The juxtaposition, bottom left, of the note about Keats, with the Shakespearean epigraph to 'Indian atrocities', top right, forms a striking visual emblem of the tug-of-war in Keats's letters between poetry and an active life.

Diligent Indolence

In an essay entitled 'On the poetry of the eastern nations', which accompanied his first published collection of poems in 1772, William Jones drew a connection between indolence, Eastern warmth, and Apollonian levels of poetic creativity:

---

1   For Strachan's later appeal against his court-martial, see 'Case of Ex-Lieutenant G. Strachan', *The Asiatic Journal and Monthly Register for British India and its Dependencies*, vol 21, Jan–June, 1826 (London: Kingsbury, 1826), 126–29.
2   G. Strachan, 'Indian Atrocities', *The Examiner* (27 September 1818), 609.
3   Leigh Hunt, 'Article and no article', *The Examiner* (27 September 1818), 609.
4   For Hunt's attack on the *Quarterly* and defence of Keats's poetry, see 'Literary notices', *The Examiner* (11 October 1818), 648–49.

THE EXAMINER.

No. 561. SUNDAY, SEPT. 27, 1818.

THE POLITICAL EXAMINER.

Party is the madness of many for the gain of a few.   POPE.

No. 546.

ARTICLE AND NO ARTICLE.

Our readers will do us the justice to acknowledge, that we very rarely indeed fail in giving them the usual article at the head of our paper ; and perhaps when it is considered that it is one and the same individual that has been in the habit of furnishing the original matter in this paper for nearly ten years, through all the various feelings of health and sickness, and the love of other studies besides politics, it may be granted by those who understand human nature kindly and wisely, that he has not failed in his regularity as often as might be excused him. We think our courteous readers exclaim, in one of the few good things that may be initiated from Parliament,—" Hear ! Hear !"

Dr. Johnson, it is true, says that an author may always write, provided he sits down to it doggedly. And write he certainly may ; but how write is another question. Not that industry in general is not sufficient ; but even setting aside the inclination, industry itself will not always do, as in cases for instance where the subject does not readily present itself, or rather where out of many subjects it is difficult to choose. A man's very industry and anxiety may then hamper him ; for he may go through so many subjects, and consider them so fastidiously as he goes, that he shall reject them one after the other from mere over-weighing and comparison. The dogged argument is very apt, we must confess, to apply to journals. There would be no excuse, for instance, for the frequent short articles in such papers as the Courier, if it were not, in the nature of things, to be found in their very brevity. The Morning Post (if it is what it used to be) is bound to be in it's place at all times, like one of it's namesakes in a street ; the Sun has no reason for not shining in all weathers, as much as it does in any ; and the Editor of the Quarterly Review would have no excuse for being behind-hand with his publication, as there is always to be found a sufficient number of better-tempered spirits, agreeable women, or promising young poets, to throw him into the requisite passion.* But in proportion as Journalists differ with these Journalists, who will deny that they become excusable?

Chance Reader. Yet after all, Mr. Examiner, what is the good of an excuse ?

Exam. To show the good-nature of those who accept it.

* We congratulate, most sincerely, our young friend JOHN KEATS on the involuntary homage that, we understand, has been paid to his undoubted genius, in an article full of grovelling abuse.

INDIAN ATROCITIES.

TO THE EDITOR OF THE EXAMINER.

" I, from the Orient to the drooping West, making the winds my post horse, thus do ride,—I speak of sudden deaths, of treasons, murders, plots, conspiracies," &c.—SHAKSPEARE.

The cause and origin of that obstinate contest between the East India Company and the Niars on the coast of Malabar, which terminated in the entire extirpation of both prince and people of that country, after a struggle of ten years, attended with a series of atrocities, the subject of my last article, may be thus collected from the concurrent testimony of the natives, as well as Europeans, who were engaged on that service.

A Gentleman of the name of Peel, lately deceased, who held the office of Collector in that district, a civilian in the Company's service (with whom I was personally unacquainted), is reported to have provoked, by his conduct towards the Rajah of the Cotiote, that oppressive system of proscription which led to the annihilation of the whole race of Niars, with the loss of an equal number of British troops, who were employed with a view to root out and destroy, as the only means of subjugating that nation to the yoke of the East India Company.

The quarrel between Mr. Peel and the Rajah of the Cotiote is alledged to have arisen from the attempting to impose upon the Rajah an additional rate of tribute to that which he had voluntarily submitted to pay to the Company. The Rajah having remonstrated at this encroachment, Mr. Peel forgot to treat him with that respect which, as an independent prince and faithful ally of the Company, he had a right to expect from their representative, or rather their servant. The refusing to pull off his shoes, according to oriental custom, on entering the Palace, was construed into such premeditated personal contempt, that the Rajah, it is said, grasped his sword, and compelled this diplomatic agent of the Company, in terms of indignation, as he valued his life, that instant to consult his safety.

The next step after this (corresponding with the measures adopted towards our late faithful friend and ally, the Peishwa*), was to obtain possession of the Rajah's person or capital. The brave prince resolved to preserve his liberty, even at the expence of becoming a desperate fugitive, in arms against his pursuers ; and the consequence was, that he and his faithful adherents, or, in other words, the whole of his subjects, were proscribed and hunted down, without quarter being given, as rebels to the power and authority of the British Government.

* A series of systematic warfare, spreading over almost the whole extent of the vast peninsula of Hindostan, has been incessantly carried on in that country before and since the year 1790 ; namely, the war in Mysore ; in the province of Trichinopoly ; the Mahratta war, which is now revived ; war in the Guzerat ; the Napaul war ; war in Cattach ; and the present war with the Peishwas Holkar and Scindia ; besides various contests with the natives of India not enumerated ; since it would be difficult to say at what period of their history the East India Company were not engaged in some war or other, for the purpose of subjugating, or of extirpating, the Indian nations.

Now it is certain that the genius of every nation is not a little affected by their climate; for, whether it be that the immoderate heat disposes the *Eastern* people to a life of indolence, which gives them full leisure to cultivate their talents, or whether the sun has a real influence on the imagination, (as one would suppose that the ancients believed, by their making *Apollo* the god of poetry;) whatever be the cause, it has always been remarked, that the *Asiaticks* excel the inhabitants of our colder regions in the liveliness of their fancy, and the richness of their invention.[1]

It is possible that Jones is deliberately countering here the negative interpretation given to Eastern indolence by Luke Scrafton in his *Reflections on the government of Indostan*, first published in 1763 and reprinted in 1770. Scrafton denigrates the Hindus as a people devoid of natural passion on account of the 'enervating heat of the climate'. He also charges that 'they are strangers to that vigor of mind, and all the virtues grafted on those passions which animate our more active spirits. They prefer a lazy apathy, and frequently quote this saying from some favourite book: "It is better to sit than to walk, to lie down than to sit, to sleep than to wake, and death is best of all"'.[2] Something of this negative flavour lingers in that letter of Coleridge's to Thelwall, in which he draws a contrast between two different kinds of intellectual discipline, one strenuous and higher, the other lazy and lower. Coleridge is already signaling his distance here from the pro-Eastern, pro-Hindu scholarship of Jones and others.[3] A measure of the hardening of cultural stereotypes about the East and Asiatic indolence can be seen in Wordsworth's *Essay, supplementary to the preface* (1815), where he argues for the importance of an active reader, inspired by the text he is encountering: 'Is it to be supposed that the reader can make progress [. . .] like an Indian prince or general— stretched on his palanquin, and borne by his slaves? No; he is invigorated and inspirited by his leader, in order that he may exert himself;

---

1   Sir William Jones, *Poems consisting chiefly of translations from the Asiatick Languages. To which are added two essays: I. On the poetry of the eastern nations. II. On the arts, commonly called imitative* (Oxford, 1772), 180–81.
2   Luke Scrafton, *Reflections on the government of Indostan*, 1763 (London, 1770), 16.
3   See Coleman 'The "dark tide of time"', 39-54.

for he cannot proceed in quiescence, he cannot be carried like a dead weight'.[1]

Keats's own idea of delicious 'diligent Indolence', developed in a letter to J. H. Reynolds in early 1818, deliberately overturns all such negative stereotypes, reverting to Jones's pro-Eastern indolence. In doing so Keats incorporates his own version of the Hindu credo:

> Now it is more noble to sit like Jove that [for than] to fly like Mercury—let us not therefore go hurrying about and collecting honey-bee like, buzzing here and there impatiently from knowledge of what is to be arrived at: but let us open our leaves like a flower and be passive and receptive—budding patiently under the eye of Apollo and taking hints from every noble insect that favors us with a visit—sap will be given us for Meat and dew for drink.[2]

The coinage 'diligent Indolence', which has its poetic counterpart in the 'ardent listlessness' of *Endymion*, occurs amidst several quotations from 'noble Books', all of which waft Keats away on a 'voyage of conception'. This voyage includes a couple of quotations from Shakespeare and a mysterious reference to 'all "the two-and thirty Pallaces"' (and Keats has "the two-and thirty Pallaces" in quotation marks).[3] After much hunting I believe Keats is referring here to a work in Bengali, *Batris Simhasan*, translated from a very popular and well-known Sanscrit work which relates the stories of King Vikramaditya. This text, its title translating into English as 'Thirty-two Thrones', was one of the earliest original works produced at the College of Fort William by the Bengali brahman pundit employed there under William Carey, Mrityunjay Vidyalankar, in 1802.[4]

---

1   William Wordsworth, 'Essay, supplementary to the preface', *The Prose Works*, ed. W. J. B. Owen and Jane Worthington Smyser, 3 vols (Oxford, 1974), 3:62–84 (82).

2   Letter to J. H. Reynolds (19 Feb 1818); *Letters*, 1:232.

3   Rollins was baffled by this reference, arguing that 'Keats could hardly have known anything about Buddhism' (*Letters*, 1:231). This claim has been repeated by later editors of Keats's letters; see *John Keats: selected letters*, ed. Robert Gittings, revised by Jon Mee (Oxford, 2002), 390.

4   For a modern edition, see *Thirty-two tales of the throne of Vikramaditya*, trans. A. N. D. Haksar (New Delhi, 2006).

That these 'two-and thirty Pallaces' might also be the 'golden palaces' of *Endymion* to which 'magic sleep' is the 'Great key', makes sense in a letter which allegorizes the creative man as a spider, spinning 'from his own inwards his own airy Citadel'. This spider takes us back to Bernier's *Travels* where the Hindu pundits are said to understand the 'real' empirical word as dream. They believe that God 'hath produced or drawn out of his own substance, not only *Souls*, but also whatever is *material* and corporeal in the Universe; and that this production was not meerly made by way of an efficient cause, but by a way resembling a Spider that produceth a webb, which it draws forth out of its own body, and takes in again when it will'.[1] Creation is spun out from the body of the divine whereas destruction entails a return to the divine.

Included amongst the noble books might also be Kauffman's *Dictionary of Merchandize*, with its long entry on opium, the finest of which is 'traded at Patna, on the river Ganges'. Described as the most valuable of all the simple medicines—'the most sovereign remedy for easing pain and procuring sleep'—it is both a narcotic and a stimulant: 'it stupefies, excites agreeable ideas, or occasions madness'.[2] That this 'madness' is the divine furor can be seen in the last of the three ghostly figures glimpsed by Keats in the 'drowsy hour' of his 'Ode on Indolence':

> The first was a fair maid, and Love her name;
> The second was Ambition, pale of cheek,
> And ever watchful with fatigued eye;
> The last, whom I love more, the more of blame
> Is heap'd upon her, maiden most unmeek,—
> I knew to be my demon Poesy.[3]

Critics usually read Keats's formulation of 'diligent Indolence' as a counter to William Hazlitt's disparagement of indolence in his lecture on Thomson and Cowper, delivered the week before Keats's letter. Hazlitt opens his lecture with the claim that Thomson is 'the most indolent of mortals and of poets', castigating his 'Castle of Indolence'

---

1   Bernier, quoted Ballaster, *Fabulous Orients*, 266.
2   [Kauffman], 241–2
3   Stillinger, *Poems of John Keats*, 376.

for pouring out 'the whole soul of indolence, diffuse, relaxed, supine, dissolved into a voluptuous dream'. But it soon becomes clear that, for Hazlitt, Thomson's 'indolence' is a catch-all word for his 'slovenliness', together with his deficient indignation 'against unjust and arbitrary power'.[1] Hazlitt had in fact given a much more positive spin on indolence the previous year in his collaboration with Leigh Hunt on *The round table* (1817). Here, in his essay 'On manner', Hazlitt praises the Hindoos as 'a different race of people from ourselves' who make it their business

> to sit and think and do nothing. They indulge in endless reverie [...]. They wander about in a luxurious dream. They are like part of a glittering procession,—like revelers in some gay carnival. Their life is a dance, a measure; they hardly seem to tread the earth, but are borne along in some more genial element, and bask in the radiance of brighter suns.[2]

That for Hazlitt India is a sign of the imagination can be seen in his mockery of James Mill's utilitarian *History of British India* (1817), reviewed in *The Examiner* in January, 1818.[3] Mill's boast that 'he could describe a country better at second-hand than from original observation' struck Hazlitt as absurd, especially when that country was as poetical as India. It was his own view that 'seeing half a dozen wandering Lascars in the streets of London gives one a better idea of the soul of India, the cradle of the world, and (as it were) garden of the sun, than all the charts, records, and statistical reports that can be sent over, even under the classical administration of Mr. Canning'.[4] Hazlitt's high valuation of Indian religion and culture at this time might well have been the prompt for Keats to think of sailing east on an Indiaman. Even Charles Lamb, who considered himself a life-

---

1   William Hazlitt, *Complete works*, ed. P. P. Howe, 21 vols (London, 1930–34), 4: 85, 91, 88.

2   Hazlitt, *Complete works*, 4:45–46,

3   James Mill, *The History of British India*, 3 vols (London, 1818); reviewed in 'Literary notices', *The Examiner* (8 March 1818), 156–58.

4   Hazlitt, 'On reason and imagination', *Complete works*, 12:51. For the dating of this essay to 'probably before April 1823' see William Hazlitt, *The plain speaker: the key essays*, ed. Duncan Wu with an introduction by Tom Paulin (Oxford, 1998), 39.

long desk slave at the East India Company, where he worked as a clerk in the accountant's office from 1792 onwards, commented that the 'dear abstract notion of the east India Company, as long as she is unseen, is pretty, rather Poetical'.[1]

Conclusion

Richard Woodhouse, in his interleaved and annotated copy of Keats's *Poems* (1817), commented: 'There must be many allusions to particular Circumstances, in his poems: which would add to their beauty and Interest, if properly understood'.[2] The cult of India and Hinduism which I have identified in Keats and his circle is (I suspect) the missing chapter from Marilyn Butler's thesis concerning the second-generation Romantics and their 'cult of the South'. If, as she argues, the revival of Greek mythology and paganism formed the *lingua franca* of the international Enlightenment—a liberal, extrovert, and sunny creed which was mobilized polemically against a conservative, gloomy, and introverted Christianity—then the same might be said for Jones's religious syncretism and his championing of the ancient Sanskrit texts. On a more personal level, too, it is clear that Keats's wider thinking about world religions such as Hinduism helped him to navigate the darker passages of the 'Chamber of Maiden Thought'. Finally, thanks to the assiduous and vigilant reporting of Leigh Hunt's *Examiner*, Keats's already strong political views on the wider world were sharpened by a sense of Britain's religious intolerance and the colonial crimes involved in consolidating its empire on the Indian subcontinent.[3] Indeed, his most conspicuous stretch of overt politicizing—the so-called 'capitalist stanzas' about the brothers' exploitative commerce in *Isabella; or, The Pot of Basil*—is centred

---

1   Charles Lamb, letter to Mary Wordsworth after his drunken rudeness to East India Comptroller (controller of stamps) John Kingston at the 'immortal dinner'. 'The dear abstract notion of the east India Company, as long as she is unseen, is pretty, rather Poetical; but as SHE makes herself manifest by the persons of such Beasts, I loathe and detest her'. *Letters of Charles and Mary Lamb*, II:228.
2   Quoted in Andrew Motion, *Keats* (London, 1997), 578.
3   An example of his strong views can be seen in his claim that the worst thing Napoleon had done was to teach 'the divine right Gentlemen [. . .] how to organize their monstrous armies'; *Letters*, 1:397.

on Ceylon's pearl-fishing industry:

> For them the Ceylon diver held his breath,
> And went all naked to the hungry shark;
> For them his ears gush'd blood; for them in death
> The seal on the cold ice with piteous bark
> Lay full of darts; for them alone did seethe
> A thousand men in troubles wide and dark:
> Half-ignorant, they turn'd an easy wheel,
> That set sharp racks at work, to pinch and peel.[1]

The dangers of diving amongst 'monstrous fishes' on the pearl banks of the Gulf of Mannar, far-famed from antiquity, was a lesson learnt by the schoolboy Keats from his prize copy of Kauffman's *Dictionary of Merchandize*.[2] The memory of this early reading dovetails here with Hunt's coverage in *The Examiner* of the recent cession of Ceylon to the British in 1815, and the subjugation of its inland kingdom of Kandy.

---

1   Stillinger, *Poems of John Keats*, 245–63 (l.113–20).
2   [Kauffman], 248–51.

Wordsworth from Humanities-Ebooks

The Cornell Wordsworth: a Supplement, edited by Jared Curtis ††

The Fenwick Notes of William Wordsworth, edited by Jared Curtis, revised and corrected †

The Poems of William Wordsworth: Collected Reading Texts from the Cornell Wordsworth, edited by Jared Curtis, in 3 volumes †

The Prose Works of William Wordsworth, Volume 1, edited by W. J. B. Owen and Jane Worthington Smyser †

Wordsworth's Convention of Cintra, a Bicentennial Critical Edition, edited by W. J. B Owen, with a critical symposium by Simon Bainbridge, David Bromwich, Richard Gravil, Timothy Michael and Patrick Vincent †

Wordsworth's Political Writings, edited by W. J. B. Owen and Jane Worthington Smyser. †

Other Literary Titles

John Beer, *Coleridge the Visionary*

John Beer, *Blake's Humanism*

Richard Gravil, *Wordsworth and Helen Maria Williams; or, the Perils of Sensibility* †

Richard Gravil and Molly Lefebure, eds, *The Coleridge Connection: Essays for Thomas McFarland*

John K. Hale, *Milton as Multilingual*

Simon Hull, ed., *The British Periodical Text, 1796–1832*

W. J. B. Owen, *Understanding The Prelude*

Pamela Perkins, ed., *Francis Jeffrey: Unpublished Tours.*†

Keith Sagar, *D. H. Lawrence: Poet* †

Irene Wiltshire, ed. *Letters of Mrs Gaskell's Daughters 1856–1914* †

† Also available in paperback, †† in hardback
http://www.humanities-ebooks.co.uk
all available to libraries from MyiLibrary.com